THREE SIMPLE WORDS

THE KINGSTON ALE HOUSE SERIES

A.J. PINE

Entangled Publishing, LLC
2614 South Timberline Road
Suite 109
Fort Collins, CO 80525
Visit our website at www.entangledpublishing.com.

Select Contemporary is an imprint of Entangled Publishing, LLC.

Edited by Karen Grove
Cover design by Sommer Stein with Perfect Pear Creative Covers
Cover art from Shutterstock
Kingston Ale House logo by Ashley @ BooksByMigs

Manufactured in the United States of America

First Edition October 2016

"While I was in love I was the happiest man on earth."
—L. Frank Baum, *The Wonderful Wizard of Oz*

Chapter One

"I think we have time for a couple more questions," Wes said as he looked out onto a sea of smiling, beautiful faces. One of the perks of the job for sure.

A hand shot up from the center of the crowd, and Wes nodded toward the woman. She stood, blond waves tumbling over her shoulders and directing his eyes right to where her breasts swelled beneath her shape-hugging sweater.

His lips curved upward. She glanced down to where his gaze rested below her eyes and offered a coy smile of her own. Then she surveyed *his* form, starting from his head and traveling lazily to just below the belt. She raised her brows with what felt to him like approval. She glanced up, and he met her stare with unabashed boldness.

"You…have a question?" he asked.

"Yes," she answered without hesitation. "Your hero, Ethan, is a very skilled lover in *Down This Road*. Tell me, do you write from experience or just base those scenes on extensive—research?"

He flashed her a roguish smile and leaned back against

the signing table, running a hand through his light brown waves.

"I like to think of experience *as* research," he said. "And I'm always looking to learn something new—for the sake of the next book, of course."

The woman narrowed her stare and pressed her lips into a knowing smile.

"The oral sex!" a petite brunette with a pixie cut blurted from her seat before he could ask for the last question, and gasps and murmurs echoed among the seated crowd. "The oral sex scenes were my favorite," she said with a slight tremble in her voice. "He wasn't just a skilled lover but an attentive one. I think that's one of the reasons why all those women were forgiving of his inability to commit. Because— because—"

"The oral sex," Wes said, finishing her thought, and she nodded vigorously.

His agent, Max, shot up from his stool at the bar. "And, that's it for questions, ladies. Let's give Mr. Hartley here a few minutes to grab a drink, and then he'll be signing for those of you who purchased books."

Max ushered him toward the bar as he thanked the crowd for their patience.

"You really are an asshole," Max said. "Seriously. You've fucking ruined sex for those of us with wives and partners who expect us to be able to do what Ethan can do. If you didn't pack houses like this with readers willing to throw their money at you, I'd cut you loose right now."

Wes ordered his drink and laughed. "I could do a how-to manual next if you want. Maybe a YouTube video? Or how about this? If you're doing it wrong, *ask* her how the hell you can do it right."

"Fuck you," Max said. "It's not that easy."

Wes raised a brow. "Have you ever asked your wife what

she likes?"

Max laughed. "You mean other than her personal shopper at Bloomingdales?" He went silent for a moment, and then his eyes widened. "Jesus, you're a genius, Hartley."

Wes took a slow sip of his drink. "True—but I don't follow."

Max pulled his phone from his pocket and began hammering out a text. When he finished he looked at Wes again. "I just told her I'm meeting her at Bloomingdale's after my breakfast meeting tomorrow. In a fitting room. Where I'm prepared to ask her what she'd like."

Wes laughed and shook his head. "That's one way to go about it. Feel free to bring the book if you want to reference a specific scene."

"Speaking of books..." Max said, but Wes cut him off.

"There's a line at the signing table. I'll catch you after?"

He didn't wait for Max's response. He was on too much of a high from the Q&A. Now wasn't the time to get into book two—or the current lack thereof. He had a line of women waiting for him, and he wasn't one to disappoint.

Wes scrawled his name across the title page along with his signature phrase, "Enjoy the journey." He slid the book back to the woman, enjoying the flush that grew in her cheeks as her hand accidentally brushed his.

"Thanks for coming out tonight," he said, lifting his rocks glass in a gesture of cheers before he threw back what was left of his scotch. The woman from the Q&A—the one so curious about his *research*—bit her lip and smiled, glancing behind her to the handful of other women still in line. When she looked back at him, she swiped a tongue over her painted bottom lip and tucked her blond waves behind her ear.

"Will you be staying for drinks after the signing?" she asked, her tone full of innocence, but her blue eyes brimming with heat.

Wes noted his empty glass and gave her one of his patented "Wes Hartley author" grins.

"It does look like I'm in need of a refill," he said.

She pressed her hands to the table and leaned forward, whispering in his ear, "Then I guess I'll see you at the bar."

"I guess you will."

No sooner had she ducked out of line than the next woman placed her book on the signing table. "Can I get a picture with you?" she asked.

"Oooh, I'll take it for you!" the woman behind her said. "If you'll take one of me and Wes with my phone when you're done!"

And there she was—the woman without a question at all who just wanted to talk oral sex—rounding the table before he had time to think. And then she slid onto his goddamn lap. Wes glanced toward the bar where Max still sat, and the man raised both a brow and a glass. Wes shrugged. This was the part of the job he'd never get tired of.

He encouraged the woman to wrap her arms around his neck, then tilted her down into an almost kiss.

She gasped. "This is just like that first time in Natasha's apartment where Ethan tells her the relationship can't move forward and then he lays her out on the butcher block table and—"

"The oral sex," Wes said.

She swallowed hard, apparently unable to respond as she squirmed against his thighs.

"Say cheese!" the other woman said, and he flashed his grin toward the phone aimed in their direction.

No. He'd sure as hell never get tired of this.

Max was gone by the time the signing had ended, no doubt only there to make sure he sold a respectable amount. Judging by the fact that the bookseller had to return to the shop to grab more stock, he'd say he had. But the text his agent had sent still hung in the air.

Don't fuck anyone who might fuck up your sales. Send me that new manuscript ASAP. And call me when you get to Chicago. I still think you're crazy as hell for leaving New York, but who am I other than the guy who sends you those big, fat checks? Just remember what we have riding on book two.

Looked like Max didn't need to continue their conversation face-to-face. All that had to be said was right there.

Wes looked up from his phone to find the blonde who'd offered to buy his next drink waiting on a stool with two rocks glasses in front of her, crystal clear liquid in each.

"I'm a vodka girl myself," she said. "I hope that's okay."

Wes smiled. "I'm not a picky man," he said, lifting one of the glasses to his lips and taking a sip. Heat spread from his tongue to his throat and straight to his core.

"You a New Yorker?" he asked, and she gave him a coy smile.

"I'm from Philly, actually. Took the train up just for your event. Heading back home in the morning." She drank. "Look, I don't do things like this. Ever. But your book—it just... You're Ethan, right? Meandering down this road and never really finding what you want? I mean, that's the title. *Down This Road.*"

"It's a story," he said, voice steady. "Make believe," he

teased. Because this was where he always drew the line, letting on how much autobiography actually seeped into fiction.

"Well...all those relationships?" she said. "All of them ending...and the hero resigning himself to being alone? Ugh." She shuddered. "So. Many. Feels."

He laughed and held up his glass. "To feels, then," he said. "To feels!"

They clinked their glasses together then drained the rest of their drinks.

"Excuse me, Mr. Hartley?"

The voice came from behind. He turned to see the brunette pixie who'd been in his lap only thirty minutes before.

He raised his brows.

"I was hoping I could buy you a drink?"

A blonde to his left, brunette to his right, and they wanted to buy more than just his books. Who was he to say no?

"I guess it's a party now," he said, and surprisingly *both* women smiled.

"Another round," the blonde said to the bartender. "Plus one." She glanced back at the other woman.

And then it was like a swarm—the bar flooded with the women who'd stayed past the end of the scheduled event. Drinks were poured, drank, and Wes was in his element, at his best when he was the star of the show.

When it was well past midnight, he finally broke from the small crowd that remained.

"I need to head out, ladies, but it has been a lovely evening."

There were audible *awwws* and visible pouts.

"You're leaving? A-alone?"

The brunette pixie's eyes were wide, and he chuckled softly at the memory of her blurting *oral sex* during his Q&A.

"Sorry to disappoint," he said, though the disappointment was really his. "But I thank everyone for a spectacular night."

He gave the small party a nod and backed away, offering them one final, appreciative grin.

Because he wasn't an idiot. He was grateful for all of the attention and knew it could end as quickly as it began. But for now the show was over, because Wes Hartley wasn't headed back to his New York apartment. He was headed home.

Chapter Two

THE PLAYBOY—WHY WE LOVE TO HATE HIM (AND THEN LOVE HIM)
by **HappyEverAfter admin** | Leave a comment

Annie tapped her finger against her bottom lip as she read over yesterday's post, pausing at the last line.

IT IS IN THE HEROINE THAT WE SEE THE PLAYBOY REDEEMED—THAT HE IS, IN FACT, CAPABLE OF LOVE. AND IT'S IN THIS TROPE WE SEE LOVE TRULY DOES CONQUER ALL. AND THAT, MY FRIENDS, IS WHY WE LOVE TO HATE—AND THEN FALL IN LOVE WITH—THE PLAYER HERO IN ROMANCE. AS ALWAYS, IT'S TIME TO SHARE, SO LAY IT ON ME. WHO'S YOUR FAVORITE ROMANCE PLAYBOY?

She took a deep breath. After all, she knew her posts were good, that they were always on point with current discussions in romance. That's how the HappyEverAfter blog was born and how she'd amassed a 5k following. Sure, it was modest in the grand scheme of things, but she'd started the blog for herself once she'd fallen in hard love with romance and found she needed an outlet. Now she had daily conversations about her favorite genre—albeit with people she'd never met—and the blog filled a void she hadn't been able to before. But the comments—it was always terrifying to read the first few. Did her readers agree? Disagree? Had a romance resistant troll hunted her down just to make trouble? While the latter rarely happened, it was an inherent truth of the book blogging community, which was why she kept a hefty folder of "Haters gonna hate" memes on her desktop—always her favorite troll reply.

COMMENTS:

HEALOVE SAYS: SO MUCH YES TO THIS POST. I ADORE THE PLAYER BECAUSE HIS REDEMPTION IS EVERYTHING. I HAVE TO SAY, THOUGH, THAT MY FAVORITE ONE IS A BIT UNCONVENTIONAL. I'M HEAD OVER HEELS FOR ETHAN IN WES HARTLEY'S DOWN THIS ROAD. LIKE, I CAN'T GET THAT BOOK OUT OF MY HEAD. TELL ME YOU'RE GOING TO REVIEW IT HERE BECAUSE I'M DYING TO HEAR WHAT YOU THINK!
11:01 a.m.

Well…not a troll, but not what she was hoping for. Annie read on.

BOOKLUVR SAYS: DITTO HEALOVE! I JUST FINISHED DTR LAST NIGHT AND UGH! TOTAL BOOK HANGOVER. ETHAN IS SO THE PLAYER I LOVE TO HATE—AND THEN FALL FOR IN THE END.
11:25 a.m.

She rolled her eyes. Surely the next example would be someone other than Ethan from *Down This Road*.

ROMREADER SAYS: OKAY, SO I KNOW THIS BOOK DOESN'T FOLLOW THE CONVENTIONAL "RULES" OF ROMANCE, BUT HOW CAN YOU NOT SWOON FOR ETHAN? EVERY WOMAN HE'S WITH THINKS SHE'S GOT EVERYTHING SHE EVER WANTED. HE'S COCKY, ARROGANT, AND AN AMAZING LOVER. SO WHAT IF HE DOESN'T BELIEVE IN THE HEA AND LEAVES THEM ALL? WHEN HE DOES, HE UNWITTINGLY LEAVES A PIECE OF HIMSELF BEHIND, TOO, BECAUSE NO MATTER HOW MUCH HE TRIES TO KEEP THEM OUT WHEN HE HAS SEX WITH THEM, HE LETS HIMSELF FEEL. SPOILER WARNING, BUT SINCE WE ALL READ (ANNIE TELL US YOU READ!!!), I DON'T CARE THAT HE ENDS UP ALONE OR THAT HE BROKE MY HEART WITH EVERY HEART HE BROKE. HE'S RIDIC SEXY, AND HE MADE ME FEEL ALL OF THE FEELS. ETHAN FTW!
12:16 p.m.

15 MORE REPLIES...

Annie stifled a scream. It would be one thing if the author was some nameless, arrogant ass. But she'd known him once—long ago. And he'd grown into this arrogant ass who was distorting her poor romance readers' views of a good love story. She pushed back from her desk with too much force, her rolling chair catching the lip of the rug and sending her toppling over.

"I'm okay!" she said, springing to her feet, only to have Brynn—her best friend and account manager—spin toward her and raise a brow.

"You read the comments," Brynn said drily.

Annie righted her chair and plopped back down into it. "I *have* to read the comments. It's *my* blog. I write the posts. I read the comments. And I reply. It's called good blogger etiquette," she said. She used her heels to scoot her chair back to the desk. "Plus, it's also free advertising for Two Stories, and you know how much we need that."

Brynn winced. If anyone knew how hard it was to keep an independent bookstore afloat, it was the woman who made the bank deposits each day.

"Okay," Brynn said. "You've got a point there. But what's got your panties in a bunch this morning? I think someone needs a caramel apple cider run."

Annie huffed out a breath. "I do need a cider, but first things first. You know that post that went live yesterday, the one about the playboy hero trope?" Brynn nodded. "Well, I always ask for a reader response at the end, so naturally I asked them to share their favorite playboy heroes."

Brynn nodded again. "I'm liking where this is going. Ready to add them all to my TBR."

Annie shook her head. "Do you remember that book by my brother's old high school friend, Wes Hartley?"

Brynn threw back her head and laughed. "The one who said he had to get out of Chicago, that only New York was the creative epicenter for young artists?" Brynn rolled her eyes and groaned. "You *hated* that one! Oh God. Don't tell me your blog is an inadvertent love fest for the book you love to hate."

Annie groaned. "You know I don't love to hate *anything*. Especially in public. I'm a bookseller. I talk about books I love but never disparage those I don't. But, crap. I guess *Down This Road* has had a resurgence in sales from the paperback release because more than half my comments were about the readers' undying love for the hero, Ethan." She cleared her throat. "And I use the term *hero* lightly. Because, duh— no happily ever after—and I can't even feel bad for him. He brings it all upon himself. I just—no. Hard no on that book."

"Tell me how you *really* feel," Brynn said with a grin.

Annie threw her hands in the air. "I know you don't share

my affinity for the romance novel, but geez!" She was up and pacing now. "You still get it."

"Get what?" Brynn asked with brows raised.

"That love can, in fact, conquer all *if* you're not such an idiot that you refuse to let it in."

Brynn crossed her arms. "Like me and Jamie were for ten years."

"Yes!" Annie halted mid-pace. "You guys were 100 percent, certifiable, bona fide idiots."

Brynn opened her mouth to protest but then pressed her lips back together. "You're right. We were the worst. But *now* we're the best." A dreamy smile took over her features.

"Exactly!" Annie pointed at her friend. "Just like all good romance heroes and heroines, when you two were ready to say 'fuck you' to fear and open yourselves up to the possibility of something more —"

"Fireworks," Brynn interrupted. "It was fireworks."

Annie held her head high. "Thanks to me giving you guys a push — and what I know was an epically romantic road trip." She collapsed back into her chair. "That's what's wrong with Wes Hartley's *not-a-romance*. This maddening character, Ethan, has women swooning for him right and left, almost all of them saying they love him — and he never returns the sentiment. Other than some pretty sensational sex scenes..." She fanned herself. After all, she would give credit where credit was due. "...Ethan, the *not-a-romance-hero*, is the most shallow, vapid, self-serving fictional human I've ever read. He takes and takes and takes but claims he cannot give."

"Except in the bedroom," Brynn reminded her with a wry smile. "Maybe that's why the women keep coming." She snorted. "Pun *totally* unintended, but I think it's one of my best."

Annie rolled her eyes. "There's no way *he's* as skilled as his character. It's gotta be some sort of wish fulfillment, right?

Compensation for the part of his life that's lacking?"

"Sounds about right," Brynn said. "Why don't you write a blog post about it? *Sex-starved Author Makes Up For Incompetence in the Boudoir With Debut NON-Romance Novel.*"

Annie blew her hair out of her eyes. "You know I can't alienate readers. They're all potential customers, too." If there was one thing Annie loved, it was finding out one of her bookshop patrons learned about the store from her blog. "But lucky you, being my friend and all, *you* get to hear me rant one on one!"

Brynn offered her a small bow from her office chair. "The honor is all mine."

"Good," Annie said. "Because I could go for hours."

Brynn raised a brow. "And apparently so can Hartley's *not-a-hero*? I mean, I'm just assuming based on those *sensational* sex scenes."

They both laughed, and Annie closed her laptop. She'd be opening the shop in fifteen minutes, and Brynn was right. She *did* need a caramel apple cider to set the morning right.

"I'm headed to Hot Latte," she said to her friend and partner in crime. "Want anything?"

"Pumpkin spice anything will do," Brynn said, and Annie made a dramatic gagging sound. Brynn rolled her eyes.

"I just don't get why autumn means *everything* has to taste like pumpkin."

Brynn spun back to her own laptop, no doubt finishing up with Friday's deposit so she could bring it to the bank this morning.

Annie knew she was setting herself up for more disappointment, but she had to ask. "How'd we do this week?" She watched as Brynn's shoulders slumped.

"We're a little short," her friend said, not turning to face her. And Annie was glad for it. Brynn had taken some side jobs lately—like helping Doug and Dan, the owners of Hot Latte, with their quarterly tax payments. Sales just weren't where they needed to be, and Annie wasn't sure if she'd be able to pay Brynn her full fee. *Again.*

Annie cleared her throat. "Right. So—pumpkin. On me." Like a latte could make up for her best friend trying to steer a financial sinking ship.

"Because life is better with pumpkin spice," Brynn said cheerily, leaning over her shoulder to offer Annie a conciliatory smile. "Hey, have you ever thought about doing something other than books?"

Annie gasped, but Brynn shook her head.

"I don't mean give up the *store*. But maybe host events with local authors. It shouldn't cost you anything other than ordering stock. I bet that would get more people in the door."

Annie grabbed her travel mug and headed for the door. "I sell books, B. I'm not a party planner."

Her shoulders slumped. It was actually a good idea. But it also meant stepping outside her comfort zone and trying something that could fail. She'd already done that opening her own bookshop, and that day three years ago was the happiest of her life. What if she couldn't do what was necessary, though, to keep the place afloat long-term?

Maybe she was overreacting. Maybe Brynn had miscalculated. Or maybe today would bring some big bump in sales. It wasn't just the steady decline in recent proceeds, though. That book, Wes Hartley's book—and the blog comments—had gotten under her skin.

Who didn't believe in happily ever after?

Wes Hartley, that's who.

Just because Annie hadn't found hers yet didn't mean it wasn't out there, waiting for the right moment to reveal itself.

She marched out of the bookshop with renewed purpose and satisfaction. A Hot Latte run always set the world back on its axis. It was also a comfort to know that, despite that year in high school when their paths had crossed, she'd never come face-to-face with Wes Hartley again, other than the caricature on the jacket of the most hopeless book that was not—in fact—a romance.

Chapter Three

Wes's phone buzzed with a text, and he blinked a few times before he got his bearings. A sliver of sunlight poked through the window, enough to illuminate the television atop the small dresser. The only other furniture in the room, aside from the nightstand and the bed where he lay, was the desk to his right. He ignored the buzz, but then he caught sight of his laptop on the desk.

There it sat, on but not awake. Why should it be? He hadn't made it do any work in months.

The phone vibrated again, this time with the text reminder, and he blew out a breath.

Deadline day.

He grabbed the device and swiped his thumb across the screen to unlock it.

Max: *It's 10 a.m. Refreshed my inbox. Nada.*

Wes: *Pages need a quick once-over before I send. Have them to you by the weekend.*

He clenched his teeth, waiting for his agent's response. Max made him sweat it out for a full ninety seconds.

Max: *Movie option rides on editor green-lighting this. You fuck this up, and you're done. We don't have room for a sophomore slump. 50 pages when I wake up Monday morning.*

"Fuck," Wes hissed. He ran a hand through his overgrown waves. Had Max just forgotten the amazing turnout they had for the paperback release two nights ago? It's not like he wasn't selling. Because shit—he was. He just wasn't exactly *writing.*

Wes: *I thought Joanne only wanted first three chapters.*

Max: *That was before you missed the first deadline. Shit is getting real, my friend. Your career can end as quickly as it began. 50 pages Monday morning.*

Wes: *Gotcha. No problem.*

Fuck me.
He tossed the phone down on the bed and flopped onto his back.
End as quickly as it began.
Most people still didn't know what they wanted to do with their lives at twenty-five, yet here he was, ready to lose it all before everyone else figured their own shit out. Was that the price of chasing a dream—having everyone else call the shots when all he needed was a little fucking space?
This was why he was getting the hell out of New York. After seven years, a change of scenery was what he needed. He wasn't *blocked.* No fucking way he was using that term. He was just in a holding pattern, one that would right itself

once he made it the rest of the way to Chicago.

He'd considered riding straight through, but he'd also left on a whim—telling Max about the decision at the signing—so he'd hoped his night in Columbus would get the words flowing. No such luck. If he got his ass out of bed now, he could make it to Chicago by late afternoon.

It was time for a phone call.

He searched through his recent calls, hoping to just hit redial. But after scrolling through a month's worth of numbers, he realized it had been longer than that since he and his father had spoken.

Well. No time like the present, right?

"It's nine in the morning," his dad said after one ring.

"Always stating the obvious, Dad."

Wes was up and pacing now. This was what fifteen seconds with this man did to him, and they weren't even in the same room.

"Do you need money?"

Wes groaned. "I paid a year's worth of your mortgage. Remember?"

"I didn't ask you to," his dad said.

"It was a *gift*. Jesus, can't I do something for you and not expect anything in return?"

The sentiment was true at the time. His parents put him through college. The only way he knew how to say thanks was to give something back. Yes, he'd spent his advance and then some, but Max said he'd earn out next quarter. Six months past release and sales were still steady, especially now that the paperback had hit the shelves. But would they be a year from now if *Down This Road* was his one and only novel?

He listened to his one living relative breathe out seven years of conversations they hadn't had. The weight of what hung between them pressed down on Wes's shoulders, and he waited.

"Well, you must need *something*," his father said. "Last time you called—"

"Was to wish you a happy birthday," Wes interrupted.

And the time before that? Shit, he couldn't even remember. And yes, he needed something—a free place to stay. But how could he ask his father for that now? He'd only prove him right.

"I just wanted to see how you were, Dad. That's all."

His dad grunted. "Work is steady. Can't complain. Actually got a commercial gig painting the inside of a new store. Sells women's clothing or something."

Wes's shoulders relaxed. He could hear the hint of a smile creep into his father's voice. He wouldn't ruin it by asking him the other question that hung on the tip of his tongue.

You been to the cemetery to see Mom lately? She was always the buffer between them. She got Wes when his father didn't, which was always. But she'd been gone five years now, and the further she faded into memory, the more it was like there was nothing left tying him and his dad together. But, shit, he was trying, even if the initial motivation was a selfish one.

"That's great," he said instead. "Look. I may be in town soon. Can I take you to dinner or something when I get there?"

"Yeah. Sure. That sounds good," he said.

This was a start. After a month, it was an opening of sorts.

"You, uh, had a chance to read it yet?" Wes asked, and the second the words were out of his mouth, he knew he should have ended the conversation at the dinner request.

"Christ, Wes. We're gonna do this again?"

Why should today be any different?

Every muscle in his upper body tensed. "Forget it. Forget I asked. I just thought you might like to know a little about your son, what he's been working on the past few years. I ask about your life. You ask about mine. That's how catching up usually goes. Only, you don't ask, Dad. You don't ask, and you don't read, and I don't know how else to show you what the hell I've been doing."

Silence. Followed by more silence.

"I'm not a—"

"Reader. Yeah, I've heard. It's fine. Look, I gotta go. I'll call you again when I get to town."

He tried like fuck to ignore the tightness in his chest but knew the only relief was in ending the call.

"When's that gonna be?"

Six or seven hours.

"I'm not sure. Probably a couple weeks or so. I'll talk to you soon."

"Wes…"

But his father didn't say anything after that.

"Bye, Dad."

Was it only two nights ago he'd been swarmed at that bar with readers who couldn't get enough of him? But dear old dad wasn't even interested in a few words on the page. He ignored the laptop but pulled up the voice recording app on his phone.

"Remember the signing—the drinks, the offers," he said into the microphone. "When you get out of your goddamn holding pattern, you got yourself quite the chapter there."

But whatever story he was trying to tell was miles away. Nope. Not yet cleared for takeoff.

Wes parked his bike with too much ease. He was supposed to have to circle the block for ten, twenty, *ninety* minutes at least, giving him time to figure out what to say. But there was no traffic, no difficulty finding a spot, and now he had no choice but to walk in or start the engine and take off again.

He let out a long breath, hopped from the bike, and tore off his helmet. The whole ride in he had used safety as an excuse to look no further than the road in front of him. But he realized now it wasn't just the rules of the road he was obeying.

He spun to take in his surroundings—red brick facades, tree-lined sidewalks, and the sun still visible above the rooftops as it made its way to the west. The last time he was home, Wes had seen nothing but the inside of his childhood apartment and the gray skies above the cemetery. At least, that's all he'd noticed.

After seven years in New York, making a life for himself in a place that made sense for his career, he was socked in the gut with something he hadn't expected. Longing. This feeling propelled him toward the door of Kingston Ale House, a place that hadn't existed when he lived here but one that held the chance for him to reboot. All it had taken was a text.

Wes: *Hey, man. I know it's been a while, but I'm coming home for a bit and need a place to stay. Got any suggestions?*

Jeremy: *Turns out I'm looking to sublet second bedroom. You interested?*

Wes: *Can't commit to a full year.*

Jeremy: *Month to month works for me.*

Wes: *You're a lifesaver.*

Jeremy: *You're an asshole for disappearing for so long.*

Wes: *Is that code for being happy to see me?*

Jeremy: *I don't speak in code. Let me know when you get here, and I'll give you the address of the apartment or the bar, depending on where I'll be.*

Turned out it was the bar. Time changed many things. Wes was older, lived farther away, and had created an emotional distance from this place he wasn't sure he wanted to bridge. But somehow a friendship he thought had been consumed by the expanse of both miles and time could be bridged with a simple text.

"Holy shit, people!" Jeremy yelled from behind the bar as Wes strode through the door. "Remember this moment as the one where you had your first brush with fame."

It was four o'clock, and the two patrons who sat at the far end of the bar barely looked up from their pints. Wes rolled his eyes at his friend.

"Well, if it isn't literary badass Wes Hartley," Jeremy continued, stepping out from behind the bar.

Wes set his helmet down on a stool and crossed his arms.

"So *you're* the one who read it," he joked.

Jeremy extended a hand to shake, and Wes gripped it, letting out a breath.

"Yeah right, asshole. Me and half a million others. But the false modesty is charming as shit."

God, could it really be this easy, falling into familiar rhythms with old friends just like that?

"Thanks," Wes said. "Been working on it."

Jeremy moved back to his place behind the tap, filling a stein with the microbrewery's Oktoberfest. Then he slid it across to where Wes's hands rested on the bar.

"You look like you need this," he said, and Wes nodded.

"You have no idea."

Jeremy looked at his wrist where a watch was nonexistent.

"I've got all night," he said. "And you're in luck. Apartment's walking distance, so you can leave the bike overnight if you need to."

Well, shit. Nothing had sounded this tempting in a long fucking time. He ran a hand across his stubbled jaw and wondered if he looked as weary as he felt. Judging by the mug in his hand and Jeremy's offer to drink away the evening, he guessed he did.

He took a long, slow gulp of his beer, his shoulders relaxing as he did. Damn, had he been holding on to all that tension for the entire ride?

No. He'd been holding on to it for at least a year. Maybe more.

"About the apartment," Wes started. "I can give you the first month up front, but seeing as I spent most of the advance on my dad's mortgage and haven't quite gotten my signing bonus for book two..."

This was where he was supposed to admit there *was* no book two. Not yet. But he'd already painted himself as a big enough asshole as it was. It's not that he was looking for a handout. His New York apartment was paid up through the end of the year, and he'd left on a whim. He had a good five months before he'd have to figure out what to do with it.

Jeremy shrugged. "If you can work with something other than a laptop, I'm sure Kingston could give you some hours behind the bar."

Wes ran a hand through his hair and let out a long breath.

"Shit, man. I don't feel like I deserve you letting me off the hook so easily. Not like I've been around much since — "

"Graduation?" Jeremy interrupted. "Yeah. Well, maybe you can do me a favor, too."

He leaned against the back counter and shoved his hands in the front pocket of his jeans.

Wes laughed. "Anything." He raised the mug to his lips for another sip. Maybe this was the turning point—things finally starting to go his way.

"My sister's shop is kind of in need of an economic boost."

Wes took another long sip from his stein. "Annie?" he asked, trying not to sound too eager at just the mention of her name. "What kind of shop?"

Jeremy grinned. "A bookshop, actually."

Wes perked up even more at this news. "How can I help?"

Jeremy scratched the back of his head. "Sales haven't been great lately, and I keep telling her she needs to host more events. You know? You sell your product by getting people in the door, and *you*, my friend, will bring people in the door. Would you do a signing for her? She'd sell a shit ton of your books, and that money gets back to you eventually. Plus—there's that dirt-cheap rent you're getting from your old friend who's not going to give you shit for dropping off the face of the earth—"

"Yes," Wes said with zero hesitation. "Whatever she needs. I'm in."

Jeremy smiled and let out a breath. "Excellent. I'll get it all set up. I just need to convince her—"

"Convince her?" Wes interrupted. "I thought you were trying to convince *me*."

Jeremy let out a nervous laugh.

"Yeah, here's the thing. I know you can take this because of all your hundreds of thousands of fans and movie options and shit…but Annie kind of hated your book."

Beer. Wrong pipe.

Wes coughed for a good forty-five seconds until Jeremy finally slid the mug away.

It's not like he hadn't received bad reviews along with the good. He'd learned quickly enough that was the nature of the beast. But no one had ever told him to his face they'd hated the work. They saved that for social media and email. He could deal with nameless, faceless loathing. In person he preferred adoration. Free drinks. Keys to hotel rooms. "Hate's a strong word," he said when the coughing had subsided.

Jeremy nodded. "Yeah, Annie doesn't hate *anything*." He took a sip of his own mug. "Except that book."

Wes raised a brow. Jeremy narrowed his eyes.

"Dude, I know what I said about fans and movie deals and shit, but what's with the Mad Hatter smile?"

"Nothing," he said. "Just—just convince her, and I'm all in." Because she hadn't said she'd hated his book in person. This was third-party information from Jeremy. Wes was sure if he found himself and Annie Denning in the same room, things would be different.

Face-to-face they always were.

Chapter Four

First Ever Author Event at Two Stories bookstore
by **HappyEverAfter admin** | Leave a comment

Hey, local readers! Two Stories is holding its first signing event this Thursday, the 22nd of September, and I hope you can make it. We have a very special guest and former Chicago local—Wes Hartley, author of the bestselling *Down This Road*. The paperback just hit stores, and we've got plenty of stock for the author to sign. We hope to see you there!

COMMENTS:

HEAlove says: OMG I AM SO JEALOUS. I wish I was in the area, but I'm calling my friend who lives in the Chicago 'burbs and ORDERING her to get me a signed copy. Post pics of the event!
9:07 p.m.

RomReader SAYS: I'M LOCAL AND—TRUTH CIRCLE—
HAVEN'T MADE IT TO YOUR STORE YET, BUT I'M SO MAKING
THIS MY FIRST VISIT. I'M SURE IT WON'T BE MY LAST!
9:30 p.m.

Bookluvr SAYS: I TOLD MY BOOK CLUB ABOUT THIS LAST
NIGHT, AND THEY ARE ALL DYING. WE WILL BE THERE.
I HOPE YOU STOCKED ENOUGH BOOKS AND THAT YOU
DON'T MIND A TON OF FANGIRLING GOING ON IN YOUR
SHOP!
8:05 a.m.

36 MORE REPLIES…

Annie blinked at her blog app on her phone then looked at the crowd.

"Brynn. You were right. Holy wow! Look at all these people!"

"Jeremy's the genius!" Brynn said, kissing the man on the cheek. "I was like, *What if we tried this?* And then *poof*—Jeremy gives us a bestselling author. This place is packed!"

Jeremy bowed, accepting her praise, while Annie rolled her eyes before going back to staring nervously out the window.

"Seriously, Jer, if this guy doesn't show…"

She'd gotten her hopes up about the extra business. The thought of losing all of these sales made her stomach roil.

Jeremy put a hand on his sister's shoulder. "Annie—turn around and look at your store. Two Stories is packed—on *both* stories. There are people standing upstairs and looking over the railing because we've filled every seat. And might I add that we pulled this whole thing off in less than a week?"

It barely took any advertising. She'd put a flyer in the window and taken out an ad in a few of the online papers.

And the blog. That was it. That was the kind of draw Wes Hartley had, and yet the man wasn't even here.

"All I know," Annie said, "is that I might have a full house, but I don't have an author, and without the author, I'm not selling those books." She nodded back toward the signing table where stacks of *Down This Road* paperbacks waited. Thank goodness for a rush order from the publisher.

"The guy was in my apartment showering when I left," Jeremy said. "He said he's done, like, a hundred of these. I don't think he's going to skip out on the one he's doing as a favor for his buddy's sister."

Annie crossed her arms. "I don't need any favors," she mumbled, even though she *was* grateful for the crowd that sat patiently waiting for the event to begin.

That's when she heard the rumble of an engine—a motorcycle engine—coming up the usually quiet, tree-lined city street. The rider slowed in front of the shop, looked up at the sign, and then promptly did a U-turn before expertly pulling into a spot along the opposite side of the street.

"Okay, that was hot," Brynn said. "I didn't think parking could be hot—but that was—"

"Hot?" Jeremy asked.

Brynn nodded. "Yeah."

"I see what you mean," he mused.

Annie gave her little brother a loving slap on the back of the head.

"*Hey*," he said, rubbing his auburn waves—the hue a perfect match to his sister's. "Don't mess the do." He grinned and raised his brows.

"You two are ridiculous," Annie said, even as she did admire the rider's adept parallel parking skills. There was something undoubtedly attractive when it happened with a motorcycle, but for some reason she didn't want to give her brother or her friend the satisfaction of knowing she thought anything about the rider was hot.

But Annie took in the rugged leather boots under the worn ends of his jeans. His black leather jacket was zipped shut. She couldn't explain why, but she couldn't look away. Something in the way he moved kept her rooted in place. Staring.

The rider pulled off his helmet and ran a hand through his hair. One corner of his mouth quirked up.

"Who's got a copy of the book?" Annie asked, and Jeremy was the first to oblige, slapping a paperback against her chest. She flipped it over to where the author bio was on the back, which included a cartoon likeness of the man but no actual photograph.

She glanced at the drawing, then up at the man striding toward them. Down at the book—up at him.

"Why don't you just ask, '*Hey, Jer? Is that him?*' Then I could tell you that's the guy who's been crashing in my second bedroom all week, and we could avoid the googly eyes."

Annie glared at her brother. She knew it wasn't him she was angry at. It was herself. Because she already knew she didn't like Wes Hartley the writer. The fact that he was attractive—that he looked nothing like that pre-pubescent fourteen-year-old who used to sit on her couch playing video games—should have no bearing on that.

And it didn't.

She glanced back down at the short bio next to the image, one that was either brilliant or pretentious, but Annie was already leaning toward the latter.

Wes Hartley is a man of little depth—just ask every woman who's ever dated him. He lives in Manhattan, where he drinks more than enough coffee, just enough bourbon, and hasn't yet run out of words. He hopes to be worthy of three dimensions soon.

She groaned just as Wes walked through the door of Two Stories bookstore.

"Hey," he said, reaching to shake Jeremy's hand. "Sorry I'm a few minutes late. It's been a few years, and this isn't exactly my corner of the city." He turned to Annie and grinned. "Guess it's gonna take me a bit to learn my way around the neighborhood."

He leaned forward and kissed Annie on the cheek, and her traitorous skin warmed at the touch of his lips.

"Nice to see you, Annie."

She opened her mouth to respond, but the right words wouldn't come. And by the time she'd thought of something as simple as *Hi*, he'd already moved on to Brynn.

"I'm sure we probably met in high school," he said, and planted a kiss square on her cheek as well. "But I was a few years behind you guys with Jer."

Brynn blushed, and Annie rolled her eyes.

"I'm thinking you've probably grown up a bit since then," Brynn said, and laughed.

"You gonna introduce him?" Jeremy asked.

Annie nodded. "Go sneak him through the stacks and wait for my cue—which will be, you know, me saying his name."

Jeremy gave her a salute and led Wes discreetly through the shelves and around the seated fans.

Brynn crossed her arms and gave her friend a pointed look.

"How did we not know he looked like that?" she asked.

Annie shrugged. "The last time I remember seeing him was when he was a freshman and we were seniors. I'd say he has probably changed a bit. I tried looking him up on social media, and it seems like other than events like this, he's pretty private. He doesn't even have a Twitter account."

Brynn gasped in mock horror. "But how will he Tweeter

without it?"

"*Tweet*," Annie said.

"Tw-what?" Brynn asked.

"Forget it. You're just fucking with me, and I have a guest to introduce."

Brynn tucked a brown curl behind her ear.

"How do I look?" Annie asked, smoothing out her T-shirt that read SAVE A WRITER. BUY A BOOK, one of the many she sold at the store.

Brynn pinched her friend's cheek. "Adorable as ever. Has the hero already swept you off your feet with his parking prowess and tousled hair?"

Annie groaned and brushed past Brynn, heading for the signing table, but Brynn was hot on her heels.

"Okay, I was teasing, but you're all ruffled up. You're attracted to him!"

Annie stopped so suddenly she and Brynn collided, the two of them nearly spilling face-first onto the ground. When she steadied herself, Annie pivoted toward her attacker.

"He's good looking. So what? That doesn't change how I feel about his story, and I cannot be attracted to someone who finds the idea of love so bleak. Did you read it?"

Brynn shook her head.

"Well, spoiler alert. His main character is a serial dater. He never connects with anyone even though each woman tries to forge a bond with him. It's like—it's like he doesn't find anyone worthy of the effort. Because it takes effort, right? You and Jamie make it look easy, but you work at it. Don't you?"

Brynn's eyes softened. "Of course we do. But Annie—it's a *book*. Not real life. Wes isn't his main character."

She didn't get it. Because books *were* real life. Books made Annie *feel*, and feelings were as real as anything Brynn could come up with.

Wes Hartley's book did not give her the *feels* it gave other readers, and if he was anything like his main character, Ethan, physical attraction was just a minor inconvenience.

"I'm going to introduce him and get this over with," Annie said, and she strode toward the signing table that was lined with books. Extra boxes sat on the floor behind the chair, and off to the side, between the tall shelves, Jeremy waited with Wes.

She smiled as she saw Doug and Dan in the front row, her favorite baristas, soon-to-be husbands, and co-owners of Hot Latte. She loved the support the independent businesses gave each other and reminded herself to be sure to thank them for coming—with a discount on whatever they bought—just like they always offered to her.

The murmuring crowd quieted when they saw her, and Annie swallowed as she looked out among a sea of smiling women. *Lots* of women who undoubtedly got the Wes Hartley feels when they read *Down This Road.*

"Good evening, everyone," she said, and the bitter taste in her mouth lessened as she realized what the large audience meant for her store—and that Wes had generously offered to do the signing on barely any notice. She sighed. "I'm Annie, and Two Stories is my shop. Thank you all for coming to this extremely special event. And thanks to my brother, Jeremy"— she strained to peek around the corner where she knew the two men were waiting—"for helping throw this little party together on such short notice." She initiated a small round of applause for her brother.

"But I know you didn't all come here to see me. You came for Wes Hartley." A few whistles and shouts rang out, but she could tell they were all behaving so she could get through her spiel and bring out the guest of honor. "Those of you who pre-purchased a paperback should have a ticket to trade for a book when you get up to the table. Those of you who have not yet purchased a book, don't worry." She grinned. "We have more, so buy two if you want. I hear books are great gifts." She pointed at the message on her shirt, and the audience laughed. But really she was thinking it should read, SAVE AN INDIE BOOKSTORE OWNER. BUY A BOOK.

"I'm not sure any of you know this, but I went to high school with our guest tonight. He was that squirrely freshman who sat on the couch and played video games with my brother when I was a senior and too caught up in my own life to know we had a burgeoning famous author in our midst. Thanks for coming back to visit, Wes." He stepped out from his hiding spot, and there was a collective gasp from the audience. "Ladies and gentlemen, I'm thrilled to introduce you to Wes Hartley."

Chapter Five

If there was ever a time Wes welcomed the ego boost, it was now. The applause, the whistles, the flirting looks from those whose eyes met his—this is what made it easier to breathe when the rest of the week had felt like holding his breath.

He'd been in town three days and had yet to churn out the fifty pages Max was expecting by Monday.

It was Thursday.

"Wow," he said, leaning casually against the table and setting down the motorcycle helmet he still held. "Thanks. I— uh—haven't been back to Chicago in a while, so this is quite the homecoming."

He shrugged off the leather jacket, and someone in the crowd yelled, "How about the shirt, too?"

He laughed as he hung the jacket on the back of the chair and looked down at his plain black T-shirt and jeans. Then he shook his head. "Annie runs a respectable business, folks. Pretty sure there's a sign somewhere that requires a shirt for service." Laughter—they warmed up to him easily, but he still felt a chill in the air. Then he realized Annie was nearby, her back to him as she walked toward the rear of the crowd.

"You know," he said, leaning forward as if about to tell the audience a secret. "This is just between us, but I had a mad crush on our bookshop owner in high school."

There were gasps and *awws*, and he watched as Annie stopped in her tracks and hesitated before turning in his direction. He knew what she'd think, that he was just trying to get on her good side—and maybe that of the readers, too. So she hated his book. That *was* a strike against him. But he wasn't lying about that high school crush. The truth was always in the words he wrote—and the ones he spoke as well.

"She was right, though. I was this obnoxious kid when she was already—well, look at her. She's gorgeous, and she was a decade ago, too."

Even from the distance he could see her cheeks go pink, and he smiled. She, however, glared at him and crossed her arms. Annie Denning was having none of it.

"But enough about me and my unrequited crush—or maybe I should write about it someday..." More laughter, but he decided to let Annie off the hook. "How about we start with a Q&A? Then I'll do a couple of readings, and then sign?"

The crowd nodded in agreement.

Then the questions started rolling in.

"When will we hear about book two?" a woman asked.

"When my publisher lets me say more about it," he said, which wasn't really a lie. Joanna wouldn't let him share what didn't exist.

"What about movie rights?"

He scrubbed a hand across his jaw. "Nothing is in stone yet, but I should have some news on that front soon."

One of the men in the front raised a hand, and Wes nodded to him.

"I'm sure you get asked this all the time, but I've scoured

interviews to find the answer and have never seen you address it in print. Are all of Ethan's lovers based on your own experience?"

Ah, yes. There it was again. The age-old question, and the one he never gave a straight answer to. He'd talked around the issue well enough in New York last week, but Annie was still watching him, and something in her stare made him want to come clean, even if he wasn't entirely direct.

He scratched the back of his neck and held Annie's gaze even though the question came from the front row.

"The story started as my senior thesis. I was young." Quiet laughter rang out. "*Younger* than I am now." He saw the ghost of a smile on Annie Denning's lips. "So—yeah," he added. "There was *research* involved. It was supposed to be an exploration of the male/female relationship, and it just sort of morphed into a book, I guess."

Her smile faded, and he wondered what he'd said wrong. That was the most up-front he'd ever been about where the material for his story came from.

His eyes dropped back to the man in the front row who wore his own satisfied grin.

"And are you—*researching* book two?"

The whole crowd erupted, and he used it as his segue to move to the chair behind the table where he read a couple of excerpts before promising to sign and take photos no matter how long the line was. He'd stay until everyone was taken care of, and then he'd stay some more and get to know the store's owner—if she'd let him.

It was the two men from the front—Doug and Dan, he learned—who were the last to get their books signed. Annie and Brynn were clearing away boxes from the books they'd sold when the blond—Doug—grabbed her by the elbow and pulled her next to him, right in front of the signing table.

"He should be your plus one," Doug said, and Annie

shook her head violently.

Wes leaned back and crossed his arms.

"I can attend a wedding without a date," she protested.

"You replied with a plus one," Dan added, and Annie rolled her eyes.

"Well, tell that to the guy who thought *attending* a wedding was too serious of a commitment. As if every woman who *goes* to a wedding wants to marry her date."

Dan stage-whispered to Doug, "She always chooses the commitment-phobes. Why do you think that is?"

"Maybe because *she* doesn't really want to commit," Doug whispered back while Wes watched, amusement on his face.

"Not until she finds someone who holds a candle to her romance heroes."

Wes laughed while Annie scoffed.

"Standing right here, guys," she said. "And I still have to buy you two a wedding gift, so you better watch what you say before I go *off* registry and pick out something myself."

Dan gasped while Doug waved her off. "She's bluffing."

"She better be," Dan said.

"When's the wedding?" Wes asked.

"Saturday," both men said in unison. "In this darling Central Illinois town called Bliss. Everything—I mean *everything* there is wedding."

Wes shrugged. "I'm free."

Again Annie shook her head. "Thanks, but I'm good without a pity date."

Doug crossed his arms. "The extra plate is already paid for. You don't want us having a table with an unused setting, do you?" He batted his dark lashes at her, and Annie groaned.

"You're not worried about an unused place setting."

Doug gave her a pointed look.

"Okay, maybe you are. Just a little. But I think you're more interested in showing off a famous author to your guests."

They both nodded.

"Guilty," Doug said.

"Totally guilty," Dan echoed.

"I feel like a piece of meat," Wes said, but he was grinning. "But I don't know. Annie sounds like she doesn't want to be seen with a—how did she put it? *Famous author.*"

Taking Annie to a wedding? He'd change her opinion of the book—and him—by giving her a night to remember.

Annie rolled her eyes and let out a breath. "Fine," she said, then turned to Wes. "You can come."

"Best invitation I've ever received," he said, then stood so he could lean over the table to kiss her on the cheek. He whispered in her ear, "I wasn't lying about that teenage crush."

When he pulled away, he could have sworn he saw her shiver.

"Okay," he said to Doug and Dan. "Whose book am I signing first?"

But all he could think about was two nights from now—and spending the evening with the fiery redhead who tried to remain cool as ice in his presence.

She had already turned and was following Brynn out a side door with her share of the empty boxes.

"Looking forward to our date," he called after her. "You can tell me about all your favorite romance heroes!"

She glanced over her shoulder and glowered but said nothing in response.

"All you have to do is give her a happily ever after," Dan said.

At that Wes let out a breath and went to work signing the books.

He couldn't give any woman what he didn't believe in. He'd never seen himself as the hero type anyway, but for one night he could play the part.

If it meant a night with Annie Denning.

Chapter Six

WHEN HEAS HAPPEN IN REAL LIFE
by **HappyEverAfter admin** | Leave a comment

So, YOU KNOW THIS BLOG IS ALL ABOUT THE HEA, SO I HAD TO SHARE A VERY SPECIAL IRL HEA WITH YOU TONIGHT. THERE'S A TIGHT-KNIT COMMUNITY OF INDIE SHOP OWNERS IN MY CORNER OF THE CITY. DOWN THE STREET FROM MY BOOKSTORE IS THE BEST COFFEE SHOP AROUND—HOT LATTE. THE OWNERS, DOUG AND DAN, HAVE GROWN TO BE MY FRIENDS, AND TONIGHT THEY ARE GETTING MARRIED IN WHAT I HEAR IS THIS CRAZY-CUTE WEDDING TOWN IN CENTRAL ILLINOIS CALLED BLISS. I MAY NOT HAVE AN HEA OF MY OWN JUST YET, BUT THESE TWO GUYS ARE PROOF IT'S NOT JUST A THING OF STORIES. TRUE LOVE IS REAL, AND I'M SO HAPPY THEY'VE FOUND IT. JUST TO GIVE YOU A LITTLE IDEA OF WHERE I'M HEADED THIS EVENING, HERE ARE SOME PICTURES OF BLISS. I SWEAR, SOMEONE SHOULD WRITE A BOOK ABOUT THIS TOWN.

COMMENTS:

ASYOUWISH SAYS: IS THIS TOWN FOR REAL? A WEDDING CAKE STATUE?
11:11 a.m.

PEPPERONMYPAPRIKASH SAYS: YOU ARE A BRAVE SOUL IF YOU'RE GOING TO A WEDDING IN A TOWN LIKE THAT AS A SINGLE WOMAN.
12:15 p.m.

BOOKLUVR SAYS: I WAS AT THE SIGNING THE OTHER NIGHT AND MAYBE OVERHEARD SOMETHING ABOUT YOU TAKING WES HARTLEY TO THIS WEDDING. IS IT TRUE? ARE YOU AND HE, LIKE, A THING?
12:30 p.m.

HAPPYEVERAFTER SAYS: HI BOOKLUVR. UM, YES. YOU HEARD RIGHT. I AM TAKING WES HARTLEY TO THE WEDDING. BUT NO, WE ARE SO NOT A THING. THE GROOMS ARE BOTH BIG FANS, AND WHEN THEY FOUND OUT WES AND I WENT TO HIGH SCHOOL TOGETHER, THEY CALLED IN A FAVOR. MR. HARTLEY WAS GRACIOUS ENOUGH TO COMPLY. BUT I PROMISE YOU—IT IS NOT A DATE.
12:33 p.m.

64 MORE REPLIES...

Umm, wow. There were a *lot* of people who seemed to care about her *non*-date with Wes Hartley. She hadn't had time to respond to more than just the one question and hoped the rest of her readers would be satisfied with that.

Annie stepped away from the mirror. Then she leaned

over the sink and nearly face-planted the glass. A step back. A step forward. And she was pretty much doing the cha-cha.

She spun to face Brynn, who stood against the wall outside the bathroom door, scrolling through pictures on her phone.

"I might have over tweezed. How bad is it? Be honest."

Brynn squinted and pursed her lips. She unclipped Annie's long, auburn bangs and let them fall over her face — and the eyebrow that was *maybe* a little thinner and arched a little higher than the other.

"There," Brynn said. "Problem solved."

Annie huffed out a breath. Then she nodded. "It's too bad I can't stand him. I mean, bookseller and writer. It looks good on paper, right? Maybe *I* should have chased Spencer Matthews across the country. The effort was wasted on you."

Brynn rolled her eyes. "Very funny. That trip to L.A. was exactly what Jamie and I needed to realize — well, to realize we never needed to leave Chicago to find happiness. Anyway, Spencer's dating that CW actress who's going to star in the movie adaptation of his book."

Annie sighed. "And to think you chose Jamie over him."

"Hey!" Brynn pushed her good-naturedly on the shoulder.

Annie laughed. "You know there's no one better than Jamie. They broke the mold with that one."

Brynn sighed wistfully. "I know."

Annie sighed louder, more dramatic, and cleared her throat. "Okay, lover. Attention back on me, please. The eyebrow isn't the worst thing ever?"

Brynn fussed with Annie's hair again, then stepped back and crossed her arms.

"Totally not the worst thing ever," she said. "And as long as you keep that dramatic part going, you won't look perpetually inquisitive."

Brynn snorted. Annie flipped her off. Then her friend's

eyes grew serious.

"What?" Annie asked, worried the eyebrow actually was terrible.

"Sales the other night?" she said. "From Wes's signing."

Annie winced, bracing herself. "You waited until now to tell me? Okay. Fine. Whatever it is, I can take it."

Brynn worried her bottom lip between her teeth. "Annie, we sold more Thursday night than the past week combined. And it wasn't just Wes's books. Tabitha had to restock the new release section, and the romance shelves were demolished. If you can start doing events like that on the regular, you'll be offering something the online retailers can't. Face-to-face time with their favorite writers."

Annie's jaw dropped. "That's amazing, but—this is the part where I remind you I'm a no-name little store. Why will anyone's favorite writer come to me?"

Brynn smiled. "Because you've got the endorsement of a *New York Times* bestseller."

Annie gritted her teeth.

"Okay. Fine. I gotta go, but think about it," Brynn said. "It's okay to ask for help, even from someone you claim not to like, and right now I need a ton of help making sure the apartment is ready for guests. Holly and Will arrive from London in an hour, and I want to be home when they get there. They're only here for two weeks, so I gotta get my little sister fill. Call me in the morning, and don't forget dinner at Kingston's next Sunday night, the whole gang!"

Brynn kissed her on the cheek and bounded toward the door.

"Bye!" Annie called after her. *Have fun with your almost-husband, your sister, and her tall, dark, and British almost-husband. I'll just be on my pity date with a guy I don't like. No big deal.*

And perpetually inquisitive.

Crap.

Annie slid her arms through the sleeve holes of her dress and stepped into the nude-colored pumps. She reached behind her back to pull up the zipper, but her hand was forced to a stop halfway up her back.

She let out a loud groan, then grabbed her leather jacket from where it lay on her bed.

Fine. I'll just have a friend zip me the rest of the way when I get there.

That was assuming whoever helped her out could also get the damn thing unstuck. Otherwise, she'd be doing the moto jacket with the dress look, and everyone else could suck it.

Whoa there, feelings. Let's settle down. It's just a dress.

Not that she was getting angry. The eyebrow and zipper — those were just minor setbacks. She'd know plenty of people at the wedding and have a great time no matter who she was there with.

She popped back into the bathroom to turn off the light and grab her clutch, checking that her house and car keys were inside. Everything was accounted for. So Annie held her head high and stepped out her apartment door, deciding to meet Wes out front. She ran down the steps to the walk-up's front door, and then down five more to the sidewalk where her heel caught in a crack and promptly snapped off.

"Shit!" she yelled, squatting down to pick up the three-inch heel that was now nothing more than a stick in her hand. "Like, throw me a freaking bone here, universe!" she added as she straightened.

Before she could turn to head back upstairs for a quick shoe change, the unmistakable sound of a motorcycle broke through the quiet of her street, and seconds later, said vehicle stopped in front of her building. Because, of course, this comedy of errors would not be complete without an audience.

"I guess I'm right on time?" he said after he killed the

engine and took off his helmet. Annie's stomach lurched.

He wasn't supposed to look so good. And that voice of his—playful and teasing with a sexy rasp—wasn't supposed to do things to her insides. But her palms began to sweat, and she felt a bit nauseous.

"Yeah." She held up her broken heel. "Just a minor wardrobe malfunction."

His smile bloomed fully now. Annie was still trying to reconcile the cartoon drawing, the ridiculous bio, and the most cynical book she'd ever read with the specimen parked in front of her apartment.

Because he didn't look like a cartoon or ridiculous, and that grin was anything but cynical. Wes Hartley wasn't how she pictured the hero of *Down This Road*. But he'd created the character and had all but admitted the book was autobiographical fiction. Still, there was the hint of something butterfly-like in her belly, and she wanted to tell the little buggers to knock it the hell off.

A leather jacket, gray pants, boots, and a body atop a Harley hadn't found their way into her fantasies before today. The heroes she read about were steadfast and reliable. She could tell just by looking at Wes—from knowing he'd fled Chicago the first chance he got—that he was more of a drifter. After all, Jeremy had told her Wes had just shown up out of the blue looking for a place to stay—unsure about when he'd leave again. But maybe tonight she could throw expectation out the window and just enjoy the view. This was not the boy she barely knew in high school. This was—a man.

A gorgeous man smiling at *her*.

She let herself study him more carefully now after spending all of Thursday night trying to avert her eyes. He was definitely taller than he was as a freshman in high school. And she didn't remember his ass filling out a pair of pants like that a decade ago, not that she'd even noticed said body part back then and *not* that she was examining it now as he hopped off the bike.

"Hey, Annie," he said. "It's good to see you again."

She rummaged through her closet, not sure what she was looking for. Annie wasn't a three-inch heels kind of girl, but tonight she wanted to be. The shoes were perfect for the dress, not that she was one to brag, but holy smokes her legs in those shoes… Brynn had insisted she try them on, and once she did, Annie was sure she'd never take them off. Seeing as she wasn't the most graceful in the inaugural donning of the pumps, though, she wiped the impractical thought from her mind.

"Gotta admit, I'm partial to the boots."

She fell from her careful squat to her ass at the door of her closet, an ankle-high black moto boot dangling from her fingertips, the other half of the pair already next to her on the floor.

His leather jacket hung open to reveal a snug-in-all-the-right-places white oxford, a navy tie hanging over the buttons.

"Sorry it's not a proper suit," he added, and the hairs on the back of her neck stood at the sound of his deep voice. Wes Hartley did not have that voice when he was fourteen. "Didn't bring much with me from New York."

Annie still sat on the floor, eyes volleying from the boot in her outstretched hand to the man in her bedroom doorway whose caramel waves seemed unruffled by the helmet he'd recently worn.

The man.

Her little brother's pre-pubescent best friend wasn't just a breakout debut author who kept himself well-hidden on social media. He was all grown up with…with this *voice,* and a motorcycle, and a five o'clock shadow she hoped he'd never shave off.

She cleared her throat.

"You were supposed to wait out there," she said, pointing with her boot. "Not watch me epically fail at finding anything close to the sexy that were those pumps." Her hand flew to her mouth. "I didn't mean sexy."

He grinned.

"Okay, I meant sexy," she added. "But not for *you*."

This time he raised a brow, and Annie groaned.

"So that maybe sounded worse. I didn't mean—"

She somehow stood without exposing her bottom half, despite the short skirt. She stepped into the boot that had been sitting on the floor, then lowered herself to her bed so she could slip on the one that was in her hand.

Wes held out a hand. Annie took it and stood, reminding herself over and over again that despite the decade that had somehow sprouted up between them, he was still her *little* brother's *little* friend, she hated his book, and he didn't even own a suit.

Okay that last one was a stretch, but her current frame of mind needed stretching.

"Take it from me," he said. "The boots are infinitely sexier than the heels."

Annie narrowed her eyes at him and stood.

"You have to say that. It's in the rule book."

Wes's brows furrowed, and she bit down on her lip, hard. If she wasn't worried about the swelling, she might have drawn blood.

"The pity date rule book," she said. "See? This is why I'm going to kill Doug and Dan. You don't even know the rules."

He laughed. The situation should have made her angry, but instead she laughed, too.

Wes stepped forward. He gripped her by the shoulders,

spun her 180 degrees, and zipped her dress so her back was no longer exposed.

Her breathing grew shallow, and she could hear Wes's do the same. His hand rested against her neck, and a current passed through them, from the tips of his fingers to the depths of her toes.

"It's not a pity date if I don't pity you," he said quietly, his voice rough.

He let out a breath, and she felt the warmth of it against her skin.

She spun to face him now, which was definitely a mistake. Because the boy who was now a man was also so close she could smell him, a mixture of outside and the clean crispness that was his cologne.

Crap. Were his eyes always that blue?

"You *want* to go to this wedding with me?"

He nodded. "Is that so surprising?"

She pursed her lips. "*You* are sorta surprising," she said. "Not exactly what I expected."

"You know there's a saying. Never judge a man by his book."

She threw her hand over her mouth. "Jeremy *told* you?"

He laughed. "He didn't tell *you* that he told me?"

She shook her head. "I'm going to kill him. God. Just when I think he's finally a grown-up, he acts like the same little shit he was in high school." She groaned.

"It's okay not to like my book, Annie."

But she could hear a challenge in those words.

"I know."

"But I bet I can prove you wrong," he said. And there it was. The challenge.

"You won't." She held her ground. "So if that's the only reason you came tonight—to try to change my opinion of your book—you should probably go."

He leaned in close, his lips an inch from hers, and her throat bobbed.

"Do you *want* me to go, Annie?"

The logical answer would have been *yes.* But she shook her head.

"I don't want you to go," she said, and he relaxed into a smile.

"That's good. Because I didn't want you to want me to go."

She backhanded him on the shoulder and let out a small laugh.

"I'm not riding your bike in this dress, though. That part is non-negotiable."

He nodded.

"Does that mean other things *are* negotiable?"

Heat spread through her. Were they flirting this quickly? That was flirting, right? Because she was suddenly thinking of what the terms of their negotiation would be, and that only made the heat grow—hotter.

Annie shrugged, wondering if he believed her nonchalance. She balled her hands into fists, then spread her palms flat against the skirt of her dress, making sure they were dry.

"I'd say that question is a bit too loaded to answer. How about we cross that bridge when we get to it?"

He held out his elbow, and she hooked her arm through it.

"Cross it, jump right off it, burn it. None of it really matters."

Annie grabbed her jacket and led him toward the apartment's front door, down the steps, and out to where his bike was parked at the curb.

"You were going to drive me there on *that*?" she asked but didn't wait for a response. "In this dress and the heels I should have had on and—"

He was doing it again. The smiling and the looking sexy and— *Stop having thoughts you shouldn't be having about people you shouldn't be thinking about.*

But it was too late. In the span of ten minutes, she'd gone from cursing the day to a feeling of lightness she hadn't expected.

Wes was unexpected, too.

"I would have been fine going to this thing on my own," she said.

"I know." He grinned. "But now you might actually have a good time."

She snorted. "You have a very high opinion of yourself. Don't you?"

He shrugged as they stopped in front of a small sedan parked a few spots down.

"You will, too...eventually," he said, and she laughed.

"Is that the happy ending to your story tonight, Mr. Hartley?"

She opened the passenger side and ushered for him to climb in.

"You already know I don't believe in those," he said as he sank into the seat.

She closed the door and made her way to the driver's side.

No, she reminded herself. *He didn't.*

Chapter Seven

"So," Wes said, deciding conversation was the best distraction for the hour-long drive. "How are we going to play this?"

Annie's eyes narrowed. "Explain yourself, please."

He shifted in his seat to face her and took a steadying breath. Even her profile was beautiful, her red hair against her milk-white skin. He had the sudden urge to tuck her hair behind her ear, but he kept himself in check by fidgeting with the radio controls.

"I mean, Doug and Dan know this is an impromptu date—situation—whatever you want to call it. But they sorta seemed like it would have been awkward for you to come alone?"

She groaned. "I thought you said you didn't pity me."

He laughed. "I don't. I was just wondering who you wanted to say I was. A friend? Your new boyfriend? Your little brother's squirrely buddy who hitched a ride?"

She backhanded him on the shoulder.

"Celebrity guest?"

She laughed hard and loud. "Do you really think of

yourself like that? I don't know, Mr. Hartley. You've changed quite a bit since you were that squirrely freshman."

He leaned against the door and crossed his arms. "And you think you knew me then."

She shrugged. "Maybe not, but I know enough to know you weren't…" She waved him off. "…*this.*"

"Charming?" he asked.

"No."

"Talented?"

"No."

"Ridiculously good looking?" He made his best attempt at a smolder.

"*No!*" she yelled, but her pale cheeks grew pink, and he grinned.

"Look, all I'm saying is that we should have a story if anyone asks. That way you can shut people down as soon as they start questioning why you're not with—"

"Brett," she said, wrinkling her nose.

"He's an idiot," Wes said, his eyes intent on her.

But she shook her head. "You don't know that. It just wasn't—we weren't right, is all. It's fine."

Annie swerved to avoid the remnants of a blown-out tire on the highway, and Wes instinctively gripped the handle above the passenger door. Maybe he should have thought twice about an hour in a car with an unfamiliar driver.

A soft thump sounded on the floor in the backseat.

"Shit," Annie said. "I probably lost my place."

Wes reached back and grabbed the fallen item off the floor—a hardcover book. He laughed softly.

"What?"

He could hear the defense in her tone.

"Nothing," he said, shaking his head. "I just get it now."

She narrowed her eyes but, thankfully, kept them on the road. "Get *what*?"

He held up the book, tapping his finger against the almost kissing couple on the cover.

"This," he said. "This is why you hated my book. You like fantasy. I like reality."

A muscle ticked in her jaw. "Let me guess. You're going to mansplain romance to me now? Your book is not a romance."

"I know," he said, matter-of-factly.

"Yeah, but everyone thinks it is. Reviewers call it a love story, and critics refer to Ethan as a romantic hero, and I don't hear you disparaging that."

He laughed and dropped the book onto his lap. "Publicity is publicity. If it sells my books, who am I to knock it?"

Her jaw tightened again. "But you'll knock it in private?"

He lifted a boot onto the dash and clasped his hands behind his head. "I'm not knocking anything. You have a right to like what you like, and I have a right to write what I write. I'm just saying that one is make-believe and the other is real life."

She gritted her teeth. "You know what? I've got our story. For the wedding. I'm here alone. Doug and Dan invited you. I've never seen you before in my life."

"*Annie*," he said, but he got distracted as she exited the highway. Wes's eyes widened as they pulled into the Central Illinois town of Bliss. They moved slowly down the small town's main street, The Aisle. And he finally felt in control enough to relax.

"This is real, right?" Annie asked, the anger ebbing from her tone. "Like, we're not on a movie set or anything?"

He shook his head. The street was lined with bridal shops, some of them even still open on a Saturday evening.

"Is that a— ?"

"Wedding cake? Uh, yeah. Doug and Dan were not kidding about this place," Annie said as they neared the end of the street. "That is a ginormous statue of a wedding cake."

"Monument," Wes corrected. "Sorry. It's just, statues are usually people, and monuments are more symbolic to memorialize—"

Her eyes were back on the road, but Annie's lips were pursed like she was keeping herself from saying something.

"Sorry," Wes said. "About that—and the book stuff, too. I kind of turn into an asshole when I'm nervous," he admitted.

She smiled. "You're nervous?" she asked, turning down a side street before she plowed right into the mammoth wedding cake.

He nodded, then chuckled as they passed a bar called Suckers. "Yeah. I get that way when I'm with a beautiful woman surrounded by bridal shops and giant wedding cakes." He said this just as they pulled up to the valet of a quaint five-story hotel with whitewashed brick and arched windows called Blissful Nights.

Annie lowered her window as a parking attendant came to the door.

"Will you be staying overnight, miss?" the young man asked.

"Overnight?" Annie asked, then paused.

Wes froze midway from stepping out of the passenger side. He didn't dare look her way, though. The drive was long enough to warrant it yet short enough to make it back to the city if they wanted. Annie hadn't mentioned an overnight stay, and he hadn't noticed a bag or suitcase or any indication that she'd planned on it, either.

"*Un*...decided," she said, and he heard her open her door.

He exited the vehicle and tried not to grin.

Jeremy was going to kill him.

His gut twisted.

When he'd told him about Doug and Dan's wedding invitation, his friend had laughed.

"God, you must be hard-up for a night out," he'd said. "But hey, all the power to ya if Annie agreed to take you. She was pretty let down about going alone, so despite her *intense* dislike of your *New York Times* bestseller, I'm glad Doug and Dan convinced her to say yes. Sometimes my sister lets her pride get in the way of other people's good intentions, but that's exactly what she needs right now. Just, you know, keep your *researching* hands off her."

Wes scratched the back of his neck and made eye contact with the guy behind the reception's open bar.

"Two red wines," he said, then turned to look over his shoulder to where Annie was talking to some friends. She stood out from the crowd, and not just because of the boots or her beautiful, coppery hair. Annie had this energy about her that brightened the room. She felt things passionately, even if what she felt was intense dislike for his book. He laughed. Maybe he'd been in the dark too long. Or maybe he'd just never known a light like hers existed, but all he wanted was for her to shine some of it his way.

He'd told Jeremy he was escorting Annie with only the best of intentions, but what did it say that he was already thinking about kissing her? He couldn't decide where this urge was coming from. Was it teenage him wanting to realize some fantasy he thought would never come true? Achieve the unattainable and prove to fourteen-year-old Wes that someday he *would* be something more? Or was it the usual—a challenge that he willed himself to conquer? In this case, charm the pants off a woman who wasn't a fan of his work.

He watched as Annie slipped her clutch under her arm so she could give a friend a hug. Her eyes crinkled at the corners, and her smile lit up her entire face. It was like her physical features weren't enough to contain the unbridled affection she had for those who meant something to her.

No. Kissing her wouldn't be proving anything to the past. It would be all about now—about doing what it took to make a girl smile like that for him. To make *that* girl smile for him.

"Your wines, sir."

But when he returned to her side, her smile was gone and her eyes no longer crinkled. The clutch was back in her hand, but her arms were crossed over her chest now as she pressed her mouth into a thin line, one he could tell she was trying to pass off as a smile to the guy facing her.

Wes had enough exes to guess that Annie was most likely in the midst of an encounter with one of her own. He took a chance on his hunch.

"Hey, babe," he said, nudging her shoulder with his. "Got your favorite." He hoped she'd play along.

"Thanks, *sweetheart*," she said as he handed her the wine, her expression relaxing. He wasn't sure yet if she was rolling with it or if she was pissed. But he decided to keep going.

The guy opposite Annie scoffed and glared at Wes.

"Right. If you knew her, you'd have a White Russian in your hand right now."

Wes stifled another laugh, but a small snort escaped. "Right," he said. "Because Annie's *The Dude*. Good thing I made her swap the bathrobe for the dress."

Annie tipped the glass against her lips and took a long, slow sip.

"That was *your* favorite drink, Brett. I drank it because you liked it. I don't think you ever asked me what my favorite drink was."

Her tone was even, no hint of anger. She was just telling it like it was, but Wes's jaw tightened nonetheless. How could someone not care what Annie liked?

The guy—Brett—sputtered, but before he could say anything, a woman sidled up next to him. Wes thought he might have recognized her from the bookstore the other night, but she hadn't been in his signing line. He would have remembered someone who bounced on her toes while everyone else stood still. She beamed at Brett but seemed to avoid looking Annie in the eye.

"What are you doing here?" Annie asked under her breath.

He shrugged. "Tabby and I are sort of seeing each other now. Doug and Dan invited her, so — "

The blond woman tugged at Brett's arm. Annie whirled to face her.

"*You're* seeing Brett?"

Wes put a hand on Annie's arm. "Hey," he said softly. "What am I missing here?"

She squared her shoulders. "What you're *missing* is a proper introduction. Wes, this is Brett, my very recent ex, and this is Tabitha. My employee."

Tabitha held her head high and looked Annie square in the eyes. "I was invited to the wedding, too."

Annie opened her mouth to say something but no words came out. Wes guessed there'd probably been some overlap between Brett's relationship with Annie and whatever he was doing with Tabitha. Annie, most likely, was thinking the same thing.

"*I* want to try a White Russian," Tabitha said, then pulled hard enough that Brett lost his footing and stumbled in the direction of the bar.

"We'll catch up later, Annie? We should talk." His voice held a hint of pleading.

Wes's gaze volleyed between the two of them until he couldn't take it anymore. He cradled the back of her head in his palm and whispered, "Slap me or play along. Either way it'll be worth it."

He dipped his head toward hers, and when she didn't

pull away, he turned a high school fantasy into reality. It was just a small kiss, his lips softly brushing hers, but there was no mistaking the hitch in Annie's breath when he pulled away. Or the way his heart threatened to burst free from his rib cage if he didn't get his shit together.

He turned toward Brett and the blonde staring at him and Annie, their mouths hanging open in small *O*s.

"I think she's gonna be busy later," Wes said, then turned to Annie to see if the act was still going.

She nodded and cleared her throat. "Yeah. Busy. I'm busy, but I hope you and Tabitha have a great night." She drained the rest of her wine and set the glass on a passing server's tray. Then she grabbed Wes by the hand and led him into the ballroom. "Let's find our table, *sweetheart*."

He raised a brow and pushed back any thoughts of how he ended up here. Jeremy had entrusted him to be a good friend tonight, and Wes could argue that by kissing her he had done exactly that. Jeremy would most likely win the argument, *probably* with a fist to Wes's face, but it would be worth it. If that kiss was all he ever got from Annie Denning, he'd risk the fallout just for the memory of it.

"What *is* your favorite drink?" he asked once the other couple had gone.

She took a sip from her glass. "This is really good, actually. I'm usually with Brynn, which means Kingston's, which means my only choices are what Jamie has on tap. And I like beer. Don't get me wrong. But this is nice. Being asked what I like is—well, it's new to me, I guess."

"No one should ever take what you want for granted, Annie. A man who'd do that sure as hell doesn't deserve someone like you."

Her cheeks flushed. "You're not changing my mind about your book through flattery."

He laughed quietly to himself. He'd almost forgotten

about the book. And her hating it.

Almost.

Annie checked their table card and weaved through the room until they found table #14. Wes narrowed his eyes and cocked his head.

"Is that an ice sculpture of—?"

Annie nodded. "The happy couple? Yeah, Doug and Dan go all out."

Wes marveled at the ice couple. Each table seemed to have them in a different pose. Theirs had one groom dipping the other as if they were Fred and Ginger. One table over had the two grooms bowling, of all things.

"They're in a super competitive league," Annie said, following his gaze. She dropped her clutch onto one of the chairs and spun to face him, her hand covering her mouth as she giggled.

"So, I guess we've got our story, huh?" she asked.

The corner of his mouth quirked into a grin.

"Depends. Does this story include me getting to kiss you again?"

"That sounds like a line from your book."

He untwined his fingers from hers, crossing his arms over his chest.

"You mean the book you hated, right? Yeah, maybe it is, but I can't help it. I write those lines. Sometimes reality bleeds into fiction. Sometimes it's the opposite. Either way, I'll try to keep it from happening again."

Shit. Talk about poking a festering wound. He hadn't realized her thoughts on his book had mattered that much to him until now. Convincing her otherwise seemed like a fun game at first, but the more he realized he enjoyed being in Annie Denning's presence, the more her opinion of him took effect.

"So, that would be me being an asshole again. This is the

part where I apologize. Again."

But she didn't give him a chance to explain further.

"Look," she said. "There's a speech somewhere in here about starting off on the wrong foot or whatever, but the truth is quite simple. Despite my feelings about your book—and your skewed opinion of the romance genre in general—I had a fun drive. And that kiss back there?" She blushed, and the sight made his chest tighten. "I like you, Wes. I don't mean I want a relationship or anything. I mean, shit. I just showed up to a wedding to find out my ex was probably messing around with my employee when he decided coming here with *me* was too much of a commitment. I'd say my own date would be smart to sneak away and ditch this craziness when I'm not looking." She paused for a couple of long breaths, then shrugged. "I come with way more baggage than someone needs for *one* date. *Not* that this is a date. Because it's not. A date, I mean."

He smiled. Nope. This wasn't a date. But it was pretty damn adorable that she was worried he'd want to bail, especially after letting his bruised ego butt into the conversation.

He shoved his hands in the front pockets of his pants.

"This *isn't* a date," he said. "Because your brother would probably murder me if it was."

She snorted, her auburn waves bouncing against her chin, a few strands sticking to her ruby red lips—lips he was dying to kiss again.

He snuck his hand behind those strands, skimming his fingers across her cheek in order to tuck them behind her ear.

"This is so. Not. A date," he said, softer this time, his voice growing hoarse.

She shook her head. His hand still rested on her neck.

"But we can pretend it is," he added. "For the sake of the ex, I mean."

Annie bit her bottom lip and grinned.

"What's in it for you?" she asked.

Being here with you.

"A story," he said instead. "I've uh—I mean, I've been—"

Okay, so this was harder to say out loud. Like speaking the words would actually make them real. But the truth was, the only thing that made this real was his inability to do anything else.

"Writer's block," he admitted. "I haven't written anything worth passing on to my editor in *months*. And if I don't get her fifty pages by Monday, well—I'm gonna be a one-hit wonder. Being here, I can observe humanity in all its basest forms because, let's face it, weddings bring out a certain kind of crazy in everyone."

She nodded. "Agreed—like that crazy kiss."

"So what if we make a story tonight?" he asked. "One for you to tell and one for me to write? Everything is fiction, which means no matter what happens, I'm not violating guy code or anything, and you're not jumping into any sort of rebound situation."

She took a step closer, and he inhaled the warm scent of vanilla and, maybe, a hint of cinnamon? He'd been too caught up in the moment to notice before. But now he began to feel drunk, wondering if one glass of wine could knock him on his ass. But he knew it couldn't have. It was this woman.

He swallowed hard, his throat suddenly dry.

"Jesus you smell good, Annie."

She leaned closer. Because apparently she was trying to kill him.

"What would the line be—if you wrote it in your book? How would you describe my scent?"

Uh, he could describe the agony of the erection straining against his pants, but somehow he thought she wouldn't appreciate that.

Christ. Words. She wanted words, now? After he told her

he was blocked? But he had to prove his plan would work, that they could use this evening—and each other—to their advantage and neither of them be worse for the wear.

Fine. Words. The girl wanted words, so he would deliver.

"He grew drunk," Wes said. "Drunk on the nearness of her, on the warm, sweet scent of home. Because that's what she was to him. She was *home*. And until he kissed her, he hadn't known what that meant. Home wasn't a place. It was a state of mind. It was her, the intoxicating scent of her skin, and his lips pressed against it."

He hadn't realized until he spoke the last of it that his eyes were closed. Maybe hers were, too, because she wasn't saying anything. All he heard was her sharp, shallow breaths. All he felt was his forehead pressed to hers. How the hell did they get here?

"I think your writer's block might be cured," she whispered. "That was way more romantic than an ice sculpture."

Wes laughed softly.

"I don't write romance," he said.

"Whatever," she countered, but she was still smiling.

"How about your ex situation? That cured yet, or do we want to give them more of a show?"

She cleared her throat. "I think the jury's still out."

Okay. They were on the same page—so to speak. He wanted this night, whatever ended up happening, and Annie seemed on the verge of jumping off this cliff with him.

He straightened and took a step back so his eyes could find hers. She chewed her bottom lip.

"One night, Annie. Whatever you want out of this evening, I'm your guy. And when we go home tonight—"

"Tomorrow," she said, and Wes's brows drew together. "When we go home—*tomorrow*…"

In his head, he had just run to the top of the steps leading to the Philadelphia Museum of Art—the Rocky Steps—and pumped his fists in the air. But Annie wouldn't know that.

He nodded slowly, making sure not to betray his thoughts with any movement that might seem too eager.

"It's—"

But she didn't let him finish.

"It's not a date. I know. Neither of us wants that. But I want a night without rules. A night where I don't have to worry what comes next. Just fun, Wes. That's all I want. I'd resigned myself to believing this night would amount to nothing more than an abundance of wine and possibly sleeping like a starfish in a king-size bed if I spent the night."

Wes scrubbed a hand across his jaw. "You can still do both of those things," he said.

She bit her lip again. He'd have to warn her soon that if she wanted to drive him mad right here in the ballroom, she only had to do that a couple more times. But like Rocky on the steps, he could write this scene the way he wanted it to go, so he offered her an easy grin.

Annie leaned forward and cupped her hand over his ear. He felt her warm breath on his skin before she spoke.

"I plan on it," she whispered. "But I also plan on doing a lot more before I pass out in that bed."

He swallowed hard, his laid-back facade disintegrating.

"Stay with me tonight," she said. "You write your story. And I'll write mine."

"But Jer—"

"He doesn't have to know," she said. "Tomorrow we head back to the city and go our separate ways. You don't have to worry about any sort of bro code or whatever. I'm not looking for anything beyond tonight, and neither are you, right?"

On any other day he would have been quick to answer. But he hesitated. He hesitated because he was violating his best friend's wishes. He hesitated because something about being with Annie made him want to think beyond tonight.

But who was he kidding? Girls like Annie Denning knew better than to get involved with an emotional mess like him. The women he dated wanted to fix him even though they knew they'd never succeed. It was the game they played. But he wouldn't play that game with Annie.

"Okay, then," he said.

She beamed at him.

"Okay."

Chapter Eight

She'd made it through dinner and had taken ample photos of the ice sculptures and general decor for a blog post later. Doug and Dan were kind enough to *not* seat them with Tabitha and Brett. That was either some really intelligent forethought on Doug and Dan's part or just plain luck. Either way, Annie was grateful. But the out-of-town older cousins they dined with were a boozy bunch, having already depleted both the red and white wine.

She turned to Wes, interrupting his conversation with Cousin Gary about whether or not his book was anything like that *Fifty Shades* they'd turned into a movie.

"Actually," Wes was saying, "I do have a producer interested in *Down This Road*, but I don't think it'll be quite like that *Fifty Shades.*"

"I'm gonna head to the bar," she interrupted. "Want anything?"

She stood and rested a hand on his shoulder.

"I'll—I'll come with you," he insisted, eyes wide and pleading. But Annie couldn't help herself.

"No, no. You stay." She patted him gently on the back, then leaned in close to whisper in his ear. "I think Gary has more questions, and I wouldn't want you to miss a single one." She straightened and winked at him, and he mouthed, *You owe me.*

She laughed as she backed away. She did, in a way—owe him, that is. Now that she thought about it, it was really thoughtful of him to come here at the grooms' request. She'd read the stupid book, so yeah, she knew Wes Hartley had no trouble finding a woman to spend an evening with. And judging by the decidedly female crowd on Thursday night, he probably didn't have to do much looking as it seemed like they simply flocked right to him.

The other man nodded eagerly, his comb-over threatening to go back to where it came from with every tilt of his head.

"Heck yeah, I've got more questions!" He slapped Wes on the knee, and the poor guy's shoulders slumped as he admitted defeat.

"Something strong," he called after her. Then he raised his brows.

She stifled a grin and weaved in and out of the path of tables until she finally made it to the bar.

"Great," she mumbled under her breath. "A line."

The woman in front of her spun on a silver stiletto to face her. Correction, to tower over her with her long, willowy frame. Severe black bangs hung just above her equally dark brows, and she smiled at Annie with bold painted lips and teeth that were a perfect white.

"Open bar," she said, her voice throaty and deep, tongue rolling on the *R*. "Always a line with the open bar."

Was that a Russian accent? Good God, it made her throaty voice even sexier than it would have been on its own. Though she sucked at mimicking them, Annie adored accents. She felt it came in handy in her line of work—which was basically reading. Every voice of every character she'd ever read had its own place in her imagination, replete with accents. This woman's was going in her repertoire for later use.

"I do love an open bar," Annie said with a smile.

The woman's brows furrowed beneath her bangs.

"I have seen you tonight, yes? You are here with the author, Wes Hartley? I hear the grooms are fans."

Okay, so maybe referring to himself as a celebrity guest wasn't really off the mark. Still. *Ego.*

"Um, yes," Annie said. "I take it you've read his book?"

She scoffed out a laugh, which made Annie flinch.

"Of course I have read it, darling. I *am* chapter six."

No. Annie cleared her throat. "You're...Natasha—the model Ethan meets in his photography class who agrees to be the subject of his final project?"

The woman laughed again and bent down to kiss Annie on both cheeks.

"Oksana. He does not use the real names in his book of *fiction*," she said. Then her lips curled up.

For a second Annie felt light-headed, even though she'd cleaned her plate of salmon, green beans, and mashed potatoes because she was squeezing every penny out of this evening. And that included the open bar.

"Do you...live in Chicago?" she asked, but Oksana shook her head.

"Paris. Milan. But my agency has me stationed in New York. The groom, though, Douglas—he is my cousin on my father's side—*Ublyudok.*"

Annie's brows pulled together.

"Sorry," Oksana said. "Bastard. My father, he is a bastard. But what were we discussing?"

"Can I help you ladies?"

Oksana pivoted toward the bar where there was no longer a line, just the bartender dressed in a white tux waiting for their order.

"Give us two shots of vodka, but don't tell me the brand. Nothing you have in your open bar is truly Russian. I will just pretend."

"Oh, I don't drink hard—"

Oksana slapped her hand on the top of the bar.

"*Na zdorovie!*"

She handed a shot glass to Annie, who shrugged.

"When in Rome," she said, raising her glass. "Or—when in Chicago with a Russian, I guess."

"*Na zdorovie,*" Oksana said again, slower this time, so Annie assumed she was supposed to repeat.

"Nose...diving?" Annie said. Ugh. She sucked at foreign language as much as she sucked at accents.

"Good enough."

Oksana tossed back her shot and didn't even flinch.

Annie followed suit.

And then thought she should probably call 911 because there was a fire—in her tonsils. But shit if she didn't leave her phone at the table, so she had to go with plan B.

She reached over the bar, ignoring the bartender's shout of *What the hell are you doing?* and grabbed the soda gun from its holster. Not bothering to check which button she pressed, Annie aimed the gun at her open mouth and sprayed.

Hmmm...Sprite. Good choice.

And thank the freaking stars for the chilled liquid to soothe her burning throat. Mission impossible? No way. More like mission accomplished. Except now she was standing there with soda dribbling down her chin and Oksana and bartender guy staring at her wide-eyed.

Annie grabbed a cocktail napkin from the bar and cleaned off her face. Then she gingerly offered the soda gun back to the guy who was licensed to use it.

"A red wine, please?" she asked as he re-holstered the

device. "Oh, and maybe some of whatever that vodka was on the rocks."

He narrowed his eyes at her, and she crossed her arms over her chest.

"Not for *me,* mister. My date said he wanted something strong, and I can verify that the vodka is, in fact, strong."

Oksana snorted, the first unmodel-like thing she'd done so far.

"Enjoy your date," she said with a sly grin.

Drinks in hand, Annie took a step back toward the tables and dance floor and her *so* not-a-date companion. "Wait!" Annie said, stopping mid step.

The woman raised her perfectly arched brows.

"Why don't you come back to the table and say hello? I'm sure Wes would—"

Oksana tilted her head toward the ceiling and laughed. "You are sweet, but no. That is not his way. He gets what he needs for his story, and then he has nothing left to give back."

"So—he's a *jerk,*" Annie said. She should congratulate herself for being right, for assuming Wes *was* his main character, and having the fact so easily corroborated. But her chest felt tight. The guy in the car—the one enduring drunk Cousin Gary's questions at their table—he was funny. And charming. And okay, *really* easy on the eyes. It didn't add up, and Annie's eyes widened as she realized she didn't want it to. Oksana smiled, and there was nothing sly or knowing or remotely model-like in the expression. It was real. Annie was sure of it.

"The passion is there when he is creating art. He dabbled in photography—with me. But when the project was over, he put the walls back up." She shook her head. "He is lost," she said. "At least that is what he was when I knew him. Does being lost make you a jerk sometimes? Yes, of course. But you go back to your table, and you look at him. Ask yourself if he will be the jerk to you, and if the answer is yes, then you either run the other way or know what you're getting into and suffer the consequences."

Annie sighed. She was already planning to run the other way, but for tonight she wanted to believe he wouldn't treat her like that—as just another page in his book.

Oksana sighed. "You cannot find the man who wants to stay lost," she said. And with that, she walked away.

Annie felt like this was some weird, other dimension sort of place where it was virtually raining exes.

So Wes had an ex-girlfriend. Who was a gorgeous, exotic model. And was represented by a whole chapter of his book.

No big deal, right? It's not like Annie hadn't just run into her own ex as well. The odds of this sort of thing happening weren't exactly in their favor, but it wouldn't ruin the evening, right? Just for one night, she wanted what Wes called fantasy—the happily ever after. Was it so strange to think that he could give it to her? She wasn't trying to find Wes if he was, in fact, lost. Because there he was, at the crazy cousin's table, still talking to Gary, except now Wes was wildly gesticulating and grinning like the most adorable goofball she'd ever seen.

"Here you go, sweetheart," she said, offering him the rocks glass as she took up residence in her seat again. "And speaking of *sweethearts*..." she said, her voice teasing as Wes excused himself from Cousin Gary to face her.

He lifted his drink to his lips and took a long sip. "I see we both have some...*old friends* at the wedding tonight. Do Doug and Dan know everyone?"

She nodded. "They really do. But I want to talk about who *you* know," she said.

He shrugged. "Ask me anything you want."

Annie pouted. "That's no fun. You're supposed to be closed off and evasive."

He laughed. "I've been known to be both." He leaned

forward and spoke softly so only she could hear. "But for you I'm an open book."

Her breath hitched. "Maybe you should go say hello to her," she said, despite Oksana wanting nothing to do with him.

"I should," he said. "It would be the non-closed-off and non-evasive thing to do. Wouldn't it?" He stood from the table and brought his drink with him. "I'll be right back, and when I return—*you*, beautiful, are dancing with me."

She swallowed and nodded as he slipped away to do what she rationalized as the gentlemanly thing in saying hello to a former lover.

She shook her head and laughed to herself. Her story tonight did not end with jealousy. It ended with a man who'd just told her the barriers were down for her tonight. They'd be back up in the morning. She was sure of it.

She watched as Wes found Oksana a few tables from the bar and kissed her on the cheek. His eye caught hers, and she quickly turned away as if he hadn't just busted her staring. After a few seconds, she couldn't take it, and she glanced his way again. Oksana's back was to her, but Wes faced her head on, looking past his ex and straight at her.

A lost man who does not want to be found, she reminded herself. Nope. Not trying to find anyone at all. Annie was just here to have fun without expectations. That was all Wes Hartley had to offer, so tonight it would be enough.

Chapter Nine

Wes had sipped his vodka slowly, so much so that it was now mostly water from the melted ice. But he wanted to stay in as much control as possible. Even more, he wanted to remember. He'd already typed a note into his phone recreating the line he'd given Annie about how fucking good she smelled.

Here was the thing, though. It wasn't a line. Something about being with her—about the familiarity of someone who knew him before he was this caricature of himself—was freeing. Well, except for her hating his book, but he could tuck that away for the night, for the girl he twirled in his arms before she spun back to face him, her free hand finding his shoulder. His landed on the small of her back.

"So," he said. "You're cool with the whole Oksana situation?"

Annie shrugged.

"You're cool with the whole *Brett* situation?"

He nodded.

"The only thing I almost wasn't cool with was the beautiful woman who'd left me to fend for myself with

Cousin Gary. Luckily, the guy was fascinating. Did you know he has issues of *Cranes* magazine dating back six years? And I don't mean *Craines*, like the Chicago business news mag. I'm talking skyscraper building, lift-a-car-into-the-air-with-a-giant-magnet cranes. The guy fucking loves cranes."

Now her eyes narrowed into slits. And her lips pursed into something between a pout and possibly the initiation of a kiss. Shit, he wanted to kiss her again.

Annie cleared her throat. "Right. I'm glad that worked out so well for you."

She relaxed back into their movement on the dance floor, and Wes pulled her closer. He dipped his head so his lips brushed her hair just above her ear.

"Gary was a good enough tablemate, but don't think for a second that I didn't watch you walk away. I'm not sure if you realize this, Annie, but I have a hard time taking my eyes off you."

She laughed softly, and he could see the goose bumps peppering her arms.

"You didn't…watch me the whole time I was over there, did you?" she asked.

"Hmm," he said. "Would have been rude to ignore Gary like that just to see you shoot yourself with a soda gun."

She gasped and took a step back.

"It's because your *Bond* girl made me drink vodka, and I *don't* do hard alcohol. I'm a beer and wine girl. Period. But the vodka burned, Wes. It freaking *burned.*"

He tried hard not to laugh, but it was a losing battle. And soon they were laughing together and making their way off the dance floor. Thankfully, Gary and the gang were still cutting footloose. So Wes collapsed happily into the seat next to Annie.

Annie chugged a glass of water and then gave him a pointed look.

"What?" he asked.

She pursed her lips. "So, I didn't realize how much of your book was autobiographical fiction. I mean, I know what you said about *research* and whatever at the signing. It was just—interesting to hear it firsthand."

She drew out that last word, and Wes exhaled a long breath.

"Is that a hint of judgment I hear?" he asked, a brow raised.

She groaned. "You're right. I'm sorry. It's not any of my business. Especially not after—"

"You told me you hate my book?" he completed. He grabbed his untouched glass of water from the table and drank it down until there was nothing left but the ice hitting his nose. Why did one person's opinion seem to matter so much when there were hundreds of thousands who felt otherwise?

When his eyes met hers again, her arms were crossed and her head was cocked to the side. She looked at him like he was a new species at a zoo exhibit.

"I was going to say it wasn't my business, *especially* not after you've been the perfect gentleman all night—coming to my rescue when Brett and Tabitha showed up and, well, coming to this wedding in the first place. I'm not sure you understand what it meant to Doug and Dan that you said yes."

"I'm more interested in what it means to you."

The corner of his mouth quirked up. The rest of the evening hinged on this—on her not caring about autobiographical fiction—on him being able to let go of the fact that this great girl who wanted to spend the night with him *hated* his life's work. Annie lifted her hand slowly and let it fall softly on his cheek. On instinct he turned and kissed her palm.

"What was that for?" she asked.

"Reflex? Teen me living out a fantasy? Because I couldn't *not* kiss you? Take your pick."

She leaned forward but stopped before she was close enough to do whatever it was she was about to do. Wes turned and looked over his shoulder to follow her gaze.

The grooms were finishing their meet and greet with the table next to theirs and had just spun in their direction. And now they approached.

"Annie! Wes!" Doug cried.

He scooped Annie into a bear hug while Dan did the same to Wes.

"We have been telling everyone—*everyone*—that our favorite author is here. You have to let us parade you around a bit!" Dan said.

Wes laughed, and Annie whispered something into Doug's ear. The man's eyes widened.

"Get *out*!" Doug yelled, giving Wes a playful push. "Oksana is *Natasha*? I'm so going back and rereading chapter six."

Dan's eyes brightened. "I have my signed copy in the suite."

Wes shook his head. "Guys?" Both grooms turned their attention to Wes. "You're not helping me impress my date."

This time Doug pushed Annie. "Get *out*. This is, like, a real date?"

Annie shook her head. "No—I mean. I don't know." She gave Wes a pleading look.

"Okay," he said. "Should we do this parade thing you mentioned?"

Not that he wanted to leave Annie's side, but he'd do anything to change the direction of this conversation.

"Right," Dan said. "Let's go to the parents' table first so I can show my mother that big things *do* happen for coffee shop owners."

Doug hooked his arm through Dan's. "Leave it to me to find a husband with mommy issues," he said.

Dan's eyes brightened. "I will *never* get tired of you calling me that, schnoodle."

"No, *you're* schnoodle," Doug said.

"Uh-uh," Dan singsonged. "You are so, totally my schnoodle."

It was like Wes and Annie had suddenly been forgotten as the happy couple lovingly argued—emphatically, lovingly argued.

Wes followed while they did the rounds, table to table. Some well-informed guests even had paperbacks for him to sign. Then, before he knew it, he and Annie were dancing in a circle to Hava Nagila as the wedding party raised the grooms in chairs above the crowd.

He was exhausted. Spent. Yet he couldn't remember the last time he'd had so much fun. When the dance floor cleared, Annie looked at him and raised her brows. He didn't need any further encouragement. So he grabbed her hand and glanced toward the lobby. She bit her lip and nodded. "Come on, schnoodle," he said as they slipped out the ballroom doors. They both doubled over in laughter as soon as they were outside.

"Please," he said. "Please tell me you and Brett—or any guy, for that matter—were never each other's schnoodles. Because I don't think I could ever see you as a schnoodle."

She shook her head, trying to rein in the giggles, but snorted instead. This only made her laugh harder, and the sound of it was infectious, like a virus swirling through his veins. This was the most he had smiled in over a year.

"Brett didn't—" she said, then hiccupped. "He obviously didn't care for me enough for silly pet names," she added.

As quickly as it had started, the laughter between them stopped.

"Don't look at me like that," she said, backhanding him softly on the shoulder. "I already told you this isn't a pity party."

How was he looking at her? Because what he was saying in his head was *What kind of asshole didn't fall for this woman if he had the chance to?* Not that he would have the chance to, but still. He'd been with her for a couple of hours, and already he'd composed a full dictionary of endearments for her.

Okay, fine. He hadn't. But he *could*. He was a writer, after all. And he'd think of something *much* more fitting to call her than *schnoodle*. What was that, anyway? Sounded like a cross between a small, yippy dog and a fruit-topped pastry.

"You're not a *schnoodle*," he said.

He smiled softly, and she shrugged.

"I'll get my happily ever after," she said. "Maybe not with Brett in a whole town built on weddings, but it's out there." She tried but couldn't even force a smile, and Wes felt something in him crack. Maybe she'd judged his book, but he'd gone and judged her right back. Even if he didn't think love conquered all, who was he to make her feel like shit for thinking it could?

Annie Denning wasn't some high school fantasy anymore. She was real and a little broken and right here in front of him, and he wanted to tell her that he was broken, too, that love— or the lack thereof—did that to people. But she had already turned from him and was headed toward the bar.

"Emerald City," he called after her, and she stopped, her back still to him. So he strode up behind her and tucked her hair behind her ear, dipped his head, and spoke softer this time so only she would hear the rest. "That's what you should be called instead of *schnoodle*." He grinned. "Not just because I've never seen eyes more beautiful than yours but because out of all the shit life throws at us, only one guy will be lucky enough to come home to you, to his Emerald City. Everyone else would get black-and-white Kansas. But not the guy who gets you."

Christ, what the hell was he saying? He may not have

asserted himself into the scenario when he spoke it out loud, but wasn't that what he was envisioning right now? How many times was he the asshole who told a girl he wasn't commitment material, and here he was with the one girl who made him wish that he was.

Silence rolled between them for several seconds, and she still wasn't looking at him. So he waited. Whatever happened next, it was up to Annie.

"You should write that down," she finally said, still staring straight ahead. "Your readers will eat that up."

"Annie—"

He placed both hands on her shoulders and gently urged her to face him. She did.

"I mean it," she said. "The story with those words? It's a happily ever after."

"You read my book," he said, brows raised. "I don't do—"

"Right, I know," she said. "You don't do happily ever after. You wrote *one* book, though, Wes. Are you sure you want to make that sort of blanket statement this early on? Isn't there a tiny little voice in your head that has some hope?"

He chuckled. "I usually try to silence that voice."

"Why?"

"Ah, yes. The age-old question." The one everyone wanted an answer to. But what if Wes didn't have all the answers? What if he just wrote what he knew?

"Maybe I'll be your muse," she added, giving him a playful smile.

"Maybe you'll be trouble," he said.

He knew they were both avoiding any further *real* talk, now. But he didn't care. He wouldn't know how to do real, anyway. Not that it was an option with Annie. But tonight? Well, tonight they could be whatever the other needed, and where was the harm in that?

"Trouble," she said. "That's something I haven't been

called before." She grabbed his hand, lacing her fingers with his. "But I think I'd like to see what that's like." She tugged his arm and started walking toward the lobby, looking back at him as she did. "I want to go to the front desk and get my room key."

He nodded and followed, for the first time this evening at a loss for words.

We shouldn't. But he knew they both wanted to.

Jeremy would flip out. But Annie was twenty-eight years old, three years Jeremy's senior. And his, too. She could make her own decisions.

This can't go beyond tonight. That was the one he knew they both agreed on.

So he walked with her to the check-in desk and waited.

"You would like a room for one night with a king-size bed. Is that correct?" the hotel employee asked.

Annie squeezed his hand and nodded to the woman.

"That's correct."

"Checkout is at eleven, but if you'd like to extend it until one o'clock, you can do so for an extra thirty dollars. Are you interested?"

The woman looked at Annie, then Wes. Annie looked at the woman, then him. He did his best to keep his expression unreadable. This had to be her decision. He didn't want to influence her any more with his stupid notions of happily ever after. But a silent prayer or incantation or whatever you wanted to call it rang out in his head.

Yes. Say yes, Annie. Make this night last as long as humanly possible.

"Can we decide that in the morning?" she asked, and the woman behind the counter nodded.

"You can just call down and let the front desk know."

Annie let out a long breath.

"What the hell." she said. "It's thirty bucks. Put us down

for late checkout."

Wes kept quiet throughout the entire transaction and all the way to the elevator. He waited until they were inside, alone, ditching the wedding at least an hour before anyone else. But as soon as the doors closed, it was like a fuse had been lit, and if he didn't do something about it soon, he would fucking explode.

"I need to kiss you," he said. "Like, really kiss you. Before we get to the room. Because if we wait until we're behind closed doors—in that room for the night—and it's an epic disaster, I don't know if I'll recover. I need to know now."

Nervous laughter bubbled from her lips.

"You think kissing me is going to be a disaster?" she asked. "An *epic* disaster?"

He grinned and took a step closer.

"For me, Emerald City? No fucking way. Kissing *you* will be nothing short of spectacular. I have zero doubts on that front. But I want to give you the chance to make a clean getaway." He glanced at the numeric display above the door, slowly rising to five—the top floor of the hotel and the floor where Annie's room was—where *their* room could be. But he needed to give her one more chance to be sure.

"So what do you say?" he asked, closing the distance between them. "Am I gonna be as much trouble for you as you are for me?"

Chapter Ten

Seriously. Who is this guy?

Wes and Jeremy were fourteen when they started hanging out. Annie never gave him a second glance. She was a senior and he—he wasn't even shaving yet. He was her little brother's *little* friend.

A boy.

Not the man standing in front of her, at least a head taller than she was, his hand braced on the elevator wall as she leaned against the rail protruding from it. Not the man whose mouth was inches from hers, so close they were probably fighting for the oxygen molecules between them. That ridiculously sexy five o'clock shadow was enough to convince her that he had made it past puberty—and then some.

He wanted to kiss her now, right here, to make sure *she* didn't want to back out? Annie was the one leading him to her room, the one with one bed. She was the one convincing him to blow off whatever guy code existed between him and her brother for one night of whatever this was.

Either he was an example of the utmost in chivalry, or he

just wanted this as badly as she did. So why the hell wait?

She grabbed his tie just below the knot and tugged him past those last few inches.

"What do I say, Wes?" she whispered, echoing his question. "I say show me what the hell you've got."

If there was magic in words other than the ones the professionals put to paper, it was in everything he said to her tonight, and everything left unsaid yet spoken with this kiss. She felt a tender ache in her chest as his tongue slipped past her lips, his movement deliciously slow and driving her mad all at the same time. His hips pressed to her belly, and she cursed her broken shoes that would have given her the advantage of extra height. Now she moaned softly against him, rising on her toes in an attempt to slide up his hard length.

"Christ, Annie," he whispered. Then his hands were on her hips, and he was lifting her so she now sat on the small railing. There was no way she could sit there on her own, but he pushed her knees open and hiked her skirt up to the top of her thighs, holding her there with his weight, his erection firm as she throbbed against him.

"Is this what you want?"

His voice was rough in her ear, and the only thing she could do was squeak out a small *yes*.

His hand slid up her thigh, his thumb skimming the seam of her panties. *Oh God, did I wear good underwear?* Annie thought she'd had her mind made up about Wes before he'd shown up tonight, so much so that what she had on *under* her dress hadn't crossed her mind. Because no way in hell was the evening going in this direction when she'd convinced herself *he* was Ethan, the not-a-romance hero.

But now it was, and come heaven or hell, she did not want him to stop. She did, however, need to do a panty check before things went any further. But Wes's lips were on her neck, hot and full of need, and one of those thumbs had just slipped *under* the panty seam, and Annie lost her train of thought as he swirled that thumb over her wet, swollen center.

She cried out softly, thankfully quiet enough that she still heard the ding of the elevator reaching its destination.

Wes withdrew his hands so quickly that she nearly toppled off the railing, but he caught her in his arms and even had the forethought to smooth down the skirt of her dress so her—*yep*—pink, Lydia Bennet YOLO boy briefs would not be on display for all hotel patrons to see. She supposed she'd have some explaining to do later, but for now she had to focus on staying upright.

The doors opened to the fifth floor and a young couple waiting to head downstairs.

Scratch that. It wasn't just some random couple.

"Annie," Brett said, and Tabitha smiled uncomfortably beside him. "You're on the fifth floor, too? Of course."

His expression was pained, and Annie could only imagine what she and Wes looked like. Her lips felt swollen from his kisses, and her lipstick had probably gone the way of scary clown at this point. Wes's stubble had rubbed against her jaw and neck, which had surely turned her pale skin a bright red.

"We're room five-eleven," Annie said, wondering what the karma gods had in store for her—or Brett and Tabitha.

Brett closed his eyes and shook his head. "We're five-thirteen."

"Next-door neighbors!" Tabitha cried with a grin. She must have quickly realized the circumstances were horrific rather than fortunate because her smile fell almost as quickly as it had appeared.

Annie stretched her arms and feigned a yawn.

"Well, we better get to our room. I'm beat after all that dancing. But you two enjoy the rest of the wedding."

Wes gave the other couple a silent nod, and Annie grabbed his hand—the one that had just snuck inside her

underwear—and led him out of the elevator. She needed him
behind closed doors again. And fast.

"Don't you guys have overnight bags or something?"
Brett called after them. She could hear the twinge of jealousy
in his voice, and she wasn't going to lie to herself. She enjoyed
it even if she had no intention of winning him back.

She waved at the other couple over her shoulder and
simply yelled back, "Don't need 'em!" stifling a giggle as she
did.

"I think you just won the breakup," Wes said as they
made it to the door.

Annie glanced back toward the elevators, but Brett and
Tabitha were gone. She shoved her clutch under her arm. With
both of her index fingers, she grabbed Wes by his belt loops.

"Actually, I consider that little interruption quite a setback
for the team. The only way I'm winning anything tonight is if
you finish what you just started in that elevator."

He grabbed her purse and withdrew the room card,
inserting it into the slot on the door. Then—*click*. The door
opened, and he backed her inside, kicking it shut behind him.

"Whoa," he said. Annie turned to follow his gaze.

"Whoa is right," she added as they both set their gazes on
the mammoth bed covered in a bright blue duvet and enough
pillows for four people.

"Pretty sure the slogan on the website was *A blissful
honeymoon in every room!*"

"Annie Denning," he said, spinning her to face him again
and walking her slowly toward the bed. "I will finish and start
again as many times as you want me to."

She swallowed. "Sounds blissful," she said, her voice a
throaty whisper.

Her legs hit the bed frame, and the mattress was so high
she had to hoist herself onto it with her hands. She reached
for his palm and pulled until it rested on her thigh. Then she

dragged his fingers up, up, until they found where they were only minutes ago.

"More, please," she said.

His jaw clenched, and his muscles ticked.

"Are you *sure*, Annie? I don't want you to have any regrets in the morning."

She nodded, then dropped to her back on the bed and kicked off her boots. To avoid any further discussion about regrets *or* her goofy underwear, she simply slid the briefs down her legs and let them fall to the floor.

"More," she said again, the word slow and drawn out. "Please."

She took his palm in hers again, placing it gingerly against her mound. He climbed up next to her so they were both sprawled width-wise across the giant bed, propping himself on the elbow of his free arm, the other waiting.

Waiting for what?

"Show me," he said, his voice gravel rough as the tip of one finger gently slipped past her opening.

Annie breathed in sharply.

"Show me what you like," he added.

So she did, her palm flat atop his, guiding him down slowly as he plunged deep and explored inside her. Then she slid his hand up toward her stomach until he had left her completely.

"Two fingers this time," she whispered, and he kissed her as he obeyed, letting her set the pace as he filled her once again—his movement slow and deliberate, her hand still leading his. Long, slow, agonizingly wonderful. She'd never felt anything like it before.

"Annie," he said softly. "This might be one of the sexiest things I've ever done."

She let out a small giggle, but they still moved in tandem. She'd read the book, the one with the *spectacular* sex scenes, and now she'd met one of Ethan's exes in the flesh. She wondered how much truth really did bleed into fiction.

"Really?" she argued. "Just *looking* at Oksana has to be the sexiest thing anyone has ever done, men and women included. And now that I know she's Natasha?" She threw a hand over her mouth, but the words came out anyway. "Now that I know she's Natasha, I'm killing the mood while you are doing perfectly lovely things to me."

He shook his head.

"Annie." He kissed her neck, and she let out a quiet hum. "I'm not letting you ruin this for yourself. This?" He tilted his head up and watched their hands perform their slow dance. "Doing this with you? It's the fucking sexiest thing a girl has ever asked me to do." He kissed her again. "No. Scratch that."

See? She was right. Oksana wins at sexy.

"It's even better because it's with the most beautiful woman I've ever had the privilege to touch."

This time, as their hands traveled back toward her belly, he paused to spread her wet heat where she ached for it most. Her back arched at the unexpected pleasure, and she decided to ride the wave instead of arguing her point further.

"Let me finish what I started, Annie."

And that was that. Wes took the reins, pumping his fingers inside her and sliding his body down the length of hers to let his mouth take care of what she needed on the outside.

Her eyes rolled back in her head, but Annie was sure she saw stars as she gripped the bedspread and bucked against Wes's extremely talented hand and mouth. His tongue circled her swollen clit while one of his fingers found the place to make her burst at the seams. She cried out when she finally couldn't take any more, her arms splayed at her sides and her legs dangling over the edge of the bed.

Wes looked up at her from where he had just performed his magic and grinned.

"If you ever argue with me again about how sexy you are,

Annie Denning, I'm going to have to do that again."

She let out a soft whimper, one she hoped conveyed that she was going to need a nap before anything like *that* happened again. But she had enough energy for him.

"I really, really should repay you," she said dreamily. "I mean, I *want* to."

She pushed herself to sitting, her limbs like Jell-O, but she was anything if not determined. She reached for him and urged him toward her.

He didn't argue, didn't say another word as she pushed him gently to his back and undid his tie. Next went the buttons of his shirt, and with each one she grew greedier, less gentle, until she tore the last one free and it popped off completely and flew to the floor.

"I'm sorry!" she said, wide eyed, but then started laughing.

"Don't be." Wes's voice was low with an undeniably sexy rasp. "I admire your enthusiasm."

That was all the encouragement she needed before flicking open the button of his pants and tugging them and his boxer briefs to his ankles. He kicked off his boots, and then his garments were no more.

She sat above him and his proud length, her throat bobbing.

"I take it all back," she said, her voice barely above a whisper.

He propped himself on his elbows, his brows furrowed. "Take what back?"

"All those things I said about your sex scenes being too good. That Ethan's—*talent* had to be you compensating for *something.*"

He tilted his head back and laughed. "You never said that."

She nodded. "Yeah, I did. Just not to you." She wrapped her palm around him, stroking him once from root to tip, and he groaned. "I'd say I stand corrected."

And with that her lips were on him, tongue swirling as her mouth followed her hand down to where it had started and back up again, her palm now slick against his erection. He hissed, and she smiled before she sank over him again, and again, and again, savoring the taste of him with slow, determined movements until her name fell from his lips like it was some sort of revelation.

And it was. *He* was.

She'd had her mind made up about him the second he walked into her bookshop. But now? Now she climbed up next to him and rested her head on his shoulder as he lay grinning, satiated—and she had been the one to put that smile on his face.

They were both spent and sprawled on the bed. And as her eyes fluttered shut, the same thought continued to dance around in her head.

Who is this guy?

And who was she when she was with him? The answer was what scared her the most.

Herself.

The whole night Annie had been 100 percent *Annie*, and she'd never felt more comfortable in her own skin.

Chapter Eleven

Wes closed his eyes and willed the punishing spray of cold water to bring him back to his senses, but he couldn't stop thinking about the way she'd shown him what she liked, how she guided him through what felt almost more intimate than if they'd had sex.

He hadn't wanted to leave Annie passed out on the bed all alone, but he needed time to think. *Fuck.* He was hard again. So he switched the water to hot since he was going to be in there longer than expected.

Release came easily. All he had to do was recall the sounds Annie made for him or the way her body moved when he touched it. The way her lips felt on his cock. He'd intended tonight to be about her, to prove... He didn't know what the hell he was trying to prove. It started with the book, but he knew it had quickly turned to something more. But what that was he couldn't define. The writer was once again at a loss for words.

He stepped out of the shower and onto the cool tile of the Blissful Nights bathroom floor. "Huh," he said aloud, rubbing the fog from the mirror to get a good look at the guy staring back at him. He was smiling, which—yes—was fucking weird. As self-involved as he was when it came to his writer life, he wasn't one for grinning at himself like an asshole. Yet here he was.

Quite the predicament.

He wrapped a towel around his hips and peeked out the bathroom door and saw that Annie had found her way to one of the pillows and was curled up on her side. His smile widened.

Shit.

He needed to get his head back in the game. This was Jeremy's sister. Jeremy—who'd not only given him a temporary place to stay but also a temporary job while he figured his shit out. He could not afford to fuck that up. Then there was Annie. She just got out of a relationship. She certainly didn't need a guy with the emotional maturity of the teenage boy she used to know thinking that he could *feel* something for her.

"You are a fucking joke," he said softly to himself. "You can't even make fictional relationships work. You think you deserve a shot at someone like her?"

Excellent. Now he could add mildly insane to his list of datable qualities.

Annie rolled to her other side and let out a sweet moan.

Tonight. They had tonight. He could keep any and all baggage from infiltrating whatever time they had left together. So he pulled his boxers back on and padded over to the bed, sliding in next to her and pulling her back to his chest. But as much as he tried, he couldn't ignore that sweet smell of home.

He lasted an hour with her pressed against him, a sweet yet

agonizing hour where sleep wouldn't come. He'd eventually gotten up, intending on jotting down a few notes as a distraction, but he was on page twenty of the hotel notepad, said pages strewn across the small table at which he sat. Some would call it a mess, but Wes liked to think of it as organized chaos. If he didn't take a break soon, his hand would cramp up completely. But the words wouldn't stop, so he kept writing.

"Do you have any idea how sexy it is to watch what I assume is a book in progress? Total book lover porn." She stretched her arms over her head and yawned. "It also helps that you're almost naked while writing. Seriously. Nothing hotter."

He kept writing for several more seconds, needing to complete the thought before he forgot it. Then he glanced up to see Annie awake in bed, her red hair adorably disheveled and the bedsheet barely covering her breasts.

He dropped his pen, massaging his cramped hand.

"I was inspired," he said, unable to hold back his grin when she looked at him like that, not just like she maybe wanted to devour him, but also like she was genuinely interested in what he was doing.

Max was interested because he was Wes's agent, and to him words were money. For both of them.

Joanne, his editor—sure. She was interested, too. But it was her job.

But Annie had no ulterior motive. Okay, *maybe,* if he really thought about it, if he wrote another bestseller and she put it on her store's shelf—yeah. Money, money, money. But that was far beyond the scribbled sheets that lay before him now.

"Can I read?" she asked, then bit her bottom lip.

Shit, she could ask him for all his earthly possessions, and if she did that little lip-biting thing after, he'd give her everything.

"I'll massage your hand when I'm done," she added. "And—maybe massage other things, too?"

This time her teeth grazed that full, pink lip, and Wes's mouth went dry. He swallowed hard.

No one read his rough drafts. Hell, *Down This Road* was basically his senior thesis, and even after he polished it and turned it in to his professor, he still spent a year after graduation editing and reworking the piece until he couldn't stand it any longer. It was the only way he survived his mom's death—throwing himself into his work so completely that everything else didn't seem real. Was this chemistry between him and Annie real? Or was it just another way to drown out the noise? Whatever it was, it seemed to be working.

He surveyed the table before him, pages everywhere, some crumpled into balls and others still intact. But even the ones he was keeping—to take home and try to use as a start to fifty pages his editor *might* not laugh at—they were in no shape to be read. By anyone, especially Annie.

"Oh my God, Wes Hartley. I just offered various types of massaging, and you are still trying to think of a way to let me down gently, aren't you?"

His eyes met hers again, and her brows raised at him in accusation. She crossed her arms and held his gaze, fierce and unrelenting.

"Seriously?" She glanced at the clock on the bedside table. "Well, it is two o'clock in the morning. I suppose I could just go back to sleep—have a nice, cozy lie in until late checkout…"

He groaned. "You *hated* my book."

Annie rolled her eyes. "Maybe *hate* is too strong of a word. I just had some issues with the choices your main character made—like *choosing* to be alone and miserable. Like, *refusing* to say three simple words that could have brought him happiness. Okay, I had some major issues with that, but whatever. I never said your writing wasn't brilliant. So what do you say? New book. New main character. New choices. Maybe I'll love it?"

He leaned back in his chair and eyed her for a long moment.

"You hated my story…but you think my writing is brilliant? I might be able to get behind that."

"Narcissist."

He laughed. "I'm a writer. Have you met me?"

She held out her hand, palm turned up. "Gimme."

Hell, he could not resist this girl.

He gathered up the pages, putting them in some semblance of order, and headed for the bed.

"They're all yours," he said. Then he grabbed his clothes and threw them on before making his way to the door.

"Wait," Annie said. "Where are you going?"

He slid into his boots and shrugged.

"Crossing my fingers there's a bar still open downstairs. Otherwise I'll just wander the halls for the next twenty minutes. Letting you read doesn't mean I have to stay and bear witness."

He winked at her and slipped out the door before she had a chance to respond—and before she saw him go into panic mode. He paced for a good ten minutes in front of the elevators. Adrenaline pumping through his veins, he had too much energy and hoped he could burn it off before heading downstairs. He was wiping his palms on his pants when he finally pressed the button. His pulse quickened every second he waited for those freaking doors to open.

"Come on," he said aloud. Being out of the room wasn't enough. He needed off this floor. He needed something cold in his palm other than his own sweat. He *needed* reality to be altered just a fraction enough for him to be able to shrug it off when she told him his words were shit. Or better yet, when she flipped out at the likeness of his fiery-haired love interest, Evie, and threatened to sue him for—for—for what? Embellishing life? Wasn't that what fiction was—a fantastical version of what happens in the normal day-to-day? Not that what happened between him and Annie in that room a few hours ago resembled anything close to normal, but still.

Where the fuck is the elevator?

He'd returned to pacing by the time he heard the tell-tale *ding*, but before he could step foot inside, he heard the click of a handle being turned, heard the soft *whoosh* of the door sliding open over the carpet. He could still step into the vessel that would lead him to safety—albeit temporarily. Or he could turn toward the sound. Because somehow he knew that open door was for him.

Elevator. Hotel room. It was like he was in the *Matrix*. Blue pill—he'd find an open bar and make himself forget how much was at stake, that his whole career hinged on the words in her hands and what he was able to turn them into by Monday. Or the red pill. He could go back to the room, take the criticism he knew was coming, and be a better writer for it. Jesus. He was already a bestseller, but somehow the opinion of this one woman meant more than spending ten weeks on the *New York Times* bestseller list.

The elevator doors closed, and Wes still stood outside them. He shoved his hands in his front pockets and pivoted back toward room five-eleven. When he got there, Annie stood in the open doorway wrapped in the sheet, the pages clutched against her chest—against her heart—beaming.

She was beaming.

At him.

After reading his words.

"She's not you," was the first thing he said, which of course made him sound like a dick. "I mean there's truth in all fiction, right? But Evie is—"

"Plucky," Annie said with a grin. "I like her. Smart girl with a good head on her shoulders. Though that soda gun incident does sound familiar…"

He laughed softly.

"You have to admit it would be a crime *not* to memorialize that in fiction."

She shook her head. "I'm not arguing with you there, sir. But—we need to talk about Jack. The hero."

Here it was—the big blow. He braced himself. Literally. One hand on each side of the doorframe.

"He's *hopeful*, Wes." Her voice was soft and sweet, just like it should sound if she was breaking bad news to him. But he was pretty sure what she'd just said was a compliment.

"That's a good thing, right?"

Hope was new to him. New to his writing.

She nodded, pages still held firmly in her hands.

"It's a really good thing. For Jack. Who certainly isn't you, right?"

Her smile turned playful, and Wes wasn't sure how to answer. Was the hope Jack's alone—a fantasy version of his own life—or was there more of himself in Jack than he knew? Jack wanted to believe in the possibility of a happily ever after with the blind date he was on at a wedding. Because he'd never met a girl like Evie before.

"No," he said, his voice firm. "Jack isn't me. Not one little bit."

Her smile faltered for a couple of seconds, but she masked it quickly. Then she thrust the pages toward him, pressing them to *his* chest so he was forced to hold them the same way she had.

"It's a really good start. I think your agent and editor are going to be really happy."

He scoffed. "Yeah, after I write about thirty more pages and clean it all up."

She hooked a finger into the top of his pants and tugged.

"Say *thank you*," she said. "Take a damned compliment and *believe* it."

He nodded slowly. "Thank you."

"You're welcome," she said with a self-satisfied grin. She gave his pants a little yank, and he crossed the threshold back into the room.

"So, do you try to change the minds of all readers who have a less than favorable reaction to your book, or am I just special?" she asked, and he laughed.

His fingertips skimmed her hairline, and she closed her eyes for several seconds.

"You're special, Annie," was all he said aloud. But to himself he added, *and it has nothing to do with the book.*

She let out a breath, settling back into the moment. "Now where were we? I do believe I owe you a hand massage," she said, walking him to the bed.

"You don't owe me any—"

She pushed him down on his back.

"Will you stop freaking arguing and just let me make you feel good? *Again.* Because I do owe you, Wes Hartley."

He grinned. "I think we're probably pretty even based on what happened earlier," he said.

Annie blew out a breath. "Yeah. But I never said thank you for coming with me tonight. It meant a lot to the grooms— and it means a lot to me. So, thank you." She climbed over him, straddled his legs and, yep—she bit her bottom lip. "I'm ready to pay up. With interest."

Chapter Twelve

Annie tried to focus on the road. She didn't drive often, only when she left the city. But when she did, she liked to think she wasn't a threat to other motorists. Right now, keeping her hands at ten and two was a struggle, not just because of her sweaty palms but because she itched to rest one of those palms on Wes's knee—and she couldn't.

"This is good," he said, breaking the ten-minute silence. At this rate, the hour ride home would feel like three.

"Huh?" she asked. Because unfocused Annie was still unfocused.

He ran a hand through his hair and sighed. But the sigh reminded her of other sounds he made last night, and Annie squirmed in her seat.

"Getting back to normal, you know? Rebooting before we get home. I think you made the right decision canceling the late checkout."

She threw her head back against the headrest. At the time it seemed like the right decision. After last night in the elevator, *out* of the elevator, reading his pages—what came *after* reading his pages, it was too much. Correction. There could never be too much of feeling the way she felt when his hands were on her, when his tongue—

Shit. She should *not* be thinking about his tongue.

This was the reason she had to put a moratorium on… on…tongue stuff. Because there's no way she would have left that room if they started things up again this morning.

"I need a cider," she mumbled. She felt Wes's eyes shift toward her in her peripheral vision.

"It's seven in the morning. On a Sunday. Even I think that might be a little too early to start drinking," he quipped, and she tried to ignore the playfulness in his voice.

"Apple cider," she corrected. "From a *coffee shop*. Not a bar. I'm not a savage. I save alcohol until at least nine or ten."

Okay, that came out more bitchy than playful, which was odd. Annie didn't do bitchy. It was a waste of energy. But she was cider deprived. Yes. The cider—or lack thereof—was most definitely at fault here.

She veered to the right, possibly cutting off a motorist or two, but she was not missing this exit.

Wes braced his palms on the dashboard.

"Jesus fucking Christ, Annie! What the hell are you doing?"

A couple of cars honked, and she was sure someone shot her the bird. But she got them off the highway in one piece, and she could already see the green and white sign—a beacon promising sanity.

Starbucks.

True, she wished it was Hot Latte and hated cheating on Doug and Dan, but for one, she was in the 'burbs. And two, Doug and Dan were honeymooning in the Dominican Republic. And what they would never, *ever* find out wouldn't hurt them.

"It's okay. I've got everything under control," she said,

glancing over at Wes, but he was still white knuckling the dash. *Shit.* Something was wrong. She waited until they were parked and the key was out of the ignition. Then she undid her seat belt and turned to face him.

He hadn't really moved yet, but his hands had relaxed. He was breathing slowly, measured breaths in and out. For several seconds she let the rhythm lull her, but a door slamming on a nearby car brought her back to her senses.

"Wes?" she asked softly. "You okay?"

He slapped his palms on his knees, and she flinched at the sudden movement.

"Great!" he said, with a little too much Tony the Tiger to sound believable. "Coffee sounds great!"

He unclicked his seat belt and bounded out of the car, not looking behind him to see if she was following. Which she wasn't. Not yet, at least. Because Annie was trying to puzzle together what the hell just happened, but she was definitely missing some pieces.

Cider. Caramel apple cider. She had to get some in her belly, warm her cranky, confused, and—to be honest—rather wanton insides. So she hopped out of the vehicle and followed Wes inside. He was already in line when she pushed through the door, and he offered her a small, closed-mouth grin when their eyes met.

"Wes Hartley? Oh my God, it *is* you!"

Before either of them could react, the barista, who moments ago was hidden behind the espresso machine, ran out from behind the counter and threw her arms around Wes.

"How *are* you?" the girl squealed, but she didn't wait for him to reply. "I haven't seen you since—since your *mom*." She backed up so her eyes met his. "God, I'm so sorry. I totally get why you didn't have enough energy to put into *us* back then. But if you're back in town for a while and still *single*…"

He let out a nervous laugh. "What are you doing in

Illinois?" he asked. "Last I saw you, you were managing that indie coffee shop in the Village."

The girl sighed. "Yeah. I decided to go back to school to get my master's in psychology. I have you to thank for that. Anyway, I got into a great program out here at Northwestern. This helps pay the bills."

Annie cleared her throat and immediately wanted to take it back. Because it sounded like she was balking at someone calling Wes single. She so totally wasn't. And what happened to his mom? And can they walk into an establishment or party without someone knowing—and possibly still pining for—Wes?

"Stacy," he finally said. "This is, uh, Annie."

Well, at least he remembered her name.

"He's still single," she said, holding out her hand to shake Stacy's.

Ugh. She needed that cider to cover up the taste of acid on her tongue. Stat.

Stacy's smile fell for a second as she gave Annie the once-over with eyes so dark they almost looked black and so big it was like a manga character was looking her up and down. Annie started paging through her memory of *Down This Road* and almost blurted out *Tracy!* when it clicked. *Geez,* he didn't even try with this name. At least Oksana was Natasha, but Stacy the barista was Tracy, the coffeehouse singer, the one Ethan—the supposedly fictional hero—met after his mother's funeral.

Whoa.

"Drinks are on me," Stacy said, interrupting Annie's mental sleuthing. "What will you and your *friend* have?"

The girl practically skipped back behind the counter, her dark ponytail swishing across her back as she did.

Wes turned to Annie, who scrutinized him with her stare. He simply offered a shrug and a sheepish grin before ordering.

"Just a grande bold for me," he said. "Annie?"

Well, the girl did say drinks were on her, right?

"A venti caramel apple cider, *with whip*, extra hot. I want it to last the rest of the ride home."

She watched as Wes stared straight ahead at Stacy filling his cup, yet he was trying to stifle a smile.

She crossed her arms. "What?"

Stacy handed him his coffee and motioned for them to follow her to the other end of the counter where she would probably make the cider.

"Nothing," he said, shaking his head as he let her lead the way. But Annie kept looking over her shoulder until they were side by side again.

"It's not *nothing* if you're trying not to laugh at me," she said. "I'm not ashamed of my beverage, if that's what this is about. I don't need to be all hipster, black-coffee-drinking cool, you know."

He let out a loud laugh.

"Here you are assuming I'm judging *your* beverage choice, and you just went and judged mine. That's cold, Denning."

Now she was the one trying not to smile. Because he was right. And he was back to his normal self—if she even knew what that was. But *this* was the Wes who rode up to her room last night, who made her feel like the Emerald City instead of a schnoodle, and her smile won out and broke through. "Black coffee *is* kind of hipster," she said. "Especially when you're only twenty-five."

She tugged at the bottom of her jacket, fidgeting as the words echoed in her ears. *Only twenty-five.* Three years wasn't that big a deal in the grand scheme of things, yet twenty-five seemed barely out of college while twenty-eight was old maid status in some societies. Okay, fine, maybe in seventeenth-century Great Britain, but honestly. He was still figuring shit out while Annie was sure she almost had all the answers.

Except the one about finding her happily ever after.

"Caramel apple cider *is* kind of adorable," he said, then licked his top lip before taking a slow sip from his cup.

Holy hell. Annie's neck warmed, and something in her belly tightened. This little detour was supposed to get her head back in the game. Instead she wondered what his lip tasted like, especially now that it had a small drip of coffee on it.

Nope. He licked that away, too.

She bounced on her toes, watching Stacy slowly drizzle caramel over the cider's whipped cream.

"I'll be right back," she said, and bolted for the bathroom, which was, thank the stars, open.

She couldn't be near him with the lip licking and the calling her adorable and the memories of last night. What the hell was going on? It's not like she hadn't had good sex before. And fine, last night was maybe better than most. Okay it was freaking amazing, but she shouldn't be losing her shit like she was now. Just like she never let herself get too broken up over, well, a breakup, Annie could also control herself in the bedroom—and out of it.

But apparently not today.

She braced her hands on the side of the sink and took in the image staring back at her from the mirror. Aside from the lack of makeup and moderate bed-head, she wasn't a complete disaster. She ran her hands under the faucet, dipping her head so she could splash the cold water on the back of her neck.

"Your drink is ready."

The voice came from behind her, and Annie gasped, her eyes darting back to the mirror. Wes stood behind her, venti cup in his hand, and she watched a small dollop of whipped cream seep out of the small opening. She spun to face him.

"Sorry," he added. "The door was unlocked. I *did* knock, but when you didn't answer…"

There was that sheepish grin again, but Annie knew what stood before her. A wolf in sheep's clothing.

She cleared her throat. "And you thought you'd just come in to check on me? I could have been actually *using* the bathroom."

Her argument was paper thin, but he nodded slowly, as if he was actually considering that she'd rushed off for anything other than the exact reason she had—the one she knew Wes knew.

He drove her absolutely mad.

"Do you need to use the bathroom?" he asked, his voice low.

Annie shook her head. Wes locked the door, then took a step closer.

"Do you want me to leave?" he added.

Her response was the same. There were no words for what she wanted right now, so if he wanted to communicate without them, who was she to argue?

He handed her the cup, and she took it willingly.

"Drink," he told her, the sound somewhere between a command and a plea.

She drank.

"Now let me taste," he said, and she held the cup out, offering it back to him.

He laughed softly, shaking his head.

"No, Annie. Let me *taste.*"

He gently pulled the cup from her hand and set it down on the ledge of the sink. Then he tugged at the bottom of her jacket, pulling her closer.

"Do you *want* me to taste?" he asked.

She nodded. God, did she ever. But even more, she needed to taste him back.

He didn't bother with coyness, just pressed his lips to hers, and she parted them immediately, inviting him in.

The bitterness of his black coffee mingled with the syrupy sweet cider. It was an odd yet delicious combination, and they both devoured it. His fingers combed through her hair. Her palms splayed against his chest. Every touch of his lips on hers made her want more, like she'd been starved of whatever this was between them and only now knew she couldn't get enough.

"I can't—" he said, his breath coming out in pants. "I can't reboot, Annie. I can't turn off whatever we started last night, and I'm not sure what to do about it."

She nodded, her head still cradled in his hands, and kissed him again. He could at least form words, but she was beyond that at this point. Words meant thinking. They meant logic. And the last thing she wanted to be right now was logical. That would mean admitting this was more than acting out after the whole Brett and Tabitha confrontation. It would mean admitting that last night was more spectacular than any chapter she'd read in Wes's book. And it would mean admitting that rebooting wasn't in the cards for her, either. But right now, she couldn't imagine moving beyond this moment.

"What if we don't?" she finally said. "What if we don't turn off what we started?" This was dangerous territory, and she knew it. But so was the thought of him *not* kissing her, of his hand *not* touching her. She flicked out her tongue and playfully licked his bottom lip.

Instead of reciprocating, he backed away and ran a hand through his still sleep-disheveled hair.

Well, that was not exactly how she saw the next phase of this situation going.

"Did I do something wrong?" she asked, and Wes groaned.

"No," he said. "I did. I did everything wrong. I promised your brother—"

"Seriously? This is about Jeremy?" She threw her hands in the air. "I'm all for good intentions and your guy code and

whatever, but that was before we knew there was this…this…
heat between us. I'm not wrong about that. Am I?"

He shook his head. "God, no. Look at me, Annie. I'm a
fucking mess for you right now, so much so that I'm ready to
take you up against a wall in a goddamn Starbucks bathroom."

She finally took notice of her surroundings and giggled.
This elicited a laugh from Wes, and his shoulders relaxed.

He backed against the wall and let his head thump against
it. Three times.

"God, I'm an asshole," he said. "It's not just the guy code.
I—I just needed out of New York for a while. And I needed
cash. Jer is giving me a place to stay *and* he got me a few shifts
at Kingston's." He let out a long breath, and Annie's fiery
need began to simmer. "I mean, I've got family in the city, but
I can't stay there. Clearly I have issues, and I didn't intend to
drag you into them."

Hello, reality. So nice of you to drop in.

"I don't get it," she said. "You're a best-selling author."

He nodded slowly. "A best seller who spent his advance
and is still waiting to earn out. And if I don't deliver on this
second book, they'll cancel my contract and that will be it. So
yeah, I can't fuck with your brother's trust. Not after all he's
done for me." He let out a long breath. "And I don't want to
fuck with you. We see—*relationships*—differently. I like you,
Annie. And I want to be with you. But I can't give you the
happily ever after you're looking for."

She reached for her drink, needing its warmth in her
hands to combat the chill spreading through her veins.

"What if I don't *want* a relationship?" she asked. "I mean,
not with *you*." His eyes narrowed, and she continued. "I
know what I said I want in the long run, but I am not in a
relationship place right now," she said. "And clearly, neither
are you. Especially not with me because—code, apartment,
job. I get it."

He laughed. "True…" But he drew out the word, like he could tell her wheels were turning and he just might buy in to a crazy scheme if she happened to have one. And she did.

She took a step forward and hooked a finger into the top of his pants, emboldened by the energy crackling between them despite the futility of pushing things further. He took in a sharp breath, and she fought to maintain control even while her skin was touching his.

"But you seemed a little inspired to write when you were with me last night. And I was—well, I was inspired to do things with you I'd never done with anyone else before."

Because you were the first guy to ask me what I wanted. And it was the first time I wanted to show someone what that was.

She stepped closer now, so their lips were centimeters from touching yet not.

"What are you suggesting?"

She grinned.

"We keep doing what we started last night—in secret. No one has to know, and no one has to get hurt. You get inspired to write, and I get—well, I get to keep sharing my cider with you."

She took another sip, then pressed her lips to his. This was the moment of truth. All he had to do was kiss her back. Which—thank the stars—he did.

All she had to do was keep her emotions out of it.

He pulled her body against his, and she felt him hard inside his pants.

"You got yourself a deal, Annie Denning."

He kissed her, and she melted into him.

Well, then. It was all set. This was exactly what she wanted. And needed. A win-win for both of them.

What guy could be safer to *not* fall for?

Chapter Thirteen

Wes wrote all day. Well, after a long, contemplative shower he wrote. And wrote. And wrote.

He'd said no when Annie invited him in and instead hopped on his bike and headed back to Jeremy's place. Jamie had given him his first shift behind the bar tonight, so whatever he was sending to Max by morning needed to happen between kissing Annie good-bye and arriving at Kingston's at six.

Fifty-five pages. If it wasn't five o'clock, he would have kept going because the words wouldn't stop. Fifty-five rough pages, but there they were. They might even be good—good enough to convince his editor he could produce a second book to rival the first. And it was all thanks to Annie.

He scrolled through his recent calls and stopped on his dad's name. *Robert Hartley*. Jesus, he didn't even have him in his phone as *Dad*. What did that say about the state of affairs between them? His thumb hovered over the contact. Then he jumped when the phone vibrated and began to ring.

"Christ!" He let out a nervous laugh and then accepted

the call.

"What's up, Denning?"

Wes could hear the brewery patrons in the background. The place sounded pretty nuts for this early on a Sunday.

"Hey, man," Jeremy said. "Sorry I missed you today. I… uh…didn't sleep at home last night and went right in to work this morning. Any chance you could get here a little earlier? Kingston just declared half-price Sunday since the Sox hit a home run, and it's like the whole city found out in a matter of minutes. We're slammed."

Jeremy had no clue Wes hadn't come home last night. Which meant he had no idea he'd stayed overnight with Annie.

He didn't hesitate. "On my way."

"You're a lifesaver," Jeremy said, then ended the call.

No, Jer. You are.

He turned back to his laptop, drafted a quick email to his agent, and attached his rough pages. So much for editing. Then he grabbed his jacket and helmet and was out the door.

When he made his way through the bar's doors, he literally had to push through a mob of people standing under one of the flat screens rooting on the White Sox who were now down by one run. What a difference fifteen minutes made.

"Hartley," Jeremy called from behind the bar. "Thank the fucking Lord you made it. You take the cash orders because I don't have time to show you the register. Pour beers. Try not to give anyone a glass full of foam. Use a pilsner for the pale ale, a pint for the stout, and a weizen for witbier." Jeremy pointed at each glass as he spoke. "But don't worry too much because most everyone here is piss drunk already and probably won't give a shit." He paused and nodded toward a table of patrons who seemed to be the only ones ignoring the television screens. "Except the hipsters in the corner. They'll fucking correct you."

Wes laughed, but Jeremy raised his brows. The guy was serious.

"You good?" Jeremy asked, and Wes guessed the correct response was to nod. So he did. "Great. Because that was your training. May the force be with you."

And that was that. Wes was on his own. Baptism by fire — or ale, in this case.

It only took him four hours to get the hang of it—four hours, three condescending hipster corrections, one broken pilsner glass, and a bandaged thumb and palm after hastily picking up the broken shards. They were thirty minutes from closing, and Jeremy had just returned to the bar after clearing glasses from a nearby table.

"Please tell me you poured one for yourself at some point this evening," he said, and Wes's eyes widened.

"No, asshole," he said. "I'm the new guy, remember? Would have been nice to know I could sample the merchandise."

Jeremy ran his forearm across his brow. The guy was clearly just as exhausted as he was, but shit. He could have used a pint of his own at least an hour or so ago.

"Sorry, man. My mistake. It's not like Jamie wants us drinking all night, but the best way to talk up a brew to the patrons is to know it intimately."

Wes rolled his eyes.

"You know anything intimately other than beer, Denning?"

Jeremy flipped him off and then grinned.

"I have my fun, Hartley. That's all I really need. And if you're anything like the guy in your book, I'm guessing that's all you need, too."

Wes grabbed a pint glass and began pouring himself

a stout. He tried to let the jab roll off his back. It's not like it wasn't true. He grew up watching his parents make each other miserable, only for his mom to die and leave his dad even more of an ass than he was when she was here. It didn't make sense. Relationships didn't make sense. So he sought out women with whom he knew there wasn't a future. It was easier when there was nothing to lose.

Now Annie was offering him the same thing, and he found part of himself wishing she wanted more — and that he had more to give.

"Yeah," he said, finishing the perfect pour. "That's all I need."

He drained half the pint. He was sweating, and hungry, and he realized he really hadn't slept much at all last night. Exhaustion swept over him like a tidal wave, and he suddenly couldn't think of anything better than sleep.

Jeremy retrieved a half-empty glass of his own from the back counter.

"Cheers, my friend," Jeremy said. "Here's to all sorts of — *fun.*"

It was quiet enough now for Wes to hear the door *whoosh* open. Brynn was the first to walk through. And then there was Annie. Her red waves framed her face under a gray knit cap. She wore the same black leather jacket from yesterday, but this time a pair of form-fitting jeans hugged her legs, and if he didn't stop staring, Jeremy was going to notice. So he gulped down the rest of his pint, afraid that whatever came out of his mouth would give him and Annie away.

"Ladies," Jeremy said. "So nice to see you."

Brynn kissed him on the cheek and then narrowed her gaze at Wes.

He lowered the glass slowly from his face. She didn't break her gaze, so he held his ground. He wasn't sure what Annie had told her, but one thing was for sure: Brynn was sizing him up.

"You're right," she finally said. He could tell she was speaking to Annie, but she was still looking at him. "I didn't have a chance to compare the other night. Way better than that cartoon on the book jacket."

Annie backhanded her friend on the arm, and Wes couldn't help but smile. Whatever she'd said, she liked the way he looked, and Brynn knew it. This gave him enough satisfaction for the moment.

Jeremy snorted.

"Right? What's with the drawing, Hartley? Not like the ladies don't like what they see. How much did you rack up in tips tonight from that table of hot grad students?"

Annie dipped her head, but not before he noticed her blush.

"It's not like my age is a secret," he said. "But the less I remind readers of how young I am, the better. It's not easy to be taken seriously in this industry."

Annie cleared her throat. "Maybe that's your problem," she said. "Taking yourself too seriously."

Wes raised his brows. "Maybe some people take what they *read* too seriously."

He'd meant it as a joke, but Annie shot daggers at him with her eyes.

Jeremy chuckled. "Nice. One wedding together, and the two of you already have each other pegged."

Wes caught Annie's eye and offered her a conciliatory grin before shifting his gaze to Jeremy. Annie forced a laugh. At least Wes could tell she was forcing it. He wondered if Brynn or Jeremy caught on.

"Pretty much sums up the evening," she said. "We even got bored and left the wedding early."

Wes closed his eyes. Shit. This was it. They should have collaborated on a lie so they'd both have the same story for

Jeremy once he found out they didn't come home last night. But Wes was too flustered after Annie's proposition and too overflowing with story to think of anything other than getting it down on paper. Or his laptop. Whatever.

Jeremy tousled Wes's hair like he was a toddler.

"Aw, I bet you had my little sister home safe and in bed before midnight."

Wes let out a nervous laugh. He definitely had her in bed before midnight.

"Yep," Annie said. "Home safe and sound before I turned back into a pumpkin."

Brynn opened her mouth to say something, but Annie cut her off.

"Isn't Jamie working the upstairs bar tonight?" she asked. "You should go let him know you're here."

Brynn pouted at her friend, but she didn't say another word before marching upstairs.

She knew.

Jeremy tossed back the rest of his pint, then laid the glass in a bus bin.

"Take a load off and let me pour you another, Hartley. You look like hell." Jeremy filled his friend's empty glass and set it back down.

Wes laughed. "Thanks. I feel like hell." He pushed the fresh beer to the patron side of the counter, then slid past Jeremy and out from behind the bar to where Annie still stood.

"This guy saved my ass tonight. He's even got the battle scars to prove it."

Wes collapsed onto a bar stool, thankful that it had a back rest because once he was off his feet, he didn't think he could support even half his body weight anymore. Annie took the seat next to him. Jeremy gave her a small peck on the cheek. He looked past her and winked at Wes.

"Hey, I'm…uh, spending the night out again. There's this flight attendant I met last year when I went to L.A. Long story. Anyway, she's in town for one night at The Four Seasons—"

"Enjoy your *fun*," Wes said.

"Ugh, Jeremy," Annie said. "When are you going to date someone I can actually meet?"

He picked up the bus bin and chuckled.

"Didn't you hear Hartley?" Jeremy asked. "I have fun. There's no room for dating there."

She backhanded him on the shoulder, and Wes barely had the energy to shake his head at his friend.

Jeremy started back toward the kitchen. "You're off the clock, Hartley!" he called over his shoulder. "Make sure my sister gets home safe."

Wes let out a long breath.

Annie spun on her stool to face him.

"I'm fine getting home, by the way. I was out with Brynn, so I told her I'd drop her off and get a cab home. Jeremy needs to stop treating me like I need a babysitter." She groaned softly. "*He's* the child, you know."

Wes smiled.

"He loves you. It's gotta be nice to have someone looking out for you like that." He lifted his glass and offered a nod of cheers. "And even if you did want a ride home, I think I'm leaving my bike here after this."

She crossed her arms and grinned.

"Well, then. While I don't need looking after, it would be economical for us to share a cab. Your place *is* on the way to mine."

"I was gonna walk—" he said, then stopped himself from going any further. Just because Jeremy's apartment was walking distance didn't mean he *couldn't* take a cab. He had ridden the bike here, after all.

He *was* practically dead on his feet. Plus, a few minutes

alone with Annie, even if it was just sitting next to her, would be a really fucking good way to end a long night.

"Yeah," he said. "Sure. That sounds good."

She hopped off the stool.

"Stay there," she said. "You look — well, like Jeremy said. So, just rest. I'll let Brynn know I'll talk to her tomorrow, and I'll pop back to let the overprotective baby brother know I'm getting home safely."

He didn't argue. He had no energy for that.

She was back in minutes, enough time for him to finish his pint, the smooth stout coating his insides and finally allowing him to relax after practically forty-eight hours of being *on*.

"Leave the glass," she said. "Jer said he'll grab the last of what's left out here."

He nodded and pushed himself up from the stool. Annie gasped and grabbed his bandaged palm.

"What the hell did you do to yourself?"

A small laugh escaped his lips.

"Broke a glass. It's no big deal."

She brushed a thumb across the heel of his hand, just below the bandage. He sucked in a breath.

"Does it hurt?"

He shrugged. "Maybe. I'm too fucking tired to know."

She reached over the bar and pulled his jacket out from the shelf where he'd shoved it.

"I know all the good hiding spots," she said. "Come on. I'm taking you home and making sure you clean this properly. *Then* I'll head back to my place, okay?"

He wanted to protest. He really did. Because that would have been the right thing to do. The *safe* thing to do. Despite their little arrangement, all he could think right now was how good it would feel to be taken care of for once. So he simply nodded and followed her out to the street where she hailed a cab, gave the driver Jeremy's address, and then sat with him in silence for the few minutes it took them to get there. It was the perfect ride.

When they got to Jeremy's place, she still didn't speak, just led him to the bathroom where she turned on the sink, let the water run warm, and peeled the tape off the gauze that covered his hand.

"It's not so bad," she said softly.

The wound wasn't deep, but it was fresh, and the skin stung when it hit the open air. He hissed softly when she pulled his hand under the water.

"Sorry." She massaged the skin around the cut, washing away tiny flecks of dried blood.

"It's fine," he said. "I can handle it. I was just—caught off guard."

Annie shook her head. "There's nothing wrong with hurting, Wes. Or admitting that you're hurt. It doesn't diminish your testosterone or anything to say ouch."

There was a hint of annoyance in her voice, but the water was off now, and she was gently patting his palm dry with a towel, taking care *not* to hurt him even though she'd just called him on something no other woman had. Sure, he'd been called on plenty of other bullshit by plenty of other women, but Annie knew him for a weekend and already hit it home.

It *wasn't* okay to hurt. Not when he had to pick up his own pieces when he did.

She rifled through Jeremy's cabinet and produced a small first aid kit, continuing to tend to his hand while he did his best *not* to let her touch get to him in any way.

"Have you always been like this?" she asked, tilting her head up so her eyes met his.

"I'm a lot of things, Annie. You're going to have to elaborate."

She sighed.

"Closed off. Emotionally unavailable. *Afraid* of your own

feelings."

He raised a brow.

"You got all that from cleaning off a cut?"

She gave him a pointed look, and he wanted to hold his ground, but the longer he stared at her, the more he was afraid she could see. He dropped his gaze to his palm. She had one piece of tape left to secure the gauze in place, so he pulled it from where it dangled on her finger, slapped it over the loose corner, and gently freed his hand from her grip.

"Thanks for the first aid," he said, making himself busy by closing up the kit and putting it away, then slipping past her and out into the hallway. "Do you want a beer?" he asked. "I need a beer."

He strode toward the kitchen, hoping she'd take the not-so-subtle hint and change the subject.

"Come on, Wes."

Nope. She was on his heels when he spun to face her at the fridge, two beer bottles in his hand. Christ, he was too exhausted to defend himself. And everything he was about to say would come out wrong, but so be it. Their comfortable silence seemed to be at an end.

He handed her a bottle, twisted the cap off the one in his hand, and then traded her for the other so he could twist the cap off that one, too. He wasn't even sure they were twist-offs, but he was too flustered to find an opener, even if it meant nicking more flesh from his appendages.

"No, Annie. I wasn't always like this, but *this* is what I am *now*." He tilted the bottle to his lips and drank it halfway down before stopping for air. When she didn't say anything else, he stepped around her and out into the living room where he collapsed on Jeremy's brown leather couch.

He threw his head back and closed his eyes, wishing he had more to bang it against other than the plush material.

Jesus, you're an asshole.

But then again, this was his M.O. He used it to keep everyone else at bay, and it always worked. But Annie—she pushed his buttons. Instead of being proactive, with her it was all reaction.

He felt the cushion dip to his left, then felt the warmth of another body in the vicinity of his.

"Are you trying to scare me away?" she asked.

He opened his eyes. She'd taken off her jacket and boots and was curled up all comfy with her beer. Next to him. Like he hadn't just acted like a total dick.

"Maybe," he admitted.

"Maybe I don't scare easily," she said, then smiled.

And, Christ, that smile was contagious. He couldn't help himself around her.

"Ahhh," she said. "There we go. I knew I could turn that frown upside down."

He rolled his eyes and laughed. "I guess I've completely blown your second impression of me."

"Second?" she asked.

"Yeah. Last night was the second. You wanted nothing to do with me at the book signing on Thursday." He raised a brow. "You're welcome, by the way. I usually get more than a couple days' notice before I do one of those."

Annie groaned. "Okay, third impression is looking more like the first." She waved her beer at him. "That—that ego thing of yours is showing."

He laughed. "Hard to keep it hidden."

She shrugged and took a sip of her beer.

"Whatever we were last night wasn't entirely real," she said. "You were your best self, and I was mine. That's how dates go. *Not* that we were on a real date." She snorted. "I guess my best self includes drinking straight from a soda gun after burning my esophagus with vodka."

She still had her knit cap on, so he pulled it from her head and brushed her hair out of her eyes.

"You're just *you,* Annie. I don't know how you do that. There's no first impression. There's simply—you."

She kissed him, just a soft peck on the cheek, but it somehow felt more intimate than what they'd done in the hotel room last night.

"We're not dating, remember?" she said. "You don't have to impress me. So how about when it's just us, you be simply— you?"

He sighed. That would be something new to try.

"Then I need to be honest about one thing," he said, setting his bottle on the coffee table.

"What's that?"

He skimmed his fingers across her cheek, then dropped his hand to his side.

"I haven't slept in two days, and as much as I want to do all sorts of things to you like I did last night, I'm about thirty seconds away from comatose."

"Well," she said, "then this is your lucky night." She set her bottle next to his, stood, and held out her hand. "Come on."

He hesitated. So she grabbed his wrist and pulled.

"You were right. About me and Jeremy," she said. "He may annoy me with the big brother act, but it is nice to have someone looking out for me. How about just for tonight, you let me look out for you."

He stood, but his brows drew together.

"I'm tucking you in, you idiot," she said and started leading him to his room.

"I'm not a fucking toddler," he said. "See? Still holding a beer."

She grabbed the beer and set it on his nightstand. "Not anymore," she said once they were in front of his bed. And then, without another word, she lifted his T-shirt over his head and unbuttoned his jeans. He was hard inside his boxer briefs. He *was* human. But he didn't have it in him, and Annie didn't try anything more than freeing him from his clothes.

He collapsed onto the mattress, and she drew the blanket up and over his chest. He could barely keep his eyes open once his head hit the pillow.

"You can stay," he said sleepily, yet in the almost fog of sleep he realized it didn't sound like much of an invitation. "I mean *stay*," he added, "if you want. I'd like you to stay."

She unbuttoned her jeans and let them fall to the floor, kicking them from her ankles. Then she did that magic trick that girls do, pulling her bra out from beneath her top. And just like that, she crawled in next to him, her body fitting perfectly in the space against his.

"Okay, then," she whispered, pulling his arm across her middle.

All of his muscles relaxed as his palm fell against her torso.

"Okay."

Chapter Fourteen

Annie woke with a start when she heard the door slam shut. She threw off the covers and planted her feet on the floor. The cold wood floor. The cold wood floor that was not *her* floor.

"Hartley?" Knuckles rapped on the bedroom door. "Are you up? I gotta tell you about this fucking hotel, man!"

Holy. Fucking. Shit.

Annie spun to see Wes still sleeping peacefully on the bed behind her. She scrambled onto all fours on the floor until she found her jeans and retrieved her phone. Nine o'clock. She had to open the shop in an hour, but right now she had to do damage control.

She shoved her clothes under the bed and pretended not to care what else lurked beneath a twenty-five-year-old guy's sleeping quarters.

"Wes," she hissed, crawling back up next to him so Jeremy hopefully wouldn't hear her. "Wes, wake up!"

He moaned softly, his eyes fluttering open, and good God the man was a beautiful sight, his lean, muscled torso exposed where she'd thrown off the blanket. When his eyes met hers, he smiled softly and leaned in for a kiss just as Jeremy knocked again.

"Dude, you're in there, right? I swear, if I don't tell someone about the shower in this room—and the things one can do in said shower—I'm not going to believe it really happened."

Wes's eyes widened, and he bolted upright, not without first knocking heads with Annie, who had to stifle her urge to cry out in pain.

"Sorry!" he whispered. "Yeah, man! I'm here. Just let me put on some—"

But the door handle started to turn, so Annie—head throbbing—dove over Wes and onto the floor where she huddled in the small space between the bed and the back wall of the room.

She couldn't tell if she was hidden well enough. Nor could she see what transpired between her brother and Wes, so she'd just have to listen.

"Hey, man," Jeremy said. It sounded like he was still in the open doorway. "You don't have to dress up for me."

He laughed at his own joke, but Wes didn't join him.

Act natural, she urged him with what she hoped was something akin to the Jedi Mind Trick.

"You woke me to tell me about a shower?" Wes asked groggily, even though Annie knew he was wide awake now. Good. He *was* putting on a show.

She could sense her brother moving, his voice getting closer as he spoke. She tugged at the part of the blanket that hung off the bed, trying to pull it over her huddled form.

"Seriously, there must have been six shower heads. All spraying from different angles…"

Her brother was right there, on the bed. Shit.

"Yeah?" Wes asked.

"Fuck, yeah," Jeremy said. "Some you could aim. Some you couldn't. And, Jesus, this girl and I were going at it with the water pouring down on us. It was goddamn beautiful. *She* was beautiful—until I must have bumped a button or a nozzle or *something,* and, dude, the sharpest stream of water nailed me right in the fucking nuts."

Annie cupped her hands over her ears, begging for temporary hearing loss, but Jeremy was too close.

Ew, ew, ew, ew, ew, she chanted in her head, but it was no use. She couldn't unhear what she'd heard, and she'd never be able to look her brother in the eye again. So that was that. She'd have to move to another country. People need bookstores abroad, right?

Wes hissed in a breath. "Game over?" he asked.

Jeremy sighed. "Game over. I thought I'd fucking been shot."

Annie heard something hit the mattress just above her head. Her brother had just flopped down onto his back.

"Sometimes," Jeremy said—and holy shit his head was right above hers. "I think I might have too much fun for my own good."

A hand flopped over the side of the bed, skimming the blanket above her back, and Annie dropped lower, flattening herself against the cold, dusty floor as she tried to inch *under* the bed to no avail.

Wes chuckled. "You are definitely not the same guy I remember from high school," he said. "Not that I begrudge you your fun, but I don't get it. You were always the steady girlfriend kind of guy."

Jeremy blew out an audible breath. "Things change, my friend. Things change."

Annie let out a soft sigh. This is where she and her brother differed on a grand scale. Jeremy had one—albeit major—heartbreak, and he swore off relationships altogether. Annie seemed to get disappointed by men over and over again yet kept coming back for more. Maybe Jeremy was on to something. Maybe that's why she hid behind what Wes thought were fantasies—those fictional happy endings.

It would also explain why she was hiding on the other side of the bed, trying to preserve whatever secret she and Wes were keeping. Whatever it was, it was her idea, and it was like nothing she'd ever done before. No commitment. No relationship. No happy ending, but also—no one gets hurt.

"Listen, man, I just woke up—"

"Say no more," Jeremy said, his voice already growing distant. "Far be it from me to keep another man from taking care of his morning wood."

"Jesus," Wes said under his breath. "You're an asshole," he called after Jeremy, but there was no response.

Several seconds later, Annie heard the shower turn on in the bathroom next door. She let out a breath. Apparently she'd been holding it whenever she could.

"Have we just completely ruined the male species for you?"

Annie straightened from her Crouching Tiger, Hidden Dragon pose, rolling her neck to smooth out the kinks.

"I know things I *never* wanted to know." She crawled onto the bed and toward him, catlike. She knew they were on borrowed time, but she needed something, however small, before she left. "Do you think there's anything you can do to help me forget?"

He smiled and pulled her to him. "How are you with first-thing-in-the-morning kisses?" he asked.

She climbed over him, feeling him hard between her legs and, *dammit*, why couldn't she stay? He groaned as she slid up his length and brought her mouth to his.

"I'm definitely pro morning kissing."

She pressed her lips to his, and he thrust his hips toward her. She sucked in a breath and then, painful as it was, slid off him and to the floor where she retrieved her hidden clothing and shoes.

"Rain check," she said, popping up and sliding into her jeans. She didn't bother with the bra, just shoved it in her pocket and stepped into her boots.

"You're killing me," he said.

She winked. "Gotta keep you on your toes, Hartley. Also—" She kissed him again quickly. "I gotta get out of here, go home to change, and make it to the shop by ten."

She straightened, but he grabbed her wrist.

"Are you sure you're okay with this?" he asked. "Our arrangement? Keeping it from Jer?"

She nodded. It had only been a couple of days, but she could tell whatever was happening was good for both of them. So what if last night she'd slept better than she had in weeks? Did it matter that as she scrambled to get out of there before Jeremy busted them, the first thought that came to mind was when she could see him next?

"When can I see you again?" he asked, as if they shared the same thought.

"Brynn comes in at noon to balance the weekend sales. Meet me at my place for *lunch* at twelve fifteen."

His jaw tightened for a brief moment.

"She knows. Doesn't she?"

Annie was almost out the door when the shower water stopped.

"Yes, but she's my best friend, and I trust her. Don't worry. She'll cover for me."

His shoulders relaxed.

"Twelve fifteen?"

She nodded and spun toward the hallway.

"Hey…Emerald City!" he whisper shouted, and she turned to him once more, her pulse racing as she imagined Jeremy throwing open the bathroom door.

"Yeah?" she whispered back.

He smiled softly. "Thank you. For last night. It was—it was nice."

She wanted to tease him, the wordsmith coming up with nothing better than *nice*. But he'd called her *Emerald City*, a nickname she knew wasn't real...because they weren't real. But it was still the best one she'd ever been given.

"You're welcome," she said. Then she heard Jeremy break into a ridiculous falsetto of Taylor Swift's "Shake it Off," and she hightailed it to the front door.

She would never look at her brother the same way again.

THE ROMCOM
by **HappyEverAfter admin** | Leave a comment

HI EVERYONE! I WAS THINKING ABOUT ROMANTIC COMEDIES TODAY, PARTICULARLY SOME OF MY FAVORITE TROPES LIKE FRIENDS-TO-LOVERS (*WHEN HARRY MET SALLY* ANYONE?)—AND MY NEW LEAST FAVORITE TROPE, BROTHER'S BEST FRIEND. I NEVER REALIZED HOW EXHAUSTING IT CAN BE TO KEEP A SECRET FROM A SIBLING UNTIL I RECENTLY STARTED READING A STORY WHERE THE HEROINE HAD TO DO JUST THAT. DON'T GET ME WRONG. IT'S A GOOD BOOK SO FAR, BUT THE CLOSE CALLS AND ALL THAT WOULD BE REALLY HARD TO SUSTAIN IN THE REAL WORLD. WHAT DO YOU THINK? FAVORITE TROPES? WHY DO YOU LOVE THEM?

COMMENTS:

HEALOVE SAYS: BROTHER'S BEST FRIEND IS MY FAVORITE. YOU'LL HAVE TO LET ME KNOW WHICH ONE YOU'RE READING. I LOVE THE IDEA OF A SEMI-FORBIDDEN ROMANCE. THE SECRECY IS GREAT TENSION AND CAN ALSO BE PRETTY DAMNED FUN.
4:00 P.M.

INSTALUV SAYS: I'M A SUCKER FOR A SECRET BABY. NOT SURE THAT ONE LENDS ITSELF TO COMEDY AS MUCH BECAUSE AIN'T NOTHING FUNNY ABOUT A SECRET BABY, BUT TALK ABOUT AMAZING CONFLICT!
4:25 P.M.

READERGIRL SAYS: ENEMIES TO LOVERS IS THE BEST. THERE IS A THIN LINE BETWEEN LOVE AND HATE AND WHEN THAT LINE GETS CROSSED? SO HAWT.
5:05 P.M.

15 MORE REPLIES...

Chapter Fifteen

Wes paced the living room floor. Max said he'd call at three. It was five minutes past. The text hadn't said if it was good news or bad news or no fucking news at all. Just that he was calling at three and that Wes had better answer.

It had been a week since he sent the pages, which meant his editor must have read them, right? She read, and this phone call was the verdict. If it was good, Max wouldn't make him wait. Would he? He'd tell him straight away. Bad news had to be face to face — or over the phone if they were in different states. That way he could soften the blow with a soothing tone.

Who the hell was he kidding? Max didn't have a soothing tone. He didn't have a soothing anything. But he was the closest person in Wes's life for the past few years, and whatever the news was, it was coming from someone he trusted. That didn't change the fact that he was ready to vomit. After all, it was only his entire future as a writer on the line.

The phone vibrated, and he almost threw it across the floor. Christ, he hadn't been this high-strung in a while.

"Hey, Max."

"Hey, Max. He says *Hey, Max* when he just made his editor cry with fifty fucking pages. He says *Hey, Max* when his publisher wants to launch the book in New York and then send him on a U.S. tour. He says *Hey, Max* after I spend an hour and a half on a call with Hollywood talking about sealing this deal on the option for book one now that you are going to blow up the bestseller lists once again." Max whistled out a breath and then laughed. "Wes, my boy, I think you just put my kids through college."

Wes collapsed onto the couch. He had to take this all in because it didn't seem real. He was blocked for weeks, had to ask for a freaking extension. He was almost ready to admit that he was a one-hit wonder.

And then there was Chicago. And Annie. A place that felt more like home each day he was there with the girl who lit up the room—and something inside of him. Everything had seemed to fall into place in the span of a weekend.

"You there, Hartley? Say something, goddammit."

Wes cleared his throat. "Yeah. I'm here. Sorry. I'm just letting this sink in. A book tour? Are you serious?"

Max laughed. "You can probably add movie premiere to that, too. Eventually. You know how slow shit goes in Hollywood."

Wes ran a hand through his hair. "No," he said. "I don't." Because he was twenty-five and still not sure this was really his life. Because the past five years had been shit. Okay, fine, the past four had gone a little better than that initial first year, but there was an emotion taking root that he couldn't articulate, probably because he hadn't felt it in so long.

He was—*happy*.

Even if the book didn't get published—even if the movie didn't get made—he was enjoying the writing. He was enjoying catching up with his oldest friend. He was *enjoying* spending time with Annie, no matter what they were doing.

He looked at the cut on his hand that no longer needed a bandage and remembered the feeling of her fingers on his palm—the warmth of her touch.

And then he realized that Max was still talking.

"...will want a detailed outline and the next fifty pages in a week. She wants to do the first pass of edits as you go, expedite the process for this book not only because we're behind but because timing is everything. We want to publish while *Down This Road* is still selling."

Wes nodded, then realized Max couldn't see him.

"Yes. Of course. I already have more pages." Even though he hadn't known what his editor would say, he couldn't stop the words now. He wrote all day and worked at Kingston's at night. But Jeremy was working, and he had tonight off. He knew exactly where he wanted to go—and who he wanted to see.

"Send me the next fifty by Monday, then. Or sooner. You're my star, Hartley."

Wes opened his mouth to respond, but he could tell by the unmistakable silence that the call had ended. It was ten after three.

In five minutes everything had changed. No. In one week, it had all changed, and he didn't want to stay in that empty apartment by himself another minute. So he grabbed his jacket and helmet and was out the door.

He didn't think, just rode. The leaves had begun to change color but hadn't yet fallen. The Chicago streets were a canopy of orange and yellow with sunlight dappled through the scattered openings between branches. He slowed to a stop and pulled out his phone, snapping a few pictures so he could remember this moment, so he could write it down later, using his words to transfer his experience to that of his characters, Evie and Jack. Manhattan didn't have trees, not like this. He could move to the outer boroughs, Brooklyn, maybe. But for the first time in years, Chicago was starting to feel like home again.

The next time he stopped, it was in front of Two Stories. He nearly tripped climbing off his bike, his eagerness to get inside—to see Annie and have her be the first to hear the good news—making him almost unaware of his own body and how to put one foot in front of the other.

He burst through the door, and when he didn't see her behind the front counter, he knew she must be in the upstairs office. So he bounded up the stairs, two at a time, and strode right toward the door in the back, knocking twice before opening it.

"Hey, Emerald City. I've got news."

But it wasn't Annie he saw. Or Brynn. It was Jeremy, sitting and slurping noodles out of a Chinese food container with his feet propped on his sister's desk.

"I found the soy sauce!" he heard as Annie emerged from the tiny kitchen area in the back of the office. When her eyes met his, they widened, and she halted mid step. Jeremy's eyes, on the other hand, narrowed to slits as they volleyed from Wes to Annie and back to Wes again.

"Emerald City?" Jeremy asked. Then he turned to Annie. "Why the hell is he calling you Emerald City?"

Annie let out a nervous laugh, which was far better than Wes was doing. He couldn't even make a sound. Jeremy was supposed to be at work. Wes didn't want to be the guy who lied, yet all he was doing at the moment was cycling through things he could say to backpedal out of this situation.

I was looking for Tabitha.

Yeah, no. Insinuating he had anything going on with the employee who was now seeing the ex might actually be worse than coming out and saying he was messing around with his buddy's sister.

Okay. Not worse. But pretty damned close.

I was looking for Brynn.

Why? He'd have nowhere to go after that one.

I was—

"Jer. Come on," Annie said. "You go to a wedding with someone, and we're bound to come home with private jokes, right? You had to be there for the schnoodle and the soda gun. It's too much to explain and wouldn't even be funny since you weren't with us. But trust me—Emerald City is the best punch line you'd have ever heard."

There it was, that nervous laugh again. Jesus, she was selling this horribly, and all Wes could do was stand and stare and see if Jeremy bought it.

"Actually," Wes said, "I just wanted to let Annie know that not only did my editor love the new pages, but my agent said the movie option is pretty much a go, so…yeah. Take *that*, the one person who hated my first book."

Wes nodded, the self-satisfied grin on his face *not* at all an act. True, he came here to kiss Annie and maybe thank her for breaking through his writer's block, but the *I told you so* also felt fucking good.

Annie's eyes lit up, but she didn't give anything else away.

Jeremy's shoulders relaxed, and his jaw unclenched. On a scale of one to Chuck Norris, his intensity dropped back down to an agitated Regis Philbin. Which was really just—Regis Philbin.

"Looks like he told *you*," Jeremy said to his sister.

"Give us the details," Annie said, and he could tell she was fighting to stay calm—fighting just as much as he was. But Jeremy kept them both in check, even though he didn't know it.

It was like there was a concrete wall between them, a concrete wall that still held a clump of lo mein noodles between his chopsticks.

"Give us the details," she repeated expectantly. "And then I have a new box of paperbacks that just came in. Maybe you'll sign them?"

He nodded. He'd do whatever the hell she asked if it meant a reason for him to linger and maybe, possibly, *not* walk out the door without tasting her lips.

"My agent just called. And, basically, my editor flipped. She loves the pages. Wants the next fifty as soon as possible so she can edit as I go. There's a lot more, but that's the gist of it. Don't let me interrupt your lunch. Show me the books you want me to sign, and then I'll head back home to work."

She nodded, then tossed a few packets of soy sauce on the desk in front of her brother.

Annie was already out the door when Jeremy turned his attention to Wes.

"I'm glad you two hit it off at the wedding, man. But that's all it was, right? Some private jokes and talking about books?"

Of course that's all it was because they'd made a deal. Whatever he and Annie were doing was exactly what Jeremy would approve of—if it didn't involve his friend and his sister. *Fun.* If no one expected a happy ending, then no one would get hurt. He wasn't going to hurt Annie, so Jeremy had nothing to worry about.

"You know she's twenty-eight years old, right, man?" Wes asked. "And probably smart enough to make her own decisions." Jeremy's jaw ticked, but he didn't have a chance to answer.

"Hey!" Annie popped back into the doorway with a stack of books in hand. "Come on. I even have a customer downstairs who wants to meet you."

He shrugged.

"See ya, Jer."

His friend nodded, but he never answered the question.

"Later," Jeremy said.

And Wes let Annie lead him back downstairs.

Jeremy, who had stopped by for a late lunch with his sister before work, lingered while Annie set Wes up in the shop's downstairs reading area, a circular rug with two plush love seats situated in an *L* formation, a wooden coffee table in front. Shelf-lined walls bordered the nook, displaying new releases and the store's best sellers, Wes's book included. He'd already greeted the reader Annie had mentioned, signed her book, and swelled a bit with pride. Until he remembered how Annie felt.

She still hated his novel—*not* that he was harping on that as she retrieved the one book still on display and added it to the pile on the table in front of him. Okay. So he *was* harping on it, silently, because a) what she thought seemed to matter a little more to him as he got to know her better, but he wasn't about to admit that, and b) Jeremy was still there, standing behind Annie as she got Wes all set up to sign, his arms crossed and a speculative glare aimed right at him.

"Jeremy." Annie spun to face her brother. "Go to work. I'm closing up thirty minutes early so I can make it to Kingston's for the big Holly-and-Will-are-back-in-town dinner."

Jeremy's eyes narrowed. "Hartley coming?" He nodded toward Wes.

Annie shrugged.

She hadn't mentioned this dinner. Or had she? Wes had been so consumed with the writing this week—along with nights at the bar—that he and Annie hadn't really had much one-on-one time other than their *lunch* date the day Jeremy almost busted them.

"You remember Brynn's sister, Holly, right?" she asked. He nodded. "She sort of moved to London with her boyfriend. I mean, he's from there. London. He's British."

Wes tried to bite back his grin, not wanting to betray

anything in front of Jeremy, but, dammit, she was adorable when she was flustered—when she was trying to figure out how to ask him out in front of her brother without really asking him out.

He nodded. "Of course. She was only a year ahead of us." He looked at Jeremy, then back to Annie. "Are you guys— inviting me?"

Jeremy gave a noncommittal shrug. Like sister, like brother.

"Leave your bike at home," Jeremy said. "Will Evans has made it a habit of bringing a bottle of high-end scotch with him whenever he and Holly are in town, and if tonight goes anything like their last visit, *no* one will be able to function by morning."

Wes scrubbed a hand across his jaw, realizing he hadn't shaved in days. Jesus, what did he even look like right now?

"Sounds dangerous," he said.

Jeremy winked. "It is."

"I'll take the bike home after I sign the books," he said.

Annie let out a breath and dropped down on the empty love seat opposite Wes's.

"Then I guess that settles it. We'll see you at six, Jer."

Jeremy seemed to be letting go of his suspicions. He was no longer trying to peel away Wes's flesh with his stare. At least that's what it had felt like. Maybe they shouldn't be keeping whatever they were doing from him, but if they told him anything, it would require defining their situation, and Wes wasn't sure he could do that.

"Yeah," Jeremy said. "Okay. See you at six."

He left them, then, but neither he nor Annie spoke for at least ten minutes after Jeremy left. Wes signed the stack of books while Annie helped a customer and then pretended to be straightening shelves that needed no straightening. It was like they were afraid Jeremy was still there, lurking behind a shelf waiting for them to slip up.

Annie pulled out her cell phone just as Wes closed the last book.

"Hey, Jamie," she said. "Is my brother there? Yeah, I just want to ask him something really quickly. Thanks."

Wes could see her out of his peripheral vision, but he didn't turn his head. He was, however, completely eavesdropping.

"Hey," she said after a pause. "Is the stout-battered fish and chips on the menu this week?" Another pause. "Great!" Pause. "Yes, that's why I was calling. You mentioned dinner, and I got hungry. You know I like to think about the menu before I order. Nope. I guess I forgot to finish my lo mein. Got distracted by — work."

Wes looked up at this, and Annie's eyes were on his. She was smiling at him, and it just about melted his insides.

"God, yes. I will so have that as an appetizer. You're the best, Jer. Bye."

She dropped her phone back in her pocket.

"You were making sure he was there, weren't you?" Wes asked.

She nodded.

"Tabitha's at the register," she said.

"So…"

"So I think there was one more book for you to sign up in my office."

Wes was on his feet and headed for the stairs before she could say another word. In fact, he practically raced her there. They were both out of breath by the time she closed the door behind them and she launched herself at him.

Wes lifted her in his arms, and she clasped her legs around his waist, kissing him hard. He stumbled but didn't fall, backing against a wall to regain his footing.

"I'm so proud of you," she whispered. "Those pages were amazing," she said. "They were so good, Wes. I *knew* your editor would love them."

She kissed him again, her tongue tangling with his.

She was *proud* of him. When was the last time anyone had said something like that? Certainly not his father, and his mom—

He swallowed hard. His mom was gone before he even wrote it. He'd had loads of people lauding his talent, from his agent to his editor to top reviewers. But most of them didn't give a shit about anything other than how well the book was selling and whether or not whatever came next would sell as well. Annie had no stake in the book. She just liked it, and that had meant more than he wanted to admit.

"What did you say?" he asked, lowering her to the ground. His voice was strained, but not from holding her in his arms.

"I'm proud of you," she said, louder this time, her tone resolute. "And I'm happy for you," she added. "I know how much you have riding on this."

He didn't know what to say. Or how to react. So he just kissed her. And kissed her. And kissed her some more.

Chapter Sixteen

Annie held up the rocks glass, examining the amber liquid inside. She'd chickened out last time Holly and Will were in town, but now even Jamie was goading her.

"Denning, you are holding about a hundred bucks right there in that glass. Don't you want to know what Ben Franklin tastes like?"

Annie wrinkled her nose. "You're disgusting, Jamie."

Brynn backhanded him on the shoulder. "Yeah, ew, babe. I don't think you're making this any more tempting for her."

Jamie had closed off the upstairs area for the night, so they had a private party of sorts. Jeremy, Wes, Will, and Holly were enjoying their Ben Nevis over at the dartboard. Jamie and Brynn were coddling Annie as she considered how many books she could buy with a bottle of the Highland whiskey and whether or not said whiskey would remove her tonsils.

"I'm sure there's a soda gun behind the bar."

The voice came from behind her, and she spun on her bar stool to see Wes, empty glass in hand.

"Holly and Will just mopped the floor with me and your

brother over at the dartboard," he said. "I need a break. And maybe a refill."

Jamie obliged by offering him another pour.

"Ha-ha," Annie said.

He clinked his glass with hers.

"It's just a drink," he said. "You don't have to if you don't want to."

She sighed. He was right. But she wanted to step outside her comfort zone. She wanted to live on the edge—just a little, even if all it meant was taking a sip of scotch.

"Jamie, why don't we go see how things are going in the kitchen—make sure your servers are doing okay downstairs."

He furrowed his brow. "We're fully staffed. I'm not even technically on the clock tonight," Jamie added, but Brynn gave him a look that Annie read loud and clear. She was trying to leave her and Wes alone.

"*James*," she said, and this seemed to get his attention.

He looked from Annie to Wes and then back at Brynn.

"Yeah, okay," he told her. "Let's check on the food."

Annie giggled softly as the two headed toward the stairs. Jeremy, Will, and Holly had taken seats at a table near the dartboard. She and Wes were sort of alone.

"She's not very subtle. Is she?" Wes asked.

"Trust me," Annie said. "Jamie's clueless. He went ten years thinking she never loved him. There's no way he knows anything about us."

Wes sucked in a deep breath, then blew it out.

"Because the whole keeping *us* a secret thing only works if it's—you know—secret."

She rolled her eyes. "I know how the game works," she said. "I needed at least one ally. I tell Brynn everything. She'd see it on my face if I didn't at least tell *her*. Don't you have an ally? Someone you can tell shit to?" She bit her tongue as soon as the words came out.

"You mean your brother?" He laughed. "My roommate and the guy whose sister I'm messing around with? Not really an ally."

"I'm sorry," she said. "I promise Brynn won't say anything."

Wes raised his brows. "I promise to reward you for her discretion, then." He glanced back over his shoulder. "Looks like the food is here. We should probably head over."

She held up her glass. "You can go. I'll be there in a minute."

He clinked his glass with hers. "You all right?"

She nodded.

"Cheers, then. See you in a minute."

He backed away, leaving her alone with her drink.

"Shit," she mumbled, then tossed back the ounce of scotch. "Shit," she whispered this time. As predicted, liquid heat slid down her throat, but she refrained from reaching for the soda gun. She didn't want to bury this feeling. Instead she savored the burn, hoping it would mask what lay beneath.

Because every time she looked at Wes, she thought about his lips on hers and his hands all over her body. How could someone whose physical touch affected her so much *not* be capable of anything more than that. Why? Why did it matter so much whether or not he believed that love could conquer all?

It wasn't like she was falling for him. Because—he didn't measure up. No romance hero *refused* the happily ever after.

Of course she wasn't falling for him. He wasn't the right guy. Annie's HEA would happen with the *right* guy. Wes was wrong. So very wrong. Anything that made her think otherwise?

That was the scotch talking.

The stout-battered fish and chips was probably delicious, more than half the table having chosen it as a main dish, but Annie was having a hard time enjoying her favorite menu item. Wes sat across from her, yet she avoided eye contact with him like he was Medusa and looking at him would give her a stony heart equal to his.

He joined in Jamie and Jeremy's heated debate about the White Sox pitcher who threw a recent no-hitter and whether or not they'd finally make it back to the Series this year. Holly and Brynn were swiping through pictures on Holly's phone of the most recent fashion show she'd produced in London. And Will—Holly's ridiculously gorgeous Brit—stared at the two women with the biggest, lovesick grin she'd ever seen.

And here was Annie—the outsider looking in. Had she ever smiled like that at anyone? What's more, had anyone ever smiled like that at her?

She took a measured sip from her glass, having now found a taste for scotch that cost more than she probably made in a week. As the liquid heat blurred the edges of conflicted emotions, the gorgeous Brit cleared his throat.

And because Will Evans was the type of guy who commanded attention on a regular basis, his gesture brought the rest of the table's activity to a halt.

"Holly," he said, his accent making her name sound like *holy*.

Wow, that was hot.

Holly looked up from her phone, still laughing at something her sister had said.

"William," she teased.

He cleared his throat again, and Annie's eyes widened. This man was—nervous.

"Holly, I wonder if you could check that horoscope app you're so fond of, see how the stars are aligning this evening?"

Annie watched as Holly's brows furrowed. She had no

idea what was about to happen, but Annie did.

"I've been so jet-lagged all week," Holly said, "I've barely checked my email. Don't tell my clients!" She giggled. "What are you up to, Mr. Evans? I thought you didn't believe in the stars aligning and all that."

Brynn nudged her sister's shoulder.

"Open the app, Holly," she said. Brynn was catching on, too.

Holly huffed out a breath. "Okay. Okay. You don't have to be so bossy."

Holly's eyes went back to her phone where she swiped and tapped. As she did, Mr. Tall, Dark, and British got out of his chair and dropped to one knee.

Annie sucked in a breath, and her eyes stung with the threat of tears. She looked at Brynn, who was just as glassy-eyed as she felt, and the two of them smiled at each other as they waited for Holly to figure it all out.

"When Gemini aligns with Taurus," she read, "you can expect nothing short of magic. If one Gemini can see fit to align with Taurus permanently, he promises to love her for as long as her constellation burns bright. He also promises never to mention last season's Jimmy Choos again."

Holly's head snapped up.

"Will, what—?"

Her voice shook as her eyes went from where he should have been to where he knelt before her. With a red velvet box open in his hand.

"I had a long talk with Sophie while you were in Milan last month." Will looked up at the table, acknowledging Wes, the semi-outsider of the group. "My daughter," he added, then turned back to Holly. "This is really all her doing." He let out a nervous laugh. "She asked me when I was going to be happy for all time, and I told her as long as I have her and you, I had all I needed." He grabbed her hand with his free one.

"I didn't think I deserved you," he said. "And I didn't think anyone could love Sophie like I do, but I see you with her—how the two of you have fallen for each other—and I know it's a lot to ask you to take on the both of us…" He kissed her trembling hand. "But, Ms. Chandler, may I ask you to be mine for all time? To be *ours*?"

Holly let out something between a laugh and a sob.

"How did you—with the app—how?"

Brynn pushed her sister on the shoulder again.

"Answer the man, Holls! Then he can tell you all his smooth-move secrets."

Holly nodded before the words left her lips.

"Yes," she said. "Yes. I will be yours for *all* time."

He slid the ring on her finger, and Holly dropped to her knees to kiss her fiancé. Brynn clapped. Annie clapped. Jeremy let out a loud whistle. Wes let a soft smile spread across his face—*not* that Annie was looking—and Jamie looked like he was guilty of a crime.

Brynn reached for her bag, but Jamie snatched it before she could get her hands on it.

"Shit," he said under his breath.

"Jamie. What are you doing?" Brynn asked.

He didn't say anything. Just sort of held onto her bag for dear life.

He didn't. He couldn't have. Not on the same night…

Brynn tugged at the bag. "James McAvoy Kingston, you are freaking me out. I just want to grab my phone to take a picture of my sister's ring."

"Um, how about your sister and her new fiancé?" Holly asked.

"Yeah, sure. That, too, if my weirdo boyfriend would just give me my bag."

Brynn tugged again at the same time Jamie relinquished, spilling the bag's contents all over the floor. Brynn dropped to her knees to collect the contents along with him, and that's when Annie saw Brynn's glasses case had popped open, but there were no glasses inside. She glimpsed something shiny just as Jamie snapped the case shut and sprung to his feet. Brynn hopped up to meet him, holding out her hand.

He didn't relinquish the case.

"Can I have my glasses?"

She reached for them, and he flinched. And because everyone was listening to them now, there was no mistaking the rattle inside the case.

Annie felt like she was in some terrible romcom—*not* that the romcom itself was terrible, but that she was that side character who watched everyone else find happiness while she again looked on from the sidelines. Brynn hadn't seen the ring, but Annie had. *Shit!* Jamie was going to freaking do it, too.

"Did you break my glasses? God, Jamie. It's one thing for you to startle me into knocking my contacts down the drain, but you *know* I can't see without my glasses."

He groaned.

"Your glasses are at home, safely hidden."

"Hidden? Is that supposed to be funny?"

He rolled his eyes, and Annie stood from the table, rocks glass in hand.

"Oh, for crying out loud, Brynn. Mr. British just had his moment, and Jamie's trying not to steal his thunder."

Holly and Will rose from their post-proposal snog fest. All eyes were on Jamie and Brynn.

"Shit," Jeremy said. "*Two* proposals?"

Brynn swiped at a tear. "Jamie?"

He let out a sigh. "It was going to be just us—tonight. When we got home. I'm not good with big, sweeping, grand gestures," he said. "But I know I'm my best when I'm with you."

Brynn reached for the case again, and this time Jamie let her have it. She opened it and lifted out the diamond solitaire ring.

"Because we both were idiots. And blind to what was right in front of us. But we're not anymore."

She shook her head. "No. We're not."

"So marry me, B. I'm not letting you get away again."

She slid the ring on her finger and wrapped her arms around his neck.

"Good. Because I'm not going anywhere."

And she kissed him.

Just like that, Holly got the proposal befitting a girl who loves the spotlight. And Brynn got her quiet promise of always from her equally quiet, but no less romantic, guy. And it was amazing and perfect yet all too much for Annie to process.

"Denning," Jamie said. "Can you go down to the kitchen? I've got a really expensive bottle of champagne I was going to sneak home tonight, but it looks like the occasion calls for sharing."

"On it, boss." And Jeremy took off down the stairs.

"Um, congratulations, everyone," Annie said, holding up her still half-full rocks glass. "Hit me up when you're looking for wedding venues, and I'll tell you all about Bliss." She could feel Wes's stare, but she stamped down the urge to return it. "I think before I imbibe anymore," she added, "it's time for me to hit the *loo*, as they say in jolly old England."

Good freaking Lord, what was she even saying? She didn't wait around for any further post-proposal lip-locking but instead hightailed it around the corner and into the upstairs *loo*. Once inside, she let out a long, deflated breath. She had to hand it to Will and Jamie, though. Proposing to sisters on the same night? Pretty spectacular. And this bathroom, with its ceramic tile and warm, wood-paneled walls—it wasn't too shabby, either.

She took a few calming breaths, then leaned against the fancy-schmancy copper sink trough and sipped her scotch, then laughed. In one week she was surrounded by a wedding and two engagements. It would be depressing if it wasn't so comical.

The door slid open, and Annie straightened, prepared for Brynn or Holly to be checking on her. But it was Wes.

He held his hands up in defense.

"Don't worry. Everyone followed Jeremy downstairs for the champagne. I said I'd wait and let you know where everyone was."

She relaxed a bit.

"Okay. I know where everyone is. Consider your duty performed." She winced at her tone, not meaning the words to come out so bitter. She blamed the scotch for her practiced even keel going all *un*even.

"So is that"—he waved his hand back toward the door—"how all your romance novels end? Double proposals, champagne, the works?"

"Is this where you remind me that romance is fantasy?" she asked. "Because I'm pretty sure all that *actually* happened."

He held his hands up again. "Hey, I'm not reminding anyone of anything. I just asked you a question."

She crossed her arms. "Fine. You want me to answer your question? Yes. Some romance novels end in proposals. Some in weddings. Some just with the hero and heroine realizing that they *can* be together, that happiness is an option. The point is that love wins. Even if it's just a happy for now, the reader is satisfied that even if the couple faces obstacles in the future, love will win."

Wes's brows pulled together. "Happy for now?"

Annie sighed. "Yeah, in books where maybe the story is going to continue with the same hero and heroine, there might be a happy for now—an ending where you know they'll face new challenges in the next book." She swirled her glass of scotch, then took a tiny, burning sip. "Why does your main character, Ethan, think he's better off alone than with one of the many—*many*—women he dates? I mean, it's not like they're all one-night stands or anything. He has relationships with them. Each woman wants to be the one to get through to him, yet he doesn't let any of them in. It's freaking maddening."

He smiled and raised his shoulders. "Maybe love doesn't always win, Annie. Maybe life gets in the way."

She shook her head. "Or maybe not opening yourself up to the possibility of love is the very thing that keeps you from it."

He raised a brow. "We *are* talking about Ethan, right? The fictional character who lives in my book."

She huffed out a breath. "It's *not* fantasy."

"Opinion," he countered. "I say it's not reality. Agree to disagree?"

He stepped closer and held out a hand to shake, but she shrunk away.

"Come on, Annie. We're supposed to be having fun, not psychoanalyzing the decisions of fictional characters or the merits of said decisions."

He closed the distance between them completely, took her scotch from her hand, and set it on top of the ledge above the sink.

"Are you no longer having fun?" he asked. "Because say the word, and we'll stop whatever this is right now."

She swallowed. "Do you *want* to stop?" she asked.

"Fuck no," he said, the words low and rough.

Sexy. God, when he stared at her with those blue eyes and that perfectly tousled hair, she almost couldn't think.

"Is fun enough for you?" she asked, then wished she could swallow the words that threatened to give her away.

He backed her slowly toward the wall and leaned in close.

He didn't kiss her, but his lips brushed hers lightly as he spoke.

"If it means being this close to you, then yes. Hell yes, fun is enough."

She writhed in her jeans. Hell. She hadn't had this much *fun* in a long time. Who was she to deny herself just because she had the type of brain that *did* want to psychoanalyze fictional characters—especially if it meant figuring out Wes Hartley.

"What do you want, Annie? Right here, right now, tell me what you want, and I'll give it to you."

He nipped at her bottom lip, and she gasped.

"What if someone comes in?" she asked.

"What if someone doesn't?"

This time when she arched her back, her pelvis rocked into the hard length beneath his jeans.

"I want your fingers inside me," she said.

He unbuttoned her jeans and lowered the zipper. Then he deftly slipped his palm beneath her panties without having to pull her pants down.

She had to admit the guy was good. Skilled. And she knew that was because of extensive practice, but she couldn't be jealous of those who came before, not when she probably had them to thank for the man Wes was now.

He slid a finger down her crease, starting at her swollen clit, and sliding with ease into her warmth.

She gasped, and he answered her reaction by kissing her, fierce and deep, and she thought she might devour him right back.

"Not too loud, Emerald City," he whispered. "They might come back upstairs."

She nodded and swallowed back a cry when he slid out of her slick heat only to add a second finger and threaten to drive her mad.

She palmed the erection beneath his jeans, and he hissed.

"Later. We're on borrowed time — and in public. There's only so much I can do and still offer us an easy out if someone walks in."

She nodded her understanding but couldn't speak as his palm rode up and he swirled a finger over her center.

She bit his shoulder — hard enough to leave a mark but not break the skin. It was all she could do to keep from moaning or crying out his name. Who was she when he touched her? Because she didn't feel like the Annie Denning she'd been for twenty-eight years. She felt like someone brand new as she gripped his wrist and shoved his hand back down, too ravenous for his touch to even beg.

"Are you having *fun,* Annie?" he whispered in her ear, and she nodded.

"Yes," she said softly. "Yes."

He plunged back inside her, and she rode him until she'd lost the will to care whether or not anyone heard them. Luckily Wes was there to think for the both of them, and when she began to climax, he kissed her hard so when she did cry out, his mouth muffled the sound.

He kissed her again before freeing himself from her jeans. "I'll walk out first," he said. "Make sure it's safe for you to make your exit."

She nodded, still coming down from the crest of that wave, and when she didn't say anything more, he pivoted on his heel and headed for the door.

"Wait!"

He sighed, and she watched the fabric of his black T-shirt stretch across his shoulder blades and expand around his biceps. *Whoa. Typing apparently did a lot for toning the upper arms.*

"Yeah, Annie?"

"I really like — having fun with you, Wes."

He grinned. "I like having fun with you, too." He glanced

down to her hips. "Button up before you come out." He winked and spun toward the door.

"Wait!" she called after him again, and he stopped. "I should probably go out first—in case anyone's there. Then I can cause some sort of diversion or something."

She buttoned her jeans, but she would be lucky if her legs hadn't turned to Jell-O.

Yeah. She was going to need a minute or seven. And the rest of that scotch.

"After you," he said, motioning toward the door.

She walked slowly, her mind racing.

Maybe she didn't need to convince him to *write* a happily ever after. *Maybe* all she needed to do was show him it existed in real life.

Brynn and Jamie.

Holly and Will.

What if—what if Wes fell in love?

She pulled open the door and almost knocked Brynn over. Her friend yelped and jumped back. Annie's first instinct was to try to pull the door shut in Wes's face, but Jamie had gone and installed bathroom doors without handles on the outside. She'd have to talk to him about that. So instead she backed up, effectively slamming into Wes's unyielding form. All this did was remind her how solid that lean writer's body was. He must do *something* to stay in shape. Typing couldn't really do much in the way of muscle tone. Could it?

"For the love of Davey Jones, Annie. It's not like I can't figure out what you two are up to. I just wanted to make sure the fish and chips hadn't gone bad or something."

Annie tried to smile, but it came out as more of a wince.

Wes just shook his head.

"Does he know I know?" Brynn asked.

"Yes," Wes said over Annie's shoulder. "I know you know. Does Jamie know?"

"*No*," Annie said with conviction.

"Well…" Brynn began, and Wes groaned. "He's my fiancé. I can't keep secrets from the guy I'm going to marry." She beamed and admired her ring.

"He's been your fiancé for all of about five minutes, B. You told him as soon as I told you," Annie said. "Didn't you?"

"Well…" Brynn said again, and Annie didn't need any further explanation. She certainly wasn't giving one about *why* their secret needed to be kept. She shouldn't have to. Brynn was her best friend and should simply have done it out of best friend obligation.

She pushed past Brynn and out into the bar area, making a beeline for the almost empty bottle of scotch.

"Whoa there, tiger," Wes said, his hand on top of hers before she could open the bottle. "Let's just *all* agree this goes no further than the four of us. Okay? I don't peg Jamie as the gossipy type, but Brynn—no offense—you do seem like a bit of a loose cannon, but if Annie trusts you, then I do, too."

Brynn pursed her lips. "No offense taken. I'm a *super* loose cannon, but I can keep it together for Annie." She looked at her friend. "Is that what you want? To keep this between the four of us?"

Ugh. With Holly and Will on their way back to England next week, that would make Jeremy the only one who didn't know—at least in their small circle of friends and family who didn't live in London. And her parents. And store patrons.

She was grasping. But really, if Jeremy didn't know, then Brynn couldn't talk to her about it unless they were alone, and if she played her cards right, Wes would be showing up more often at the bookstore, not giving her much time to *be* alone to get Brynn's third degree. In fact, he could even write there. God, she was full of brilliant ideas, but at the moment the only real justification she could think of for not telling Jeremy was that once it was out there with him, it was *out* there, which meant all the questions and expectations Annie didn't want to deal with. This wasn't really a relationship—not when Wes didn't believe in anything other than its eventual end. There was also the danger of Jeremy's reaction. Despite Annie already knowing her ABCs and 123s by the time Jeremy was born, he could turn on the alpha big brother persona quicker than she could blink. Not that she worried about Wes holding his own with him. She just didn't want there to be a situation where either guy had to hold his own against the other.

"Yeah," Annie finally said. "Just between the four of us. For now."

Wes started backing away.

"I should probably head down before you. Just in case."

Annie smiled at him. "I'll see you downstairs?" she asked.

He nodded. "See ya, EC."

And with that he was on his way down the stairs.

Brynn put her hands on her hips, her dark, wild waves bouncing on her shoulders.

"*EC*?" she asked.

Annie sighed. Yeah. No more black-and-white Kansas. No more status quo. She was finally shaking things up, adding a little color.

"Yes," Annie said. "Emerald City. Please don't ask."

Brynn held up her hands in surrender but then gave her a knowing grin.

"Have you asked him yet?"

Annie's brows furrowed.

"About helping us out—getting some of his author friends to host signings at the shop. I'm glad you're enjoying whatever is going on between you two, but I just don't want you to forget about Two Stories."

Annie's gut twisted. She *had* forgotten—or at least, she hadn't let herself remember. He'd already been her pity date at the wedding. She didn't want him to see her as *poor Annie who can't find love or keep her store above water.*

"I promise I'll get some names from him," she said, forcing a smile. It must have worked because Brynn smiled, too.

"You comin', *Emerald City*?" she asked.

"In a sec," Annie said, and Brynn's smile softened before she turned and headed down the stairs.

Maybe it was cheesy, but so what if she thought *Emerald City* was the nicest thing any guy had ever called her? So what if her heart sped up just because he'd said it? So what if she was starting to hope he might want more than fun when, at the moment, all he worried about was others finding out they were sneaking around like a couple of horny teens?

This wasn't a relationship. It was an arrangement. Silly things like hoping for more were erased from the picture before things even began. Stricken from the record. So what if it was her brilliant idea in the first place? All that meant was that if and when this backfired in her face—and let's face it, she was Annie Denning, so the odds were high—she'd have no one to be angry at other than herself.

But if she messed things up for the store—for the working relationship with her and Brynn? She'd never be able to forgive herself for that.

She glanced at her distorted image in the whiskey bottle and mumbled under her breath.

"Be careful what you wish for."

SECRET FRIENDS WITH BENEFITS
by **HappyEverAfter admin** | Leave a comment

HI THERE, EVERYONE! SO, I'M BETA READING THIS BOOK, ~~WHICH ISN'T A BOOK BUT IS ACTUALLY MY LIFE~~ WHERE THE HERO AND HEROINE HAVE AGREED TO A MUTUALLY BENEFICIAL SECRET SEXUAL RELATIONSHIP. THE HERO DOESN'T BELIEVE IN HEAS AND THE HEROINE WHOLE-HEARTEDLY DOES. SO—THEY'RE TOTALLY WRONG FOR EACH OTHER, RIGHT? ~~EXCEPT THE HEROINE IS ME, AND I'M AFRAID I LIKE THIS GUY MORE THAN I'LL ADMIT, WHICH MEANS IT'S GONNA HURT LIKE HELL WHEN THIS BACKFIRES.~~ THE HEROINE HAS A SECRET AGENDA TO MAKE THE HERO FALL IN LOVE—YOU KNOW, TO PROVE TO HIM THAT HAPPILY EVER AFTER DOES, IN FACT, EXIST. BUT TO MAKE HIM FALL IN LOVE WITH HER MEANS ADMITTING SHE HAS FEELINGS FOR HIM AS WELL. IT'S—MESSY, TO SAY THE LEAST. ~~UNLESS HE REALIZES THAT LOVE CONQUERS ALL, THAT ALL YOU NEED IS LOVE, AND WHATEVER OTHER LOVE CLICHÉS I CAN COME UP WITH.~~ I'D LIKE TO TAKE A POLL, READERS. CAN A HEROINE FORCE HER HERO INTO BELIEVING LOVE IS ALL YOU NEED, OR DOES THE HERO NEED TO CHOOSE LOVE HIMSELF BEFORE HE CHOOSES HER? ~~BECAUSE REALLY I JUST WANT YOU TO CORROBORATE THAT I CAN DO THIS AND NOT GET HURT. THAT'S NOT TOO MUCH TO ASK, IS IT?~~

COMMENTS:

HEALOVE SAYS: IMO, HERO HAS TO FIGURE IT OUT FOR HIMSELF FIRST. CAN'T WAIT TO HEAR HOW THE AUTHOR DEALS WITH THIS, EVEN IF IT IS A BETA READ AND NOT AN OFFICIAL REVIEW YET. BECAUSE THE HERO CAN STILL FALL IN LOVE BUT NOT CHOOSE LOVE, YOU KNOW?
6:02 p.m.

ROMANCINGTHESHELF SAYS: A STRONG HEROINE DOESN'T HAVE TO TRICK THE HERO INTO FALLING FOR HER. HE WILL BECAUSE SHE'S THE ONE HE'S SUPPOSED TO FALL FOR.
6:44 p.m.

BOOKSWINEFEELS SAYS: SOUNDS LIKE THE HERO NEEDS TO GET KNOCKED ON HIS ASS BY LOVE. I HOPE SHE'S THE ONE TO DO IT!
7:17 p.m.

11 MORE REPLIES…

Annie decided to stop reading the comments right there. That's all she needed—one loyal reader to be in her corner. She'd just have to be the girl to knock Wes Hartley on his ass—a man who, to her knowledge, had never let any other woman do that before.

But Wes was different with Annie. She could feel it. Even if she didn't truly know him before now, she'd felt a shift ever since the wedding, like she was her truest self with him, and maybe—just maybe—he was the same with her. If that wasn't the best recipe for proving there was such a thing as happily ever after, she wasn't sure what else was.

Challenge accepted.

Chapter Seventeen

"It was *so* good seeing you, Wes." Lindsay hugged him tight, and he tried not to squirm. "I thought it was you, and I just happened to have my book with me…"

Dog-eared on the page where his hero kisses the character named Becky, a girl who was clearly on the rebound and just needed something to fill the void. Becky, who looks a lot like the curly-haired brunette he was trying to step away from now.

"What are you doing with yourself these days?" he asked when she finally set him free.

She batted her eyes, and her cheeks grew pink. "I finished nursing school. And Kevin and I are still together." She flashed a ring. "Engaged, actually. He flipped when he read your book—when I showed him how much you wanted me, but I wouldn't let you truly *have* me because I still loved him."

Wes made a choking sound and looked around for Annie, hoping she was still unpacking stock in the supply room.

"I'm happy for you, Lindsay," he said. And he meant it. But he also meant to end this exchange, like, *now*. He scratched the back of his head and looked longingly at the couch behind him. "I should really get back to work, though."

She gasped. "Oh, of course. I'm meeting Kevin for dinner soon. I just wanted to thank you—and have you sign my book." She winked. "*Our* book." Then she backed away and out of the store.

Wes wiped his palms on his jeans and let out a nervous laugh. Who knew coming home could be so—confrontational? He dropped back down into the spot that had become his over the past few weeks.

The couch? Comfortable. The lighting? Perfect. The sugary sweet warmth of the apple cider sitting on the table next to his laptop?

The worst. Like, the absolute worst. This was no writer fuel. It wasn't fuel at all. It was candy, and Wes didn't do candy. Or sweet. Unless he was tasting it on Annie Denning's tongue. *That* was a whole other story.

Annie materialized out of nowhere and plopped down on the couch perpendicular to his, picking up the now cooling cup.

"You hate it," she said.

He was caught so off guard he wasn't even going to try to lie.

"I really hate it."

But he couldn't stop smiling, especially not when Annie looked adorable in that green T-shirt that read READING IS MY SUPERPOWER. It was cut so that whenever she reached for something on a high shelf, he caught a glimpse of the skin between the shirt's hem and the top of her jeans. *Not* that she was reaching for anything right now. But he was imagining her reaching, and well—he was a writer. He could do a lot with his imagination. Plus, the shirt made those green eyes of hers even greener, and he got a little lost when he looked at them.

But he still hated the cider.

"I drink coffee, Annie. With nothing in it. Strong and bitter."

She huffed out a breath. "That should be your author bio. *Strong and bitter.*"

He chuckled, then reached for her wrist and tugged her over to his couch. There were no patrons in or around the reading nook of Two Stories at the moment, and while he was enjoying the quiet time to write, he enjoyed this distraction even more.

She landed on his lap and wrapped her arms around his neck.

"You could probably sue me for sexual harassment or something," she said, nipping his bottom lip.

"Hmmmm," he hummed. "I'm not your employee, so that probably wouldn't hold up in court." He nipped her right back, and she gasped. "Besides," he added. "I tend to think of it as exceptional customer service rather than harassment."

He licked her bottom lip, and she took in a sharp breath.

"Wes?" she asked, as they continued with not kissing but almost kissing, which was driving him out of his mind more than actual kissing might do.

"Annie?" he said, his voice raspy and deep.

"I think we should maybe—you know. We haven't actually…"

God she was adorable when she was flustered, even more so when he was the one doing the flustering. He leaned back and crinkled his brow, feigning confusion. "We haven't actually…what?" He bit back a grin.

She groaned. "Look, I'm not shy about this. It's just different with us. We've done the whole naked thing and the orgasm thing, but we haven't actually—"

"Tamed the one-eyed monster?" He spoke softly and raised a brow. She opened her mouth to continue, but he cut her off. "Tickled the pickle?"

"Wes…"

"Pillaged your castle? Slytherined your Hufflepuff? Opened the gates of Mordor?"

"Wes!" she cried, and an older woman's head peeked out from behind a nearby bookshelf. Annie clapped her hand over her mouth, but tears were streaming down her cheeks as she stifled the sound of her laughter.

She whacked him on the shoulder.

"Mordor?" she whisper shouted. "You have simultaneously ruined both Harry Potter and Lord of the Rings for me!"

He sighed.

"You're right. I'm sorry. I'd probably be Ravenclaw anyway, and you'd end up being Gryffindor. Ravenclaw your Gryffindor doesn't sound as hot."

"It sounds downright painful," Annie said. She snorted, and the spying woman poked her head out from the shelf again.

This time the woman's eyes locked on Wes's, and recognition bloomed. He cleared his throat and gently slid Annie from his lap so he could stand.

"Mrs. Forster," he said, striding toward the woman and holding out his hand.

But she swatted the hand away and wrapped him in an unexpected hug.

"I've known you all your life, Wesley. Cut the crap and call me Sarah."

• • •

Annie didn't want to eavesdrop, but Wes didn't exactly invite her over to meet whoever this Sarah was. Other than walking straight past the two of them, there was no way *out* of the reading nook, the spot Wes had been coming to write on nearly all his free days for the past three weeks. Even Jeremy couldn't question it since he'd been having spotty internet access at his place and Two Stories offered free wifi. It meant she could see Wes several times a week—in public—and not have her brother question it.

But now she was trapped in her own place of business. Tabitha was at the register, so Annie decided to straighten shelves and try not to listen.

"Does your father know you're here?" the woman—Sarah—asked him.

Wes let out a long breath. "I tried to tell him I was coming home. Even called him from the road. But you know how he is."

She sighed. "He's your father, Wes. I think he'd like to know you're in town. I read about the book signing a while back, but luckily your father didn't see. How long have you been here?"

The tone in her voice told Annie that this woman knew Wes well, well enough to ask that question. Annie had known Wes needed a place to stay, but she didn't know it was because he didn't want to let his dad know he was home.

"A month," he said, his tone flat.

Annie stilled in the long silence. Her back was to them, and she fought the urge to turn, but her resolve didn't last long, not after Sarah spoke.

"Hasn't he lost enough?" she asked. "He loved your mom, Wes. I did, too. And we *all* miss her. But if he knew you were so close yet didn't call? If he *knew*? It would crush him."

Annie spun to face them, her heart in her throat. At least this wasn't another ex. Annie hated pretending like she hadn't seen the other girl. But this seemed even more intimate—family drama that Wes hadn't shared with her, and she wanted more than anything to escape.

Wes stared at the woman, his jaw tight and his hands fisted at his sides.

"If you really knew her like you think you did...if you knew *them*, you'd know how fucked-up that sounds," he said.

"Wes—"

He shook his head. "No. Sarah. Don't. Just don't. I appreciate your good intentions, but my father and I are way beyond that. Robert Hartley doesn't get crushed. He doesn't even shed a tear for the woman he supposedly loved."

Shit. Annie needed to abort this mission and fast. She shouldn't be here. This wasn't her conversation to hear.

She pulled out her phone and quickly texted Tabitha, asking her to come looking for her in the reading nook. It was terrible and awful to put her employee in the middle of this, but the way Annie saw it—Tabitha kind of owed her one.

Fifteen seconds later, Annie heard her name.

"Hey, Annie? Can you come help with something up at the register?"

Wes and Sarah froze as Annie emerged from where she was hidden.

She gritted her teeth and painted on a smile. The woman must have seen her and Wes earlier, but now wasn't the time for introductions.

"Excuse me," Annie said, walking past them as if she didn't know either one. And the more she thought about it as she made her way toward the front of the store, the more she believed that to be the absolute truth.

Chapter Eighteen

Wes checked his phone. One thirty. Jamie thought they'd be dead tonight, a Thursday with no important games on or anything like that, but at eleven o'clock an unexpected bachelorette party on a pub crawl burst through the door, and his chance of getting off before midnight disintegrated into thin air.

"Hey," Jamie said, wiping down the bar. "I'm really sorry I had to keep you so late."

Wes shrugged, doing his part and wiping off the taps now that last call had turned into *Finish your drinks and pack it up, ladies.*

Wes's phone buzzed with a text, and he pulled it from his pocket. He tried to keep his reaction neutral.

"That Annie?" Jamie asked.

"Am I that obvious?" Wes countered.

"I—uh—" Jamie continued. "I know you were probably banking on taking advantage of Jeremy being out of town for the weekend."

Actually, he'd just planned on taking advantage of the

fact that Jeremy had already left this afternoon. The rest of the weekend was still in question.

"We really don't need to do this," Wes said. "Annie's a smart girl. I trust her to make her own decisions."

Jamie nodded. "So do I. And if it was anyone else, I'd stay out of it. But Annie's my friend. I owe her a shitload of gratitude for what she did to help me and Brynn figure our crap out. So if I need to step in on her behalf, I will."

Wes nodded in response. Guess they were really doing this. Talking about it out in the open. He didn't think that was the way of men, at least not men he knew and certainly not himself. Besides, maybe Annie would still be awake when he got there. Tabitha was opening the shop tomorrow, so she could sleep in.

Wes sighed. "You probably think I'm a huge asshole," he finally added.

This time Jamie shrugged, and Wes wondered if they'd ever make it further than noncommittal gestures in this so-called conversation.

"I don't make it a habit of taking advantage of my friends or sneaking around. But this is what Annie wants right now, and I'm honoring that," Wes said. "Just so we're clear. I know what Jeremy thinks of my past, but it's not like that's a secret from Annie. She knows where I'm coming from, and she's okay with our arrangement."

Jamie nodded.

"Annie and Jer are more than friends to me—to *us*," Jamie said, and Wes knew he meant Brynn. "They're family. And while I respect that this is what Annie wants right now, I won't stand by and watch if you do anything to hurt either of them."

Wes clenched his teeth and let out a forceful breath through his nose. He really was on his own here. Wasn't he? If this whole thing crashed and burned, Annie and Jeremy would have Jamie and Brynn to help pick up the pieces, and Wes would be, once again, flying solo.

Never mind that he'd been in town for nearly a month, that he and Annie had finally found a rhythm, even if it meant only seeing each other one-on-one once or twice a week. He still hadn't called his father, the one person who *should* have his back yet never really did.

"I care about Annie," Wes said. More than he was willing to admit out loud. But it didn't mean he couldn't be careful with what they were doing—with doing his best not to hurt her even if he was starting to feel things he hadn't felt with any other woman.

Jamie stopped what he was doing and turned to face him now.

"I know she's smart. I know she can make her own decisions. But I also know she's got these...expectations when it comes to relationships, and maybe I worry about her wanting more than you might be willing to give."

Jamie did have a point, but Wes's instinct was still to go on the defensive. He did his best to hold back. Jamie was the guy who signed his paychecks, after all. It would only be another month before he got that first royalty check, and then he wouldn't have to play it so safe anymore. And if the movie thing panned out? Well, then he wouldn't even have to wait. He could stay or go. And the closer he got to finishing his manuscript, he wondered how welcome he really was in the place that used to be home.

"Noted," Wes said.

The last of the patrons were filing out, including the very drunk group of women for whom Wes had already called a cab to make sure they got home safe. He and Jamie finished closing up in a thick, tense silence. Wes locked the front door and followed Jamie out the back where he set the alarm and made sure the place was secure.

"She likes you," Jamie finally said before he hopped into his truck and Wes onto his bike.

"I like her, too."

Jamie shook his head. "Every other guy she's brought around—she never lit up for them like she does for you."

Wes laughed quietly. "Because *you* notice these things."

Jamie crossed his arms. "When it comes to those who matter, Hartley, I notice."

Though he knew neither of them would say it, he wondered if Jamie noticed how he lit up when Annie was around, too.

• • •

Annie woke to the sound of her phone, and she couldn't remember what she'd set an alarm for or why she'd wanted to wake up at one in the morning. Or why she was sleeping fully clothed on the couch.

She squinted at the phone until her eyes adjusted and realized it wasn't an alarm but a text response from Wes.

Sorry our night got ruined. Maybe tomorrow after you get off work? Or...I guess tomorrow is today, huh?

Shit. She'd meant to wait up, even pulled out her favorite book, *The Wonderful Wizard of Oz,* to keep her awake. This was supposed to be their night. *The* night, actually. Because despite the fun they'd had since that fateful wedding weekend, they hadn't actually gone the distance. The whole nine yards. And now that Annie was awake and thinking about it, she *really* wanted Wes to hit a home run.

Oh, screw the freaking euphemisms. She wanted sex. With Wes Hartley. Tonight. It wasn't just that they'd discussed it the other day in the shop. Annie had a plan. A seduction plan. And now all she had was bed head and her heart beating a mile a minute.

The text was time stamped a minute ago. Double shit. Had he just texted as he left the bar, or was he already home?

I'M UP! she texted back, hoping the all caps would somehow make his notification louder.

She was up and pacing the room now, and when he didn't text back immediately, she groaned. In fact, it was a full seven seconds before his reply came through.

Good. Because I was starting to feel like an ass sitting out here on your front step.

Her heart leaped, even though she thought it was just that other part of her that didn't want to call off tonight's festivities.

Huh. She wasn't expecting that.

She raced to her door and then to the main door of the walk-up. And there he was. Beer-stained T-shirt under his leather jacket. Five o'clock shadow that begged to rub across her jaw. And blue eyes that searched hers for something.

"What?" she asked, as if his expectant gaze warranted a response.

He shook his head like he was shaking off a thought.

"I'm just—I'm really glad you're still up," he said.

She laughed. "I wasn't. I even missed the initial text but not the reminder. That's what woke me."

His brows knit together.

"I just wanted to see you," he said. "But I should let you get some rest."

She threw her arms around his neck and kissed him without warning. He sighed against her, then ran his hands up her back, pulling her closer, like he couldn't get enough of what was right in front of him.

"I don't want to rest," she said, breathless against his lips. "Unless you do."

He backed her through the open door and then up the stairs and into her apartment.

They kept moving until they hit her couch, and then they

toppled over the arm of it together.

"Don't. Want. To rest," he said, his voice strained with need.

She wrestled his jacket free and then his beer-dampened shirt.

"Tough day at the office?" she asked. But then there he was, kneeling above her in just his low-slung jeans, all lean muscle and ragged breaths and those eyes—still searching. What was he trying to find?

She unbuttoned his jeans, and he stopped her, his hands on top of hers.

"Are you sure you want this, Annie?"

Her brow furrowed. He could have just been asking about the moment, about the immediate future. But something made her think it was more. She wouldn't ask. Because either way, her answer was the same. But she wasn't so sure what his would be.

Although his hands still rested on hers, he didn't try to stop her again when she answered by lowering his zipper, then pulling his jeans and boxers over his hips. Good God, this man was a sight. And damn puberty for not letting their paths cross a decade ago. Because maybe if she and Wes had connected as teens, they'd have what Jamie and Brynn have now.

She groaned softly, inwardly scolding herself for stupid *what ifs* that could never have been. Three years back then was huge. Three years now? Maybe Wes was done maturing physically, but he was the first to admit he was emotionally stunted.

Stop thinking. Just do what you've been dying to do with this guy for weeks.

Except they were on her couch, and it's not like she had a condom in her back pocket.

"I don't suppose you brought anything with you?" she

asked, and he shook his head.

"I wanted this to be on your terms," he said. "Kind of alleviates the temptation if I'm not constantly prepared."

Huh. She wondered if he learned this from experience, from being *too* prepared too often. She didn't want to know.

"Then—we're going to have to switch locations."

He sat up, his eyes darting to the coffee table, and he picked up her book.

"Still your favorite, huh?" he asked.

"Still?"

He nodded. "Confession. I saw it on the bookshelf in your house when we were in high school. Your brother mentioned it being your favorite, so I borrowed it and read it that night. Returned it the next day so you wouldn't know it was gone."

She took the book from him and leafed through its pages, eyes wide with recognition.

"You read *this* book? *My* book?"

He nodded again. "I mean, I'd seen the movie. Who hadn't? But I wanted to see if what our teachers at school always said was true."

"What's that?"

"That the book is usually better than the movie."

"Consensus?" she asked, her heart beating too wildly for just their shared love of a book.

He looked down for a second, then met her gaze again with a guilty-looking grin. "It's what made me want to write," he admitted. "Which means I was maybe trying to impress you with the whole Emerald City thing," he said.

Annie swallowed. "And now? Are you still trying to impress me?"

He shrugged. "Is it working?"

She kissed him. "Yeah. I'd say it is."

The kiss felt different than just a few minutes ago. Did Wes feel that, too? It was like his admission had just closed a ten-year gap, and she wasn't sure what that meant. But it meant—*something*.

He cupped her cheek in his palm. "If I'm going to be completely honest, I don't think my impression will last if I don't take a quick shower." He looked down at his naked body. "I'm a mess, and I don't want to be a mess for you."

Ha. A mess. Not from where she stood. Still, who was she to deny him?

"Yeah, sure," she said, needing a few moments to think anyway. "Towels are in the cabinet next to the sink. See you in a few?"

He smiled. "Don't fall asleep."

She crossed her heart and held up the book, then headed into her room while Wes stepped through the door across the hall and closed it behind him. She opened her small, top dresser drawer, the one meant for jewelry and loose change and, in her case, condoms. She pulled a couple from the pack—just to be safe, or maybe it was wishful thinking—and backed up to her bed, flopping down on her back.

What he'd said to her that night in the Blissful Nights hotel—it wasn't off the cuff. He'd read her book, shared her love of it. Hell, he'd become a writer because of it. This changed everything, didn't it?

She pretended to fan herself with the small foil packets. She thought this night seemed born out of a physical need. Initially she'd planned on answering her door in nothing but the emerald green bra and panty set she was wearing. But she'd fallen asleep, and in the confusion of waking up, all plans of seduction were lost to making sure he didn't leave.

She hungered for Wes just the same now, but there was something insatiable in her need. Annie peeked under the collar of her T-shirt. She *was* still wearing the sexy undergarments.

Her legs swung back and forth off the foot of the bed as

she tried *not* to think about what it would mean if she finally opened the gates of Mordor. If he Slytherined her Hufflepuff.

She laughed, but suddenly their funny euphemisms weren't as funny as they were before. Because this *would* mean something. And while this wasn't part of the plan—this attaching meaning to what was happening between them—she wanted him just the same.

No. Annie had wanted men before. She *needed* Wes.

"You are a little slow on the uptake, Denning," she said to herself in the mirror above her dresser. A beautiful man was in her shower. And maybe he needed her, too.

She stripped down to nothing but the demi-cup bra and lacy, boy-cut briefs. She gave the girls one quick adjustment, gathered all her gusto, and strode across the hall. She knocked softly on the door, her nerve wavering, but Wes answered immediately.

"Yeah?"

Ugh. He didn't say *Come in.* Did that mean she had to try to yell through the door over the shower water? Or did that mean he knew she wanted to come in and was inviting her to do so? If she hemmed and hawed another few seconds, would he doubt he even heard a knock at all and then be startled if she actually walked in?

She blew out a breath and whispered, "Get yourself together, Annabeth Louise Denning." Then she rolled her eyes at the thought of how proud her mother would be that she was talking to herself as if she *was* her mother.

That was it, the final straw. When *Mom* started entering her thoughts… Well, there was only one way to erase that.

She burst through the door and slid on a patch of wet tile before hip checking the counter with a thud.

"Shit!" she yelled, hunching over and rubbing the skin that would be purple in a matter of hours.

Wes threw back the shower curtain.

"Are you okay?" he asked, nothing but sincerity in his tone as she stood—though doubled over—with her palm on the throbbing wound.

"I'm fine," she said, straightening. "This is me doing sexy seductress. You like?"

He stood there, curtain open and his slick, toned body in full view. She might not have the skills in the seduction department, but based on what she saw in front of her, Wes liked something he saw.

"I can't think of anything I like more," he said, water dripping off his lips—water Annie was desperate to taste.

His eyes had that playful glint she loved, all the hesitation from before having melted away. She held up the condoms and fanned them in her fingers, a tentative smile playing at her lips. Annie realized she needed Wes to be sure about this as much as he had questioned her feelings back on the couch.

"Two?" he asked.

She shrugged. "We don't have to use both. Or either, really. It's your call. But I want you to know I want this. I want *you* like this."

His chest rose and fell. He combed his fingers through his soaked hair, pushing it back as it fell over his forehead.

"Show me what you want, Annie. Like that night in the hotel room. Show me."

He stood there, bare and exposed and offering to give her what she wanted. All she had to do was articulate it. Or point him in the right direction.

She stepped toward him, careful on the wet tile this time, and lifted his hand to her breast. Her nipple pebbled beneath the lace of the bra, and he dipped his thumb inside the demi-cup to rub the sensitive skin.

She gasped, then reached past him to drop the two foil packets in the soap dish.

"Use your mouth," she said. "Please." She still wasn't used

to having a say. Not that any guy had ever taken advantage of her. It was just—with everyone else there had been a rhythm. A routine. But Wes seemed to take pleasure in *her* pleasure more than anything else, and she still wasn't sure what to do with that.

He unclasped her bra, spreading it open so it hung off her shoulders, exposing her breasts with two hard, sensitive peaks. He dipped his head and flicked his tongue against the right and then the left.

Annie's knees buckled.

"Whoa there," he said, catching her around the waist. "Maybe we should take this elsewhere?"

She shook her head. Sure, it was probably safer for both of them if they continued this in her bed, but Annie didn't think she'd last long enough to get there at this point. She wanted his hands on her, his lips, his teeth—she wanted every part of him to tease every part of her. And then she wanted him to slide between her legs and make her come.

But she couldn't formulate the words. Because they were words she'd never said to anyone else. She'd never known she wanted what Wes was offering until he asked.

"The water's warm," he said. "Do you want to come in?"

"Yeah," she whispered, her strained voice unrecognizable to her own ears. There was something animal in her tone, something Wes Hartley was about to unleash.

He held her arm as she stepped over the lip of the tub, bra still dangling off her arms and panties still on. She didn't care. The water felt good against her skin, heat mixed with heat. He pulled the curtain closed and let the steam envelop them.

"What's next?" he asked, the corner of his mouth quirking up.

"Mouth and hands," she said.

He lowered his head back to her breasts, and she grabbed one of his hands and placed it at the seam of her panties, hoping he'd take the wheel from there.

His mouth went to work on one breast. She wasn't even sure if it was left or right because her brain was scrambled already. She couldn't be certain, but she thought there was a finger teasing the inside seam of her underwear, sliding along the place where leg met pelvis.

When he reached the bottom, went as far south as he could, that's when he snuck beneath the fabric and entered her with one slick push.

For the love— There went her knees again.

Somehow she righted herself, managing not to slip down to the base of the tub, and Wes continued to slide in and out, his movements slow and controlled just like that night at the wedding when she guided his hand where she wanted him to go—where she *needed* him to go.

She grabbed the base of his shaft and stroked the hard flesh from root to tip. He groaned, his finger exiting her so he could tug at the wet lace. She helped him, shimmying out of the briefs while managing to keep one firm hand on him. She shook off the bra, throwing it outside the curtain.

Once she was finally free, she urged him back toward the spout. He maneuvered them into the corner so no one got impaled, and she lifted a foot onto the small porcelain ledge and pressed her swollen center against his erection.

"I don't think I have any more foreplay in me," she said, a note of disappointment in her tone. "I can't—I just need—"

She didn't have to say another word. He was reaching past her, grabbing one of the condoms and tearing it free from the package. She'd no sooner uttered her inarticulate plea when he'd rolled it down his length, lifted her thigh to get the right angle, and entered.

He sank deep, filling her completely, and she cried out.

"Am I hurting you?" he asked, his voice deep and laced with concern.

She shook her head. How did she say what couldn't be said? *He* was the master with words. She only read them. How did she tell him he was doing everything right, that she hadn't known what right was until he'd touched her? How did she tell him that he'd entered deeper than she knew he would, filling the depths of her too-long protected heart? How did she tell him she was falling in love when she wouldn't even hold his hand in public?

Annie was shit with words and timing and choosing a guy who could promise happily ever after.

How did she say *anything* when words couldn't do justice to the burning ache in her belly as he moved inside her, slowly building toward a release she knew would come, but not the way she'd anticipated?

"It's perfect," she managed to whisper before he was kissing her so hard and deep, those wet lips as delicious as she'd anticipated.

Because in this moment he was—perfect. *They* were perfect. Did he feel it, too, or would he let his stubborn belief keep him from admitting that maybe, just maybe, *she* could make him happy?

She could show him what happiness was, but how could she make him claim it?

The answer was simple. She couldn't.

Chapter Nineteen

Jeremy slid the flyer across the bar. Wes slid it back. It was like they were doing a little dance. Back and forth. Back and forth. Until Wes finally used too much force and knocked it to the floor.

"Dude, what the fuck is your problem?" Jeremy asked. "It's for a good cause."

Wes shrugged. "I'm all for donating. I'll even match the highest bidder for the evening. But I'm not doing a bachelor auction."

Jeremy groaned. "Don't you get it? You're a local celebrity. If you are on the list, *you'll* be the one to earn the highest bid. Unless you have some secret woman stashed in your closet—in which case, I'm charging her rent—you have zero reason other than pride to say no. And pride is highly overrated."

Wes finished the last of his pint and stepped back from the bar, turning toward a table that needed bussing. He was off the clock in a few minutes, ready to escape to his manuscript, though he was avoiding Two Stories today. It had nothing to do with bumping into Sarah on Thursday—though his past did seem to find its way to the present whenever Annie was around. He just had to deal with tonight, with seeing his father, on his own. The easiest path was always to keep others at an arm's distance, which meant avoiding Annie—just until he got through the evening.

"Count me out, Denning," he said before Jeremy forced a confession out of him or before the guilt ate him alive. He gathered the empty glasses from the high-top table and deposited them in the bus bin at the nearest server station. "I've actually got a date right now," he lied, slipping behind Jeremy to wash his hands in the bar sink.

His friend slapped him on the back.

"Shut the fucking door. You've been holding out on me!"

Wes dried his hands on the towel next to the sink. "It's either *shut the front door* or *shut the fuck up*," he said. "The whole point of the first phrase is to use it as a euphemism for the second."

He pivoted to face his friend who had his hands crossed over his chest. Jeremy gave him an *I give zero fucks* grin.

"I'll shut whatever the hell I want, Hartley, and you're going to tell me about this well-kept secret of yours."

Wes pushed past him, grabbing his helmet and jacket from the spot where he'd stashed them behind the bar.

"I'll fill you in if anything comes of it," he said. "But it's still too early to tell."

Because he didn't want to put himself on the auction block for other women. Despite his and Annie's arrangement, it just felt wrong. He wasn't ready to fuck things up between them. It had been so easy to walk away from the others, and though he and Annie held each other at a distance in public, there was an invisible tether between them, one he wouldn't sever with something as ridiculous as a bachelor auction.

Then he was out the door and on his bike.

Wes had an hour to kill before he had to make good on his promise for his dinner date, and the only place he felt even remotely sane these days was in the writing. He was a dick for not stopping by the shop today — or the two days before that. It was, after all, on his way. But he couldn't shake the intensity of what happened between him and Annie Thursday night. So instead, he sat down at his laptop and hammered at the keys.

It was Jack and Evie's first time, too, but he was going to do for his hero what he wasn't able to do for himself. Jack would keep it casual, stay detached. Wes wouldn't burden him with the confusion of wanting someone so much he physically ached when he wasn't with her. He wasn't going to put Jack in a position of letting Evie demolish him.

Annie said the book had hope, unlike *Down This Road*. In the early pages, she'd said Jack was opening himself up to the possibility of something more with Evie, something she hadn't seen in the first book. But Wes suddenly felt his hope spring was tapped. Tonight would prove that, when he came face-to-face with the one person who'd had the power to restore that hope for years yet never had.

He set his alarm on his phone since he knew he'd get lost in the words, so when a knock sounded on the door, he startled and thought he'd missed the warning bell.

"Christ," he whispered, then laughed softly to himself. He checked his phone. He'd been writing straight for the past forty-five minutes, but he wasn't late.

"Just a sec," he called to whoever was on the other side of the door, expecting to find a parcel delivery or some other benign visitor. But Annie stood on the other side of the door in her leather jacket and a green cardigan over a black T-shirt that said WHEN I THINK ABOUT BOOKS, I TOUCH MY SHELF in white lettering. He wanted to chuckle at the shirt, but she was going to kill him with the green, reminding him of that emerald bra and panty set, the material soaked against her body as she stepped into the shower with him.

He cleared his throat.

"Annie. Hey. I was just on my way out."

She brushed past him and into the apartment, so he closed the door and followed her in. Apparently she was on a mission.

"I could have used my key, you know," she said.

Right. This was her brother's apartment.

"Okay..." he said, crossing his arms over his chest.

She tugged at the bill of her knit cap but didn't take it off.

"I'm just here to grab this apple cider mix Jeremy got for me when he was in Wisconsin this weekend. Don't let me keep you."

She slipped into the kitchen and came out a few seconds later with a small shopping bag in her hand.

"Tabitha's closing tonight," she said. "So, I guess I'll see you when I see you."

As quickly as she'd breezed in, she was practically out the door. The words left his mouth before he could think them through.

"I'm having dinner with my father," he said. "That's where I'm going."

She spun from where she stood in the already open doorway.

"Oh," she said, her expression softening. She was clearly upset about something, but she wasn't about to say it.

"It's a lot to get into right now," he said.

"It's fine," she blurted. "Not my business. Have a nice dinner."

She turned to the open door again, but Wes grabbed her hand.

"Come with me," he said.

She stopped and let him pull her toward him. Fuck. It had only been a few days, but he missed having her this close— close enough to touch. To smell that sweet vanilla.

"That sounds kind of like a date," she said, her expression unreadable.

He let out a bitter laugh. "If it is, it's the worst date imaginable. I'd turn me down right now. Robert Hartley can cook spaghetti as well as anyone else, but I promise he'll probably burn the garlic bread and serve it with a side of bitter resentment."

The ghost of a smile tugged at her lips.

"And you want me there for spaghetti and resentment?"

He nodded. He really did. It wasn't just because he wanted a buffer. Being next to her calmed him. He'd been dreading walking out that door yet knew he had to man up already. It wasn't a battle of Hartley wills if one party didn't even know the game was being played.

"Yeah," he said. "If you can't think of another way to spend your Monday night."

She shrugged and took a step closer. He could dip his head and kiss the top of hers if he wanted. And he fucking wanted. But he hadn't seen her since she left him in her bed to go to work late Friday morning. Like an asshole, he'd feigned sleep until she left.

"Annie—" he added, but she slapped a hand over his mouth.

"You don't owe me an explanation, Wes. Our arrangement doesn't require explanations."

Except it did. Especially after that night—after telling her about the book. He owed her so much more than disappearing for three days, but he was a chickenshit when it came to her— to what he knew he felt but couldn't say. She was letting him off too easily. And because he liked easy, he was going to let her.

He pressed his lips to her open palm. When she didn't flinch, he laid his hand on top of hers, kissing her warm skin again.

"Is that a yes?" he asked, lowering her hand.

She nodded.

"You got yourself a date," she said, her lips parting into a soft smile.

"The worst date ever."

She laid her hands on his cheeks.

"Silly, silly boy," she said. "How can it possibly be bad if it's with me?"

He blew out a long breath and let his shoulders relax, not realizing how tense he was until that moment.

"Gimme two seconds. I just have to save this file."

He turned back toward his laptop on the coffee table. He did a quick save and closed the computer.

"Getting close?" she asked, following him over and resting on the chair.

He nodded as he stepped past her in the other direction, grabbing his jacket from his room. When he was in front of her again, he did what he'd been wanting to do since she walked in. He kissed her, and she didn't hesitate to kiss back, opening her mouth and inviting him in. He let himself have these few moments of peace before he walked into the lion's den.

God, she tasted good, like cinnamon, vanilla, and warmth—and Annie. She had a flavor all her own; one that even though she was here, in his arms, giving him exactly what he needed, he craved more of.

"I really don't want to leave this apartment," he said, groaning at the thought.

"If I didn't think it was beyond important that you did," she said, her breathless voice driving him fucking mad, "then I'd be talking you out of it so quickly you wouldn't know what hit you."

He laughed, forcing himself to take a step back.

"I know exactly what hit me," he said. "A fucking tornado called Annie Denning."

Her cheeks were flushed and her lip gloss smeared just outside the line of her plump lips. She grinned at him, and it struck him that he put that smile there, that he had the power to make someone else happy. That he *wanted* that responsibility—of making Annie Denning happy.

"Maybe you're not in Kansas anymore," she said.

She was teasing him. He knew she was. But her gaze held something more than the playful glint he was used to. Or maybe that was him—*feeling* more than he expected.

Because ever since she blew into his life—or, he guessed he kind of blew into hers—he'd been knocked so far off his axis he wasn't sure he could right himself.

And now he wasn't sure he even wanted to anymore.

"No, Emerald City," he said. "Kansas is long gone."

Chapter Twenty

Annie had thought of every excuse in the book to avoid riding *the bike*.

Not in a cocktail dress.

She preferred walking.

She liked to ride the L.

Taxis were fun!

The helmet wouldn't fit over her hat.

She only rode motorcycles every other Monday but never twice in the same month.

Also, Wes needed to stop referring to it as a bike. A bike had pedals for your feet. Colorful tassels that hung from the handles. And possibly a cute little basket up front to carry your books. Who cared if her perfect version of a bike sounded like something off a five-year-old's Christmas list? At least it was a legitimate definition.

But what she stood before now had only one similarity to her Huffy. A kickstand.

Sure, she showed up at the apartment to pick up her cider from Jeremy, but she chose a time when she knew Jeremy wouldn't be there and hoped Wes would. She wasn't sure what she was expecting, but dinner with his father was definitely not on the list.

Yeah. She had nothing at the moment. No witty comeback or madcap excuse that might work.

"How much does it weigh?" she asked.

Wes grinned. "Five hundred sixty-five pounds of pure, sleek, leather-topped beauty."

Five hundred sixty-five pounds of metal beneath said leather that would crush her when they crashed. *If* they crashed. No, she was pretty sure it was *when*.

He handed her a helmet, but before she could argue, he snagged the knit cap from her head and stuffed it in a case that was strapped next to the seat.

Guess his bike does have a basket.

"You don't have to ride," he said. "I'll take a cab if it makes you more comfortable, but there's no way I'm getting in *your* passenger seat again."

She grabbed on to the helmet and stared at it for several seconds. He was teasing her about their drive home from Bliss, but there was a slight edge to his tone, one she could tell he was trying to mask. She remembered how freaked out he was when she pulled into the Starbucks lot. Whatever was going on that morning, he sucked it up for her. She'd do the same, now, and suck it up for him.

Their eyes met again.

"But, Annie," he added, "you're safe with me. I would never let anything happen to you."

Her stomach plummeted. It was as if she was on the Giant Drop at Six Flags, freefalling from hundreds of feet in the air. Yet the last time she checked, she was on solid ground. Something about Wes Hartley, though, pulled the rug out from under her.

She believed him, that he'd keep her safe—on the bike.

She just wasn't so sure about her heart.

"Okay, then," she said. "I trust you."

He helped her fasten her helmet before putting on his own. He showed her how to position her legs so they stayed clear of the muffler. And then he climbed in front of her and reached behind to grab her arms and wrap them around his waist.

"Don't let go, okay?"

She squeezed him tight and pressed her helmet to his back. No way in hell she was letting go.

Whenever they hit a red light or stop sign—which felt like every thirty seconds—Annie sucked in a breath and gripped Wes tighter. At least the weather was cooperating, a balmy fifty degrees even as the sun set. At the light just before Lake Shore Drive, he did a quick check-in, making sure she was okay. She lied and nodded, though she was sure he knew it. Annie just had to remind herself that once they got on the drive, it was only about five miles north to Edgewater. And to Wes's childhood home.

Suddenly she wasn't so afraid of the journey. The destination, though. *That* sure as hell freaked her out.

The light turned green, and Wes rubbed her thigh before grabbing the handles of the bike and opening it up onto the expressway.

The force of the movement threw Annie back against the tiny seat rest and she gasped. She'd lost her grip and had to scramble to gain purchase, but she did in seconds.

You're safe with me.

She repeated the words inside her helmet like a mantra. Wes knew what he was doing. He'd stop the bike if anything was wrong…right?

She pressed her cheek to his back. Well, as much as she could while wearing the cumbersome helmet. When she realized she'd been squeezing her eyes shut, she forced them open and understood what her fear was doing. It was making her miss out.

Come to think of it, she'd been missing out on a lot. Like feeling the way she felt about the man in front of her. And admitting it to herself.

Lake Michigan rolled out before her eyes, a blue blanket spread as far as she could see. It was early October, which meant daylight saving time hadn't yet stolen their sunlight. So she breathed out a long sigh and took it all in. The beach where she'd spent her summers for as long as she could remember. The path where people took advantage of the lingering autumn warmth to jog along the water or walk their dogs. She wondered if she and Wes had ever been on that same sand at the same time, clueless that a decade later he'd be spending nights in her bed. Or that she'd be here, on the back of his motorcycle, on their way to a family reunion he had clearly been avoiding.

But he wanted her there. And she wanted to *be* there. And she certainly didn't want to miss out on anything anymore.

She relaxed against him for the rest of the ride. When they finally pulled up in front of a narrow, yellow brick building on a quiet tree-lined street, Annie had forgotten she was on the bike. She also forgot that once the vehicle stopped, she was supposed to let go.

Or maybe it was just that she didn't want to.

Wes took off his helmet and ran a hand through his hair. Then he rested that free hand on top of the two that were still clasped around his waist and squeezed.

And that's all it took, one tiny gesture to make her see that as much as she'd thought him the one with the walls to break down, she'd constructed barriers of her own. Annie loved the books she read—the happily ever afters and the hope that love could conquer all. But in the back of her mind, no man could live up to her expectations. She saw that now—the reason why she seemed to play it safe, always ending up with men she wasn't sad to see leave. Did Brett hurt her? *Yes*. Did she miss him? *No*. It was like a tiny part of her always knew he wasn't the one, but wasn't it safer to know she'd survive the fallout of however their relationship ended?

Her eyes widened under the helmet, and she was grateful for the privacy, grateful for a private moment to have her revelation.

She'd never let anyone in who was *real*. What a hypocrite she was for giving Wes shit about a book that didn't end in a happily ever after when Annie preferred the fictional heroes to reality. What did it matter that she'd dated men, that she'd lost them, when she didn't care for them like she should have in the first place?

Like she cared for Wes.

Shit, she was in trouble.

She unsnaked her arms from his torso and removed her own helmet. He hopped off and grabbed it from her, fastening both to hooks on the back of the bike, while she just sat there wondering what her next move should be.

Did she tell him she loved him before they headed into the building? He'd just avoided her for three days, and now she was going to barge in on important family business and drop this kind of news? Probably not the best idea.

But when he stood before her like that, his hair tousled from the helmet and his recent finger combing, leather jacket now unzipped and exposing a well-worn but fitted gray T-shirt, she had to do *something*.

It's not like he was saying anything, either. So the moment hung in the air, ignorant of time, until he or she released them from this suspended animation.

Annie reached for his face and pulled it to her own, kissing him hard and deep, his stubble scratching her jaw. She slipped her tongue between his lips, and he clasped his hands behind her neck, fingers tangling in her hair.

This. This was the moment she'd like to infinitely suspend. She felt his kiss from her lips all the way to the tips of her toes and back again. She let him fill all the spaces she'd kept locked away, hoping that maybe he was letting her do the same. A kiss like this couldn't be one-sided, so she crossed her fingers that everything they were leaving unsaid was being spoken without words.

You're brilliant and talented, she said as her tongue tangled with his.

You're broken, and that's okay. I won't try to fix you, but I'll be here for you when you're ready. She brushed her lips along his jaw.

You're sexy and delicious, and I want to kiss you every time I see you. She laughed softly as she did just that.

And finally, because she knew they'd have to part and face what they came here to face, *I'm in love with you.* That's what her lips spoke with the last kiss.

"Are you ready?" she said aloud, and Wes backed up enough so she could see his blue eyes blazing into hers.

"I am now," he said, his voice rough and at the same time full of something she hoped was recognition.

I just gave you my heart, Wes. Please be careful with it.

He helped her off the bike and onto the sidewalk in front of the building.

"You're my parking good luck charm," he said. "This is it."

He nodded toward the yellow brick.

She laughed again.

"What?" he asked.

She shook her head, trying to talk herself out of connecting dots that might not be there.

"A yellow brick building," she said. "Are we following the yellow brick road?"

He scrubbed a hand across his jaw, smiling as he looked from the building back to her.

"Isn't the Emerald City at the end of the yellow brick road?"

She nodded.

But he shook his head. "Then no. We're not." He kissed her once more, soft and sweet this time. "Because, Annie— I'm already there."

Chapter Twenty-One

Wes was trying to process what had just happened on the curb. Something had shifted between him and Annie the other night. He knew that. He'd been trying to wrap his brain around it for three days.

But that kiss? Christ, that kiss. If he didn't know better, he'd swear he had just polished off a bottle of that imported scotch. But he was stone-cold sober, standing in the entryway of the apartment he hadn't seen in five years, not since he lost the one person who held their small family together.

He braced his hand on the wall, grateful he'd just walked in instead of knocking, so his father wouldn't see him like this.

"Hey," Annie said softly. "You okay?"

"Wes? That you?"

A gruff voice sounded from around the corner, so he forced himself to stay upright and follow the sound, Annie thankfully by his side.

When the small hallway opened into the living room/dining room combo, Wes found his father opening a bottle of wine at the dining room table—and *Sarah* standing next to him with an empty glass waiting to be filled.

His dad stood tall, a good two inches over his own six-foot frame. His hair was light brown like his, but it was threaded with more gray than the last time they'd seen each other. And he had a beard. He'd never seen his dad with a beard. He and Sarah were oddly matched, his father in a cream cable-knit sweater and jeans while the dark-haired woman wore a navy cardigan and khakis.

"You brought someone with you," was his dad's greeting.

No *Hello* or *How ya doing?*

"So did you," he responded, not expecting the words to sound so bitter. He liked Sarah. She'd lived in the building as long as they had. "Will Mr. Forster be joining us as well?"

Sarah's face went white.

"Wes," his dad said, his voice low and soft yet with the hint of warning it carried so well. "Joel passed away two years ago. A heart attack."

Wes staggered back. Annie tried to grab his hand, but he pulled free before she could get a good grip on him.

"You've got to fucking be kidding me," he said.

"Watch, it, son," his dad said.

"Robert, honey, it's okay," Sarah said. She grabbed the bottle of wine and filled a glass, handing it across to Wes as if it were a peace offering.

He took it, but that *honey*—that's what did him in, what pushed him so far over the edge he wasn't even going to try to climb back up.

"I need a minute," he said, and strode across the hardwood floor to the open balcony door. As soon as he was outside, he breathed in the Lake Michigan air. Despite them living a few streets inland, he knew the lake was out there, and he took comfort in knowing that just a few miles east was freedom.

He drained his glass of wine in seconds, only then realizing he'd basically thrown Annie to the wolves. He turned and found her standing on the balcony just outside the door, arms crossed and her eyes narrowed.

She pursed her lips, and Wes readied himself for the onslaught. He deserved it.

"Tell me about your mom," she said, her tone soft and tentative.

"Wait, what?" he asked.

She stepped out onto the small, metal balcony and met him at the ledge.

"*Down This Road* starts with the hero, Ethan, at his mother's funeral. He and his father barely speak, and then Ethan leaves town for three years. How much of Ethan's story is yours? I mean, I've met Oksana and Stacy. I saw you with Lindsay."

His eyes widened at this. Looked like they'd both kept Lindsay a secret.

"How much of that book is really you? How much of that bleak, hopeless, I-accept-my-lonely-existence stuff is Wes?"

He braced his hands on the ledge in front of them and sighed.

"The correct answer is *none of it*, right? The story belongs to Ethan, not me."

She shook her head. "You're deflecting. And I'm not going anywhere, so you may as well lay it all out there, Hartley. I told you I don't scare easily."

But her voice was uneven, maybe even a little shaky. He knew it wasn't about his past. She could handle whatever he told her. But could she handle what it meant, this kind of intimacy? Because she was asking for it, and he was about to comply.

"Five years," he said. Her brows furrowed. "Five years," he echoed. "I've been gone for five years. Since the funeral. I was home for her birthday weekend, the first time I'd been here since I left for school. She and my dad had just argued about something, and she'd stormed out saying she needed to go for a drive." He shook his head. "I should have never let her get behind the wheel," he said. "I should have fucking stopped her. Instead I hopped in the passenger seat to keep her company." Annie put a hand over her mouth and shook her head.

"Why didn't you tell me? God, that day on the highway when I drove like a lunatic to change lanes and get off at the Starbucks ramp—I didn't know."

Her gaze softened, and she reached a hand to his cheek, but he didn't let himself press into her warmth.

"I don't even remember the accident. I blacked out and woke up on a stretcher in the ambulance. According to the accident report she swerved to miss a fucking pothole and lost control. The driver's side wrapped itself around a light post. I walked away with a few stitches and a fucking concussion."

She pressed her palms to his chest, and a tear slid down her cheek. But he shook his head.

"I don't want your sympathy," he told her. "I was gone for two years before that, too," he added. "No matter what I say about my father, I'm an equal opportunity shitty son."

"You were away at school," she said. "If you're dealing with survivor's guilt, I get that. If you feel guilty for avoiding your dad since your mom passed, *fine*. But don't punish yourself for being a kid who loved being away. That was most people I know."

He shook his head.

"I liked school, Annie. But I stayed away because it was easier." He ran a hand through his hair. "They were good people," he said. "I mean, she always told me what a great guy he was. But it was like they existed purely to push each other's buttons, to get a rise out of each other. I didn't want to get caught in the middle of it anymore. My father had to plead with me to come home that weekend—promising it wouldn't be like it was before. Instead it was a whole lot worse."

She tugged at his belt loop and pulled him close, reaching on her tiptoes to kiss him. Just once — soft and reassuring.

"You were a kid. Cut yourself some slack." She kissed him again on the cheek. "And the accident wasn't your fault. God, Wes. I'm so sorry. Maybe it's time you got to know your dad as an adult. Man-to-man and all that. You guys need each other."

He laughed softly and unexpectedly. "I've never actually heard someone say that. Man-to-man."

She swiped a tear from under her eye and shrugged. "Well…he's a man. You're a man. Go be men together. Or whatever." She cradled his face in her palms. "Where were the stitches?" she asked.

He took her left hand by the wrist and raised it to the hairline just above his temple, pressing her fingers to the raised scar beneath his hair. She kissed the wound he knew she couldn't see, one that had been sealed for years. Only now it felt like it was finally starting to heal.

He skimmed his fingers across her forehead, wondering what he did to deserve her and how he was going to keep from messing this up.

"I'm really glad you're here," he said. "Thank you."

She rested her palms against his chest, and he could feel his heart beating against her touch.

"I'm glad I stopped by to pick up my cider — that I totally left in your apartment *not* completely by accident."

He grinned. "Maybe it wasn't the cider you really wanted?"

Her cheeks flushed pink. "Don't get too cocky, mister," she said, backhanding him softly on the chest.

He caught her hand before she pulled it away. "I know what *I* want, now, Annie. And I think — maybe — you were right." But he didn't take it any further than that. Instead he grabbed her hand and pulled her back through the door.

"Everything was delicious," Annie said, raising her wineglass to toast Wes's father. "Thank you so much for letting me join you."

Sarah gave her a look from across the table, one Wes didn't miss.

"Annie, why don't you come help me with dessert while we let the boys have a few minutes alone? It's warming in the oven over at my place."

Aha, Wes thought. *Here comes the man-to-man part.*

"I'd love to," Annie said. She reached a hand under the table to grab his and squeezed. And then she was up and following Sarah to the front of the apartment.

Wes topped off his glass of red and took a few healthy swigs.

"Place looks great," he said, deciding on small talk. "You put in crown molding."

His dad gave a gruff, "Mmm-hmm," and then took a few gulps from his own glass.

Well, this was going well.

"Tell him you're reading the book," Sarah whisper shouted, popping her head out from around the corner before she and Annie walked out the door.

His dad set down his glass and crossed his arms over his chest. He stroked his short beard with his fingertips, like he was still getting used to it. Must be a new look. Not that Wes would know. Jesus, how did he not know things like whether or not his father had facial hair? Probably the same way his dad didn't know he was writing a book all those years ago.

"Are you really reading it?" Wes asked.

"Mmm-hmm."

Shit. It was like he was some preprogrammed toy that only had one response—the one that was most maddening.

"Do you—like it?" he asked.

His dad shrugged.

Wes tapped two fingers against the inside of his forearm.

"Two words. Sounds like—" He raised his brows, knowing he was being an ass. But he guessed it took one to know one. It had been six months, plenty of time for a man to sit down and not only read his son's published novel, but to have something to say about it.

"Still a smart-ass after all these years, huh?" his dad said.

Wes let out a bitter laugh. "After how many years, Dad? The five since I've been gone? Because you haven't known me since then, and I'm not sure how much you really knew me before."

His father's jaw clenched. Even beneath the beard he could see it.

"Your mother could relate to you. I never knew how."

Wes shook his head. "Why? Because I wasn't an athlete? Because a score at a speech tournament wasn't as exciting if I didn't have to get busted up to earn it?"

His father slammed his glass down on the table, red wine sloshing over the rim and onto the white tablecloth.

Wes ground his teeth together and forced himself not to react. He just held his father's fiery gaze.

"You really are the guy in the book. Aren't you?" his dad asked, his voice low and rough. "That Ethan who thinks his parents had a loveless marriage, that his father *never* knew him? What a load of shit."

His dad got up and went to the bookshelf tucked into the corner between the fireplace and the balcony doors. He pulled a thick, leather-bound book off the top shelf and brought it back to the table, dropping it in front of Wes. More wine sloshed out of his father's unattended glass, but the man didn't seem to care.

"Your mother and I—we had a rough time of it, trying to have kids. You came along when we had just about given up on the idea. You didn't know us when we were younger. And you don't remember me from when *you* were younger. You want the story that's missing? Here you go."

Then the man simply walked past him and out the front door.

Wes decided not to let his father's wine go to waste and transferred it into his now empty glass. He drank it down as he pored over the photos in the album, an album he'd never seen before. Many pictures were of his parents before he was born, vacation snapshots. Some with destinations like Hawaii and San Francisco. Another of the two of them ice fishing. There was a section dedicated to a surprise thirtieth birthday party for his mom. His stomach sank, and his eyes grew hot with the threat of tears when he turned the page to find his dad staring at the camera with three paint brushes in his hand—one that had the word *Mommy* stenciled on it. One that said *Daddy*. And the third read *Baby*. The day he found out they were having a child.

Why had no one ever shown him these photos? Why had he never known they were like this? Or had he blocked it out with everything that came later?

His dad's cheeks were tear-soaked in the photo, the whites of his eyes pink. With each second he stared at the image, Wes found it increasingly harder to swallow—to take in enough air to fill his lungs. He turned the page one more time and saw himself at four or five years old, sitting on his dad's lap while the man read him *Where the Wild Things Are*.

Wes pushed away from the table, his movement so quick and so sudden that his wineglass fell over, the remaining liquid sloshing onto the open pages of the album.

"Fuck!" he growled, grabbing a napkin and blotting up

the wine as fast as he could, but the photo was already stained red, the image itself beginning to smear. "Fuck!" he said again, and suddenly there was another set of hands helping his own.

"It's okay," Annie said softly as she gently pushed him away while she continued damage control.

"No," he said, practically tearing at his hair. "It's not okay. It's not okay if I've had it fucking wrong all these years. I always blamed him for pushing me away, for us being too different that we couldn't connect. But what if I pushed just as hard?"

He thought about all the Sundays he'd walked in on his dad watching a football game, assuming they'd have nothing to talk about if Wes didn't give a shit about who was playing. He thought about the speech tournaments his mom came to and wasn't sure if he'd even asked his dad to join, if he would have canceled a weekend painting gig to watch his son wipe the floor with the competition. And he remembered the argument between his parents before he left for college—his dad asking his mom if she was going to cut her hours at work after she'd just made partner at her law firm and his mom maintaining that it was more important than ever for her to be a visible presence in the office.

At that point it wasn't about the money. He'd earned scholarships, and they'd been putting away for years to send him to school. It was one of the reasons they never left their tiny apartment.

Maybe his mom had done her best to put Wes first. But if he tried to see it all through his father's eyes—she'd put her career above everything else. Then Wes. Then him.

"I fucked up," he said, his voice rough.

He was leaning on the back of the couch now, Annie's hands on his cheeks. Her thumbs swiped at the wetness under his eyes, but she didn't say anything.

"This is the guy I never wanted you to see," he said. "This

is the guy in the book who blamed everyone else for his fucked-up life when it was always in his power to fix it."

She smiled softly. "Like clicking your heels together and saying *There's no place like home*?"

He shook his head. "There is no magic. And I'm sure as hell no fucking wizard."

Annie kissed him.

"No," she said. "You're not. You're the brilliant, beautiful man I'm in love with."

She didn't wait for him to respond, just kissed him again.

And for the first time in what felt like hours—he could breathe.

Chapter Twenty-Two

"The accident," Sarah had said as the two of them had waited for the apple pie to cool. "Victoria—Robert called her Tori—worked ridiculous hours in the suburbs. Her commute was an hour each way. He'd planned a surprise party. Tori was so late that some of the guests had to leave. When she finally got home, they both just blew up at each other."

"Wow." Annie hadn't had anything more articulate to say.

"He's still working past the guilt that the last time they spoke was an argument," Sarah had told her. "And it looks like Wes is working through quite a bit, too. I'm glad he has you."

Now Annie and Wes rode in silence. Wes had insisted they walk to the nearest train stop, which was several blocks away. And despite the chill, Annie had complied. After an hour alone on the balcony with his dad, during which the two had made a dent in what she hoped was the beginning of reconciliation, he was in no shape to drive. She got it, now, his reluctance to step into a vehicle driven by anyone else.

"The only place I'm in control is on the bike."

That was all he'd said before asking if she wouldn't mind taking the train.

She didn't ask him if he wanted to go back to his place. It was like they'd decided without saying it out loud that he was going home with her. Because when they got to her door, he said nothing when she ushered him inside. Neither of them spoke a word as she peeled off his jacket and T-shirt. As he did the same with her until they were chest to chest. Skin on skin. And she could feel his heart beating against hers.

He hadn't told her he loved her. He hadn't responded at all to her confession. But that was okay, right? It was there. She could feel it. He'd just had one hell of an emotional roller-coaster ride. She could give him some room to process it all.

But right now she let him guide her to her bed, undress her completely, and himself as well. Every other time they'd been behind closed doors, he'd catered to her every need—asked what she'd wanted and given it to her. But what she wanted now was for him to take the lead. He'd lost control, and she wanted him to know he could get it back—or that at least she was in this with him, that they'd get a grip on it all together.

She laid on her back and reached for an unopened condom left over from the other night, still sitting on her nightstand.

"Show me what you want, Wes," she said, handing it to him.

He tore it open and handed it to her to roll on. She did.

He lowered himself to her, nudging his tip at her opening. Without any foreplay, it took several moments to ease his way inside. He was gentle, waiting for her body to ready itself, and when it did, he thrust inside her, and a tear leaked out the corner of her eye. Not because it hurt. But because it felt so right. Because she was so devastatingly in love with this man, and she wasn't sure she'd survive if it ended.

This wasn't a game anymore—no secret arrangement between two people who claimed they only wanted fun. This was her heart, and she had given it to him without the guarantee of the happy ending.

When she opened one of her favorite romance novels, she always knew the couple would find their way. But this wasn't fiction. It was real life, and she realized there were no guarantees, and that was the scariest part to admit.

His movement was slow at first. Long glides in and out, each time sinking deeper. No, that wasn't possible. They were as close as they could get when he entered her the first time. But she felt it deeper. With each thrust—each arch of her back and tilt of her pelvis, she loved him further, harder, without limit.

But she couldn't say it again. She couldn't say anything, too terrified of her own emotions. So she made love to this man and hoped he was doing the same. She tangled her fingers in his hair as she kissed him, raked her hands down his back as he filled her again and again.

"You can let go," she whispered against his lips. "Let go, Wes," she said again.

"Annie, I—"

"Yes, you can." She cut him off, not letting him doubt her anymore. "You can with me."

He nodded and kissed her hard, his movements speeding up. He was so close. She could feel it. And when he slipped a hand between them, swirling his thumb over her swollen center, he brought her there, too. Annie cried out in glorious release while Wes let out something akin to an angry, frustrated growl as he plunged deep inside her again and again and again before he finally collapsed against her, his head resting on her heaving chest.

She kissed the top of his head and ran her hand through his hair, along the temple where his scar was buried, to the strands at the nape of his neck that were drenched in sweat.

Annie had broken through. She knew she had. Tomorrow everything would be different.

Annie had expected Wes to have a revelation. If not that, maybe a little morning delight and *then* that revelation—the one where he realized he hadn't reciprocated in the *I love you* department.

What she *hadn't* expected was the imprint of Wes on the sheet next to her but *not* the man himself.

"Come *on*!" she yelled aloud. But exasperation quickly turned to a sinking feeling in her gut. She'd told him she loved him. And maybe he hadn't said it back, but last night wasn't just sex. It was her proving the words were real and him responding without any words at all.

Or was it all an act? After all, how many of Ethan's lovers in *Down This Road* thought that *they* were going to be the one to change him? How many of them fell for him just to find an empty bed the next morning?

She'd broken through. Hadn't she?

Tears pricked at her eyes, and she swallowed back the threat of a sob. *This.* This was why she played it safe. But she hadn't seen it coming—hadn't seen *him* coming. All this time she thought she'd be the one to knock Wes Hartley on his ass, but maybe he'd done just that to her first.

Her phone vibrated with an incoming call, and she filled with her last shreds of hope that it was Wes, that there was a perfectly logical reason why she'd professed her love to him last night and woken in an empty bed. Because things couldn't be worse than what her mind was dreaming up.

Then she looked at her phone.

Things got worse.

"Mom. Hi," she said. "Is everything okay?" The last person she wanted to talk to when she was having trouble keeping her emotions in check was her mother, but the woman didn't randomly call on a Tuesday morning, which meant one thing only. Something was wrong.

"Hi, honey. I wanted to catch you before you went to work. Are you working today?" Annie opened her mouth to answer, but her mother kept going without pause for her to do so. "Anyway, I figured this would be best heard in the privacy of your own apartment, so enough beating around the bush. Your father and I are divorced."

Annie shook her head, like she was trying to clear it to process what she'd just heard.

"What? When? Does Jeremy know?"

Her mom sighed. "We got divorced your senior year."

Annie was pacing now. "My senior year of college? Mom, that was—that was six years ago!"

She listened for her mother's response, but instead a long silence rolled out between them, and the world Annie thought had just flipped on its axis fell out of orbit completely.

"No," Annie said, eyes wide in recognition. "Tell me you're joking, Mom." Still no response, so she filled in the blank. "*High school*? You and Dad have been divorced since freaking high school?"

"That's it, sweetheart," her mom finally said. "Embrace what you're feeling. Let it all out."

"Let *what* all out, Mom? What the hell am I supposed to feel about this news?"

Her parents had a happy marriage. They were what she aspired to—longevity. Proof that what came after *The End* in a book could last beyond the honeymoon phase. *They* were the bridge to reality, that it could be done. And now that bridge crumbled to dust in the revelation of a lie. She thought she'd found her chance at the same happiness with Wes.

And now he was gone.

"This is good, Annabeth. You're angry. *Feel* it. Really get in there and roll around in that ire. You've spent too much time burying your nose in that unrealistic fiction. Take a bite out of reality and savor the bitter taste of freedom."

Annie let out something between a groan and a scream. "Freedom? What about commitment? About love seeing you through the good and the bad?"

Her mom laughed. "My therapist says that's a bunch of bullshit. She says we both settled but didn't realize it because we'd gotten so used to the routine. But one night over your father's cedar plank salmon and a bottle of wine, we both realized we needed to spread our wings, and we've never been happier."

Spread her wings? Who the hell is this woman?

"Okay, okay," her mom continued. "I owe you an explanation. Look, I was your principal. Your father was a teacher. We didn't want there to be—" She paused. Dramatically. Because apparently her mother was all about drama now. "*Talk*," she continued. "We just didn't want to tell you until you and Jeremy were out of the house for good, and after grad school and your brother's failed engagement, we feared he'd move back in, that we might not get rid of him until he was thirty. Then your father would have had to move back in and—let me just say it would have been odd. But look at our boy! Twenty-five and independent. We're so proud."

Annie's hands clenched into fists. "Odd?" she cried. "Odd is faking a marriage and retroactively fucking up your kids!"

Her mother sighed. "Oh, sweetheart. We did what we thought was best for you and Jeremy at the time. Newsflash—adults don't have all the answers. We're really all imposters, messed-up teens in the bodies of those who should be wiser. But I'm still figuring it out, you know? Life and all that. You're so young, honey. Maybe you can figure it out earlier than I did."

Annie opened her mouth to say something, but no more words would come. She had to sit and digest the lie that had been her life since she was a teen.

"We've both been very happy, you know," her mom said, more quietly now. "He's been seeing a very nice young woman for a few years. We play Bunco together, actually. Her name is Theresa. And I have to tell you—I've been enjoying being single for the past decade. I have my fun. I go home. And no one's nagging me to pay more attention to them. There's this app called Tinder—"

"Ew, Mom. *No.* You may be used to your divorce, but I'm not. I need a minute here. Or a lifetime, really. Please don't ever tell me about your singles escapades. Like, *ever.*"

When she realized *she,* herself, was still naked, Annie pulled on a pair of yoga pants and her hoodie that read DON'T JUDGE A BOOK BY ITS MOVIE. She brushed her teeth and threw on her knit cap while her mother was going on about an anger retreat she was attending this weekend and that Annie should join her so they could howl at the moon together. *Howl at the freaking moon?* Oh, she was going to howl all right. Only with ten years of repressed emotion, she might go full-on werewolf if she wasn't careful.

"I gotta go, Mom," she said when she was ready to walk out the front door.

"Okay, sweetie. Good talk. I'll call you after the retreat. But let me know if you change your mind. Oh, and I haven't told your brother yet, so let's try and keep this between us until I track him down, okay? Whenever I call it goes right to voicemail."

Annie nodded but knew her mother couldn't see.

"Bye, Mom." She ended the call.

She swiped open her blog app and readied herself to type but realized she couldn't fake reading a book about a woman's parents who were divorced ten years without her knowing—or the man she'd fallen in love with making love to her and then disappearing. She had enough to worry about without wondering how her brother was going to react to her parents—or her and Wes for that matter—and she sure as hell hoped her brother wasn't home. Because she was going to head over to his apartment, use her key, and march right in, demanding an explanation.

She just hoped it was one that wouldn't break her heart.

Chapter Twenty-Three

Wes had already ordered when he got the text.

Max: *What are your plans for lunch?*

Max: *Like I give a shit. You're having lunch with me and Leslie Alexander from the studio. She's making us an offer.*

Max: *Yes, I'm coming to Chicago. I'm on a fucking plane right now.*

Max: *I'll meet you at that piece of shit bar you're "working" at. 11:00.*

Max: *Don't argue with me. I live on the Upper East Side. Everything, by comparison, is a piece of shit.*

Max: *Joanne loved the new pages, the hero getting ready to fuck things up again. Now give her the happy ending you wouldn't in the first book, and we're gold, Ponyboy. Print out what you have and bring it for Leslie to read. If she likes it, we may be looking at a two-title option.*

Max: *11:00. Don't be late.*

Wes shook his head. Incoming texts from his agent were no different than a face-to-face conversation. Max only listened if he needed information from you.

"Double espresso and caramel apple cider for Wes!" the barista called.

He checked the time on his phone. Ten fifteen. *Shit.* He wasn't going to make it back to Annie's—and he barely had enough time to make it home, shower, and print his three-quarters finished manuscript.

He grabbed the drinks and held the cider in the air.

"Free cider!" he called out. "My plans just changed."

A woman and her teenaged daughter took him up on the offer, and Wes hustled through the door and in the direction of his apartment. Of *Jeremy's* apartment.

Shit. Everything was happening out of order. He was supposed to sneak out for the coffee and cider, bring it back, and tell Annie what he'd been too overwhelmed to say last night. Then they'd go to Jeremy together and tell him the truth—and everything would be fine because Wes wasn't messing around with his best friend's sister.

He was in love with her.

She was passed out asleep when he left, so chances were he had time to get home, get done what needed to get done, and then call her on the way to Kingston's. But when he got to his apartment door, Max was there waiting—in what looked like one of his signature tailored Italian suits, wingtips, and his overgrown dark hair just barely holding its intentionally tousled style. The guy would have been a movie star himself if it wasn't for the unfortunate case of his five foot, six inch frame.

At least, that's what Max would tell you.

"Where the fuck have you been, Hartley?"

He snagged the Hot Latte cup from Wes's hand, finished the espresso like it was a goddamned shot, and pushed through the door as soon as Wes turned the key in the lock.

"You look like shit, by the way."

Wes laughed. "Yeah, well, for the first time in a long time, I don't feel like shit."

Max tossed the empty coffee cup on the counter and crossed his arms. "You know, that makes a fuck load of sense," he said. "You're so fucking gorgeous when you're cynical, makes sense that happiness would suck some of that away." The man chuckled. "I'm sorry for your loss."

Wes toed open the door to his bedroom and undressed, wrapping himself in a towel.

"Make yourself useful," he said to Max as he walked out of his room and into the doorframe of the bathroom. He nodded toward his laptop on the coffee table, hoping it still had some juice in it. "I have a wireless printer on the kitchen counter. Just wake it up and print the file that should still be sitting there. That's the manuscript."

Max scoffed. "Did you just give me an order?"

Wes was the one crossing his arms now. "I suppose I did. You *do* work for me, right? If I don't make money, *you* don't make money, and I think you want me to make money. So print the manuscript. Please."

He closed the bathroom door behind him, turned on the shower, and laughed quietly before stepping in. He let the hot water wash away the years of grief and guilt and blame.

Things were far from perfect between him and his father, but last night was a start in the right direction.

Everything was different. *He* was different. Last night kicked the shit out of him, and he might not have survived it if Annie wasn't there. It's like she knew exactly what he needed at every turn. Or maybe it was just that she knew *him*. Because as hard as he may have tried to keep that from happening, he couldn't keep Annie Denning out.

She loved him, and it was time to start believing that he deserved someone like her in his life. It was time to start believing that it didn't have to get as messy as it got for his parents. He just had to let Annie know he felt the same way — as soon as this meeting was over.

He laughed quietly to himself, imagining the satisfied grin of the woman who'd finally proven his outlook on life wrong.

"Three hundred pages in four weeks, huh? You find your muse here in the Windy City, Hartley?"

Wes had just emerged from his room in a clean pair of jeans and a black button-down with the sleeves rolled past his elbows.

"I think I did," he admitted. Though he wasn't quite ready to tell Max he was staying.

"Once we sign this option deal," Max said, "the tour stops are going to multiply. Joanne has fast-tracked this one to launch next summer. You get her those last fifty pages, and we're set. Then get that apartment sublet because after we kick this baby off in June, you are on a two-month tour — possibly three. My inbox is exploding with booksellers who are already hearing buzz about the new book. They want you, Wes. They fucking want you. If we play our cards right, we can tack on a European tour after the U.S. one ends. We could have you booked through the new year."

Wes cleared his throat. A couple weeks ago, this all seemed too perfect. Even now he was still happy about the buzz his publisher was generating—about the possibility of both books being optioned for film. But it wasn't just about *him* anymore. Annie was part of the equation, too. How did he tell her he was in love with her, that he wanted to move back to Chicago *because* he was in love with her, but that in eight months he was going to leave? Possibly until the end of the year?

He checked his phone, which was almost dead. It was a quarter to eleven.

"We should go, yeah?" he asked his agent.

Max nodded, manuscript tucked away in a leather messenger bag. "But I'm not getting on your Harley," he said. "Some men need to ride around on a replacement for their manhood. I got mine right here."

He shifted his junk.

"Jesus, you're an asshole," Wes said.

Max winked. "You say that as if I'm not proud."

"We're walking," Wes told him. "My bike's in Edgewater, and you know I like to avoid the taxis when I can."

He'd work on that, too. But for now, he'd start with his relationship with his dad. His relationship with four-wheel motor vehicles would be next. Baby steps.

Max narrowed his eyes at Wes.

"*You're* walking, then. I'm heading out to grab a cab. Don't be late."

Max was out of the apartment before Wes could answer him. He woke up his phone again. Or at least he tried. It was dead. He threw on his jacket and shoved the charger in his pocket.

Just stay asleep, Annie. He wasn't sure if she was in the store today or not, but the fact she was still asleep at ten was promising. He was exhausted from last night, emotionally and physically. All he had to do was make it through this meeting. Then he'd head back to Annie, wherever she was.

• • •

Annie hesitated, key in hand, as she stared at the lock to her brother's apartment. She knew she wasn't going to walk in on Wes and another woman. That wasn't his style. He seemed to have exes all over the city—even though he'd been in New York since college, everyone who found their way into his first book was back here, lurking. But that didn't mean he wanted any of them.

She loved him. Annie *loved* him, and she was finally ready for the one part of the happily ever after she'd always protected herself from—the risk. Because her heart beat so savagely in her chest that she thought it might explode. And Wes—he was simply scared. That was the only explanation that made sense. But she'd show him they could be scared together.

Last night was indescribable. Annie had never felt more connected to another human being as she had with Wes. But that didn't explain the empty side of her bed where he'd fallen asleep—the fact that he was gone without a note, a text, anything. What if everything was different for him in the sober light of day?

What if she got the hell over herself and just walked into the apartment? She wasn't going to answer any of her questions standing out here.

Annie groaned. Why did her inner monologue have to get so logical?

She shoved the key in the deadbolt lock first, then unlocked the handle. Before she could plague herself with more questions, she just walked in.

The living room was empty. She poked her head into the kitchen, both bedrooms, the bathroom. It was like she was on some crime show and she was checking each room for a perpetrator. But no one was here. If she had a partner, she'd look back over her shoulder and yell, "Clear!" And then they'd get on with their search warrant or whatever.

But Annie didn't have a search warrant. She didn't have permission to be here. And she felt like an idiot for trespassing. For not trusting him. Just because her parents were a hot mess didn't mean the apple couldn't fall far, far from the tree. She wasn't her mother, and Wes wasn't either of his parents. They were something else entirely, the real deal. There had to be a reasonable explanation for his absence this morning after what they'd experienced last night. She would just grab the cider she'd left here when he'd unexpectedly invited her to his father's house. He probably had the opening shift at Kingston's and just didn't want to wake her. She'd casually pop in and say hello. That was it. She just had to see him to know that whatever happened last night wasn't a fluke. That what had been brewing between them for the past month was real from the moment his lips touched hers.

Where had she left the cider?

Ah. There it was. On the chair in the living room. Annie strode over and grabbed the bag, ready to spin back toward the door. But Wes's laptop was open. And awake. Which meant he *was* here, right?

She took a quick peek, just at the page count, and saw there were at least thirty pages more than the last time she'd read it.

"He gave me all his other pages to read," she mused aloud. "He'd probably want my input on these, right?"

It's an invasion of privacy.

But he's writing our *story.*

It's me on the page, so it's my right to read.

What the hell else do I have to lose?

She would have continued the rationalization in her head, but she swallowed her guilt and scrolled through the pages of Jack and Evie's story until she came to the first chapter she hadn't read.

The hero and heroine's first night together. Like *really* together. Like *opening the gates of Mordor* together.

She let out a nervous laugh.

"Sex, you idiot. Just say the word *sex*," she chastised herself. And then she read.

It was every bit as emotional as that first time with Wes had been. She grinned when she read Jack's internal reactions.

For the first time after returning to the place where he grew up, Jack finally felt like he was home.

Every kiss from her felt like a promise, and he wanted so badly to be the man to keep it.

As much as he tried to protect himself, Evie had found the crack in his walls and had burrowed her way in. This was when he knew it was time to mess things up, to do something beyond repair so she'd have no choice but to send him packing. He'd have to hurt the woman he was falling for in order to protect himself. Jack hated this side of himself, but it was an unavoidable truth.

Happiness wasn't in the cards for him, even if Evie let him imagine, if only for one beautiful night, that it was.

"You've got to be fucking kidding me!"

Annie was on her feet now, hand clasped over her mouth. Then she reminded herself that no one was there to hear her. And she didn't give a shit because the kettle was about to blow, and there was *no* way she was holding back.

Annie had never fought for her own happiness because she always thought it had been just out of her reach. But she knew now it was fear—fear that loving so big and so fiercely would backfire. Maybe tragically, like it did for Wes's parents. Or maybe like it was about to end for them—with Wes choosing his own realistic vision of the future over Annie's ideal one where love conquered all.

He'd once told her that the stories she loved were fantasy

while the one he wrote was reality. She had vowed to prove him wrong, and now was as good a time as any.

Tears pricked at her eyes.

"Enough," she said aloud. "Enough already. I don't want to be that girl anymore."

Safe had kept her from loving—from being loved in return. Wes had loved her last night. She was sure of it. And if she had to be the one to prove it to him—well, that's exactly what she was going to do.

E—nough. Annie was worth a hell of a lot more than sitting on the sidelines.

She opened the internet and logged on to her blog.

Stranger Than Fiction
by **HappyEverAfter admin** | Leave a comment

How much of the author is on the page? I'll tell you firsthand. All of him. And consequently, all of me. Those of you who thought the heroine was too presumptuous to think she could change the hero's views on love? You were right. I was wrong. About so much. I always thought the books I read taught me the power of love—that they reminded me not to settle for anything less than spectacular. Guess what? I found spectacular. But it wasn't enough, not for the hero who doesn't choose love.

(draft)

She slammed the laptop closed, clutched the bag with her cider tight in her fist, and left.

Chapter Twenty-Four

"Jer's not on until noon," Jamie said when Wes asked where his roommate was.

"Huh. Guess he didn't sleep at home last night," Wes mumbled under his breath. That meant he wouldn't give Wes the third degree about who *he* was with last night since he'd have no clue he hadn't come home, either.

"What's that?" Jamie asked, filling a pitcher for Wes to bring to the table where he hoped a celebration was about to happen.

"Nothing," Wes said. "I just need to talk to him about something."

But maybe this meant he'd be able to get to Annie first, and they could tell Jeremy together. Soften the blow, so to speak.

He sat down at a table against the front windows with Max. Leslie would be there any minute, and his whole life would be flipped upside down. Hopefully in the best possible ways.

"Let's not jump the gun," Max said as Wes poured him a

pint of Jamie's chocolate stout. "We're not celebrating yet." Max pushed the glass back toward Wes. "Jewish superstition to celebrate too early."

"I thought you were Italian," Wes said.

"My mother's maiden name is Goldberg. She'd have a *kina hora* if she caught me celebrating a deal before it was signed."

Wes burst out laughing. "Is my badass agent a mama's boy?"

Max leaned closer to Wes. "You don't fuck with tradition," he said softly, and Wes did his best to compose himself.

"Am I interrupting an intimate moment here?"

The two men looked up to find a tall, lithe blonde in a fitted cream sweater, skinny jeans, and brown leather boots up to her knees.

Max sprang to his feet. The woman was a head taller than him, and she bent to kiss him on both cheeks.

"Leslie. So good to see you. This is my client Wes."

Wes stifled a laugh as he saw Max morph from his crass, everyday self to someone—well—appropriate to bring out in public. He had to hand it to the guy. He knew how to play the game, and that's why they were here, about to sign away the film rights to his books.

Max pulled out the seat opposite Wes, and Leslie sat down, reaching across the table to shake Wes's hand.

"I'm a huge fan of your work, Mr. Hartley. And I want you to know that I was green-lighting this project from the get-go. But I needed the studio to sign off on the deal. The higher-ups are a little skittish about book adaptations if there isn't another book in the works. Now that they've heard about book two and all the hype it's generating, I'm happy to bring you the news that we'd like to purchase rights for both books and get right of first refusal for book three."

She opened a leather folder onto the table, exposing the

contract that was already signed by the president of the studio and Leslie herself, who was listed as executive producer.

Wes wasn't one for contracts—that's why he had an agent—but there was no mistaking the numbers printed on the page. This contract would make him financially independent for years to come.

"I want to write the screenplays," Wes blurted, not aware of this desire until he spoke it aloud. "I want to maintain the integrity of the stories. I know some things will have to change for the big screen, but it's really important—especially for book two—that the essence of my characters remains."

"Leslie," Max interrupted, "we can negotiate this. I understand this wasn't part of our initial discussion—"

She smiled and focused her gaze on Wes. "Done." She flipped to page three of the document. "It's already here."

Wes shook his head, waiting for the other shoe to drop, but Max was already standing.

"I'm just going to take this where there's better light so I can scan the pages and send them to my contract specialist. She should have any last-minute changes to us within the hour. But, Ms. Alexander, I think we have ourselves a deal." He glanced at Wes. "Unless, of course, the talent has any objections."

Wes was still shaking his head. This was real. This was fucking real.

"No," he said, laughing. "No objections. None at all." He shook Leslie's hand again and looked up at Max. "Will your mother object if I celebrate before we officially sign?"

Max flipped him off, but he was out of Leslie's line of sight, so Wes just laughed.

"I'll be back in a few minutes," Max said. "You two do whatever the fuck you want."

And there was the Max Wes knew and loved. The man who took a chance on a twenty-four-year-old kid and was now giving him a career.

He poured a fresh pint for Leslie then held up his own.

"To us," he said.

"To us," she echoed.

Something caught his attention. Or rather, it was just an uneasy feeling. Wes followed that feeling and turned his gaze to find Annie standing to his left, just in front of the bar, her green eyes blazing.

"You asshole," she said. "Here I was giving you the benefit of the doubt, thinking you just got cold feet or something." She let out a bitter laugh. "I was coming here to give you a chance to tell me you loved me, too." She swiped at a tear escaping down her cheek. "You didn't even leave a note," she said, with such finality in her tone.

"Annie," he said, but she shook her head.

"I read the pages, Wes. I *know* Jack leaves Evie after their amazing night together. After she tells him she *loves* him. I thought I was more than just your muse," she said. "I thought *we* were *more*." She looked at him, at the woman sitting across from him. "Let me guess—she's another one of your *fictional* characters. I can't believe I told you I loved you."

He stood to explain everything, to tell her how much he loved her, too. But Annie picked up his pint and threw it in his face. He squeezed his eyes shut against the torrent of liquid, and when he opened them, it was too late. Jeremy came out of nowhere, or maybe he'd shown up while Wes was being blinded with beer. Either way, he never saw it coming. Wes heard the crack before he registered the pain as his best friend leveled him with a sucker punch to the face.

The last thing he remembered hearing before he blacked out was Max.

"This is so going in the book, pretty boy."

Wes heard the shouting before he opened his eyes. And then he decided he didn't want to open them because the shouting was loud, and his head was throbbing. Then he *tried* to open them, but only one would actually cooperate.

Amid the audible chaos, he reached a hand toward his left cheek and winced when he touched the swollen skin. Then he winced again because, *fuck,* it hurt to wince. There was something soft under his head, and for a second he imagined he was lying on Annie's lap.

And then it all came flooding back.

His books were going to be optioned for film.

Annie loved him.

Annie threw a beer at him.

Jeremy knocked him out cold.

Before he signed the papers.

Wes pushed himself up on his elbows to a chorus of gasps. Out of his good eye he could only see people from their knees down to their feet. Either he was lying on the floor, or he had more than just a swollen eye to worry about.

"Easy, there, champ."

Wes recognized Jamie's voice, especially now that the place had gone silent, and grabbed on to the outstretched arm, letting the guy help him up.

"How long was I out?" Wes asked, stumbling but not falling. Then he gained his footing.

Jamie shrugged. "A minute, maybe? Which is apparently long enough for that eye to swell up."

Wes eased himself back into his chair, and Jamie handed him a towel to dry off. Only then could he focus on the scene before him. Annie stood next to Jamie, looking like she wanted to both hug him and clock him in the other eye. Max had his arms crossed and a shit-eating grin on his face. And Jeremy stared at him from a bar stool, his expression unreadable.

None of this could be good.

"Someone tell me what the *fuck* just happened." He pointed at his agent. "You first. Did we lose the deal? Where's Leslie?"

Max barked out a laugh.

"She stepped outside to take a call. And lose the deal? Are you kidding? This shit is Hollywood gold. Leslie wants this scene in your final pages. Make it part of the hero's grand gesture or something." He pulled the leather folder off the bar. "Contract's all ready for us to review, but I think you better get your ass to the ER to make sure you don't have a concussion or something. Can't have you signing legal documents if you're not fit to do so."

Wes shook his head at this, but the slight motion felt like someone was using his skull as a hockey puck, so he decided to give the whole ER idea careful consideration.

He swallowed hard and met Annie's gaze.

"I know you probably think I left you this morning, but I have a logical explanation. Still, not sure it warranted"—he motioned to his soaked torso—"*this*. Did you really think—after last night—that I would bail?"

Annie opened her mouth to say something, but she was interrupted by Jeremy attempting to launch himself at Wes again and Jamie stepping in to hold him back.

"Go take a walk, Denning," Jamie ordered in an authoritative tone Wes hadn't heard before from his mild-mannered employer.

"Wait," Wes said, standing to meet Jeremy's lethal stare. "I lied to you," he added. "And there's no excuse. So maybe I deserved that. But I'm in love with her, man."

He heard Annie take in a sharp breath, but he didn't break his friend's gaze.

Jeremy just shook his head and brushed past him, apparently following Jamie's advice to walk it off.

"I didn't think you were the type to jump to conclusions,

Annie," he said, his eyes—or *eye*—back on her now.

She fidgeted with the bill of her knit cap.

"I thought she was another one of your—I mean, after I read your pages and Jack was hell-bent on self-sabotage—and you left and didn't call—and now my mother's on Tinder and my father is dating Theresa from Bunco—*Dammit!* This is what *not* playing it safe did for me. It made everything come crashing down at once."

Annie crossed and uncrossed her arms.

Wes scratched at the back of his neck.

"Who's Theresa? What pages?" Because he hadn't shown her anything new. Because the only way she'd know about Jack's plan to fuck everything up is if she read them without his permission.

"I went to your apartment before coming here—to confront you for leaving."

"I didn't *leave*, Annie. I was getting you a fucking cider when I got called to this meeting."

"You...*what*?" Her hands fisted at her sides. "Let me finish."

So he did.

"I went to your apartment...and let myself in with the spare key. When I didn't find you there, I remembered my cider. And it was right by your laptop that hadn't gone to sleep, so I knew you'd just been there."

A muscle in his jaw ticked. "So you read my pages without asking me? And you assumed that was *us*?"

"It *is* us," Annie said. "Wasn't that the agreement? I let our *situation* get you through your writer's block, and I get to have fun without worrying about my stupid expectations?"

He shook his head and stood, ignoring the growing headache.

"Jesus, Annie. It was more than just fun. It was always more than that, and you knew it when we started—" He motioned back and forth between them. "When we started *this*."

"But the book…"

"It's *fiction*. Just like all those books you read where love conquers all. Did you ever stop to think about what comes after that *happily ever after*? Or even at the end of a book you found so hopeless you assumed the writer was a lost cause, too? The book ends, but in real life the story doesn't." He ran a hand through his hair, tugging at it. This whole time he'd been thinking himself unworthy of her love. What he hadn't expected was her thinking the same. "Maybe I draw from my own life, but that doesn't matter. It's never *my* story. It's Jack and Evie's. It's their choice what happens next. Maybe I was scared when I wrote that scene, but that doesn't mean it's us. Because us, Annie? I thought after last night we were *better* than them. I thought that even if Jack didn't get his shit together and admit he loved Evie, at least *I* had." He shrugged. "Maybe I was that guy before us, but everything was different the moment I first kissed you. A book is just words on a page. And maybe I fucked up by not *saying* the right ones at the right time. But I felt them. Jesus, I felt them, and I know you felt them, too." He shook his head. "But you never really trusted me. Did you?"

"Wes," her voice cracked, and something deep within him cracked, too.

"I loved you, too, Annie," he said, grabbing his jacket from his chair and throwing it on.

Past tense. Shit. That was a lie. He loved her now with every pulse of his blood through his veins. But was love supposed to wreck you this hard so soon after figuring out you were capable of the emotion in the first place? If that was the case, fuck it. Maybe he *was* better off before.

"Tell Denning if he still needs me, I'll do that damn bachelor auction. I owe him," he said to Jamie. Jamie nodded.

Max was filling Leslie in, explaining that she'd have a signed contract after his client was cleared by an ER doc. And that was Wes's cue to leave.

"Where are you going?" Annie called after him as he headed toward the door.

"To make sure your brother didn't do any real damage."

But he knew what Jeremy had done didn't go any further than skin deep. He might not have said the words to her when she said them to him, but she had to know, right? He'd let her past every fucking barrier he'd put up, and she still assumed the worst of him.

Maybe he'd earned that. At least, an earlier version of himself had. But he wasn't that guy anymore. And if anyone should have been able to see that, it was Annie.

So he kept walking, counting the seconds it took him to exit the bar.

One. Two. Three. Four. Five. Six. Seven. Eight. Nine. Ten.

Ten seconds for him to walk out the door.

Ten chances for her to tell him to wait.

Ten opportunities for her to fight for them instead of conceding defeat.

But the only person who followed him out of the bar was Max.

Annie let him go.

Throbbing head and swollen eye? That was just the prologue. The real pain—gut twisting and chest collapsing—was now.

Chapter Twenty-Five

"What'd I miss? Something good? What happened to him?"

Brynn breezed through Kingston's front door, nodding back toward Wes who'd just exited.

Annie clutched her torso. She thought she was going to be sick.

Jamie pulled Brynn into a kiss, and Annie hugged herself tighter while Jamie filled his fiancé in on what he knew.

"I think—" she said. "I think I just lost him."

Brynn pursed her lips. "Had you—*found* him?"

"I messed up," Annie said. "It was only supposed to be fun. And then it was more. I jumped to conclusions because of who he was, but it turns out he's not that guy anymore. People *can* change if they want to, B. Yet I'm still the same scared person I've always been."

Brynn shook her head. "Oh, honey. You just came in here ready to fight for something—even if you were a little off base." She gave her a soft smile. "If that's not something new, then tell me I'm wrong."

Annie tried to swallow past the lump in her throat. "I

didn't just lose Wes," she said. "I also lost *us* the line-up of authors who were supposed to do signings at the store. I never—I never asked him. I'm so sorry, B. I put my feelings for him before the store, and *shit.* I am in way over my head here."

Brynn's eyes widened.

"Because you're in *love* with him!" she shouted. Then she jumped up and down and squealed. "This is the best news ever!"

Jamie put a hand on Brynn's arm and shook his head slowly.

She pouted. "I missed a lot, huh?" she asked. "I think you better spill the rest, Denning."

Annie sniffled. "Did you miss the part where the store is still in trouble?" she asked. "Aren't you going to talk to me about fiscal responsibility or something?"

Brynn waved her off. "Let's take care of you, first," she said. "Then we'll take care of the store."

So Jamie went behind the bar and poured them each a pint while Annie and Brynn perched on two stools so Annie could tell her—and a pretending-not-to-listen Jamie—about last night and this morning. About her crazy parents and Wes's. She didn't go into any intimate details about Wes's situation with his father, deciding she'd already invaded his privacy enough. But Brynn got the gist of the emotional caliber of the evening. And everything that came after.

"You *are* in love with him," Brynn said, squeezing Annie's hand.

She nodded. "But I believed the book instead of him— and messed up."

Brynn laughed.

Annie scowled.

"Oh, come on," Brynn said, shoulders still shaking. "We all get wrapped up in our own safety nets sometimes. For

Jamie and me it was convincing ourselves it was better to stay friends than to risk losing each other completely. But we were idiots."

Annie forced a laugh. "I told you that," she said. "I called Jamie that a lot, actually."

Brynn raised her brows. "See? And I get how important books are to you—to a lot of readers. But you were so caught up in seeing him as the guy in the book—instead of just, well, a guy."

Brynn was right. There was a lot of Wes in *Down This Road*, but there was much of him that wasn't. The reader never knew how Ethan's mother had passed away. They never knew the passionate yet volatile emotions that made up his parents' relationship. They didn't know of Ethan's guilt over not being around—over not being able to stop his mom from getting in that car.

Because that wasn't Ethan's story. It was Wes's, and that wasn't for the world to read. But Annie knew. He'd let her in on all the secrets he didn't share with anyone else.

Because he loved her.

Her epiphany was interrupted by her brother's return. Jeremy stepped back through the door, shaking out his hand. Annie could see his knuckles were bleeding.

"Jeremy, *no*. Please tell me you did not do anything else stupid."

She grabbed his hand to inspect it. The wounds were superficial, but if they were a result of him going after Wes...

He shook his head.

"I maybe got into it with the wall out back," he said, forcing a smile. "It gave me shit for blaming my buddy when my sister had also been lying to me for the past month."

Annie let her head fall against her brother's chest.

"Yeah. Well, wait until you hear about Mom and Dad."

He held up his phone. "Just talked to her. We're so messed

up. Aren't we?"

She nodded. "I can't speak for Mom and Dad and their lies, but I *can* defend me and Wes." Annie sighed. "I love you, Jer. I really, really do. But *I'm* the big sister, here. And you forced us to lie by forbidding Wes to do anything other than escort me to and from the wedding."

"But I—" he said, stepping away.

She shook her head. "I'm twenty-*eight*. And I love that you want to protect me. I really do. But you know what? I've been doing such a good job of it on my own that I didn't even know I *could* fall for someone until Wes came along."

She laughed out loud as recognition bloomed, the pages of Wes's manuscript replaying again in her head. Maybe Wes contemplated self-sabotage on the page, but Annie had just done it for real. *She* was the one infusing truth into fiction—or fiction into truth.

"Oh my God," she said aloud, covering her mouth with her palm.

"What?" he asked.

"What?" Brynn echoed.

"What?" Jamie added. "Actually, I don't *really* care that much. I just thought it would be funny if I—"

Brynn backhanded him on the chest, and Jamie shut up.

"I'm *Jack*," Annie said.

"Who's Jack?" Brynn and Jeremy asked in unison.

They all turned to Jamie, but he held up his hands.

"The hero in Wes's book. The one Wes's agent said had to work the knockout punch into his grand gesture or something."

Annie was grinning wide now, and Brynn and Jeremy were looking at her like she'd grown a third eye.

Jamie grumbled something under his breath that sounded like, "Grand gestures are overrated."

"Hey!" Brynn said, backhanding him again. "I grand

gestured *you*!"

He laughed. "Yeah, well, I tried to grand gesture you the night of our ten-year reunion, but you thought you were meant for someone else."

She groaned and turned back to Annie.

"You want to perform a grand gesture?" she said.

Annie nodded. "And since you have experience, B, tell me what the hell I should do, and I'll do it. No more playing it safe. I'll do whatever it takes for him to forgive me."

• • •

Jeremy crossed his arms and uncrossed them. Then he paced the runner that separated the kitchen from the living room. Wes pulled the bag of frozen peas from the left side of his face so he could see his friend more clearly.

Were they still friends? Wes had been home from the ER long enough to pack up the few things he'd brought with him from New York, settle himself on the couch, and try to combat the swelling. Jeremy had walked in at least a minute ago and still hadn't said anything.

He opened his mouth to start, but Jeremy cut him off.

"I've never done that, you know. Hit anyone."

Wes noticed the broken skin on Jeremy's knuckles.

"So today you went balls out?" He motioned to his own knuckles insinuating Jeremy's. "Pretty sure my face didn't do that."

Jeremy dropped into the chair perpendicular to the couch where Wes sat. He forced a smile.

"A brick wall looked at me funny." His face grew serious. "She's my *sister*, man. I've watched her get the shit end of the relationship deal too many times. I couldn't protect her from guys I didn't know. But I trusted *you*."

"I know."

Wes rested his elbows on his knees and dropped his head into his hands. Then he looked up, expecting more disappointment, but Jeremy only looked apologetic.

"Annie told me she was equally to blame for keeping this from me. And I get how *maybe* I didn't make things easy for you two."

Wes blew out a breath. Maybe she didn't fight for him, but at least she was trying to salvage his friendship with her brother.

"I'm still an asshole for lying to you, but your sister's an adult who makes her own decisions."

Jeremy nodded. "I'm still a dick for hitting you. And I know she's an adult," he said. "Doesn't mean I'll stop feeling protective of her." He scratched the back of his head. "What did the doctor say?"

"No concussion. Nothing's broken. Just some pretty bad bruising."

Jeremy winced. "Yeah, I can see that. You know, you could press charges or something. I probably deserve it."

Wes laughed. "Ow. Fuck, that hurts. And no, asshole, I'm not pressing charges. I had it coming. But I will amp the shit out of the situation if it goes in the book."

Jeremy let out a nervous laugh, and Wes tilted his head back, placing the bag of peas where they rested before.

"Are you really in love with my sister?" Jeremy asked.

Wes groaned. "Yeah," he said softly. "But I don't think I'm cut out for this love thing."

Jeremy laughed again, this time the sound bitter and knowing.

"I'm the first one to agree with you there," he said. "But I feel inclined to counsel you otherwise, only because it's my sister who's involved."

Wes shook his head slowly, so as not to upset the peas.

"She didn't trust me, Jer. She didn't trust me, and she

didn't fight for us. I don't know what else I'm supposed to do."

What a fucking sight he must be, broken inside and out.

"So you're signing yourself up for a bachelor auction?"

He sighed. "It's for a good cause, right?"

"You mean you didn't say that just to throw it in my sister's face?"

He leaned forward on his knees again, ready to head to the freezer for a fresh bag since the one in his hand was starting to thaw.

"Maybe in the moment. Yeah. But we're getting close to the holidays, and you said it was for a good cause. The prize is a date—so I'll buy the winner a drink after the auction, and we'll call it a day. I'm not looking to throw anything in anyone's face anymore if you're not."

The right side of his mouth quirked into a grin. He was careful not to aggravate his wound this time.

Jeremy rolled his eyes. "Fuck you," he said, but he was smiling now, too. "You would get us the biggest donation," he said. "Especially with that wounded look."

"You're pushing it," Wes said.

"Yeah. I know. But there's this girl at the food bank I'm trying to impress. She's coming to collect the donations and MC the event. When she sees I've got you on the roster?" Jeremy whistled.

"Hey," Wes said. "I thought you don't believe in love."

"I don't. But I sure as hell believe in fun." Jeremy raised his brows. "And speaking of fun… Did I tell you it's a costume theme? I mean, it *is* October."

Wes barked out a laugh. "Of course it is."

His face still hurt, but the laughing felt good.

"You really moving out?" Jeremy asked.

He nodded. "It's probably best."

"Probably," Jeremy echoed.

"Can you do me a favor?" Wes asked, pulling a folded-up

piece of paper out of his back pocket. "Can you give this to your sister?"

Jeremy took it and read. "What the hell is this?"

"A list of authors—local and out of town—who'd love to set up signings at Two Stories."

Jeremy's eyes widened. "Brynn might have called to check in—make sure I wasn't suing Kingston's or anything." He forced a smile even though it hurt to do so. "I know the store needs some help and I—just, give it to her, okay? She's done an amazing job over there, and if I can do anything—"

Jeremy nodded. "Thanks, man. I'll tell her." He let out a long breath. "You going back to New York?"

He glanced at his phone. No missed calls or texts. No Annie. His dad was here, and they were just starting to repair their relationship. That in and of itself was reason enough to stay. But how could he be in the city where the woman he loved let him go so easily? How could he and Jeremy stay friends when Annie was between them?

At least with the distance they had an excuse *not* to see each other. Maybe in another five or ten years Wes could come back to Chicago and not worry about his heart dropping through the floor if he bumped into Annie Denning. Men were good like that, not seeing each other for years and picking back up where the friendship was the last time they saw each other. He and Jeremy would be fine.

"I don't know," Wes finally said.

Because he didn't know what was worse. Bumping into Annie while he was trying to get over her—or never seeing her again.

Chapter Twenty-Six

"You look like an ass," Brynn said, giggling.

Annie pulled off the headpiece portion of her costume so Brynn could see her glare.

"Is it because I'm dressed like a donkey? Also, are you going to be lobbing jokes like this all night?"

Brynn gave her a fervent nod. "All night."

"And he has no idea I'm coming to the auction, right?"

Brynn's smile faded.

"I feel really shitty keeping this from Wes, Annie. And before you ask, *no*. I haven't told anyone. Not Jamie, not your brother. This is your thing. So it's not my place."

Annie nodded. "Thank you."

She'd tried calling Wes once, the day after the ale house situation. But when it went right to voicemail, she didn't know if it was because of bad reception or because he didn't want to answer, and her nerves got the best of her once she heard his voice on the recording. So she said nothing.

Now it was time to do something big. Because who could ignore big? And even if he rejected her after this, at least she could say she tried. She could say she fought. Annie had never fought for someone before, but then again, she'd never loved someone like she loved Wes.

"I'm scared," she added, after letting her nerves get the best of her. "What if I'm too late? This isn't like Brett or anyone before him. I feel like I got over those relationships the moment they ended. This is—different." She loved Wes too much to admit this could still be the end.

Brynn grabbed the donkey head from her and rested it on the foot of Annie's bed.

"Sorry," she said. "I didn't like the way it was looking at me. But here's the thing, sweetie. Being scared is part of the fun."

Annie wrinkled her nose, and Brynn knocked her softly on her donkey shoulder.

"I'm serious," she said. "Any relationship that doesn't heighten your emotions—that doesn't get your heart racing for one reason or another—it's just filler. A placeholder, really. The happy ending is just the beginning."

Annie plopped down on her bed. She wondered if her parents ever got each other's hearts racing or if they were always just placeholders until something better came along. She didn't want to follow in those footsteps. And if the rapid drumbeat of her heart was any indication, she was far, far off that course.

She narrowed her eyes at her friend who was dressed in a Chicago Cubs baseball uniform.

"You're such an expert?" she asked. "Jamie won't want to get near you tonight if you're wearing that."

Brynn laughed. "*Or*," she said, "he'll want to tear it off me the first chance he gets." She waggled her brows. "And yes—to answer your question, I am an expert now. Because I was just like you, filling the space until I realized Jamie was the only one who fit. But you've got the advantage, here. You *know* who fits. But you doubted him. You didn't trust him, and that's a hard thing for someone to take."

Annie forced a smile. "Like Jamie doubted your feelings for him."

Brynn nodded. "He had every right, even if he was stupid enough to think I could have wanted anyone else after that night in Amarillo."

Brynn's eyes got all dreamy and far off.

Annie held up her hands in surrender. "I love you guys. I really do. But if I have to hear about Amarillo again…"

Brynn crossed her arms and gave her friend a knowing grin. "You could tell me about the Blissful Nights hotel," she said.

Annie bit her lip, remembering her first night with Wes. And she'd enjoyed keeping the details of said night to herself, like it was something just for them.

"I think I'm going to hold on to that one," she said.

Brynn shrugged. "Hold on to hope, too. A good-looking ass is hard to resist."

Annie shook her head at her friend, then picked up the headpiece that completed her costume.

"I'll have you know that Bottom, in *A Midsummer Night's Dream,* was actually one of the wittiest characters, even if he didn't know it."

Brynn offered her a hand to pull her up from the bed.

"Then let your witty words win back your hero," she said.

No. Annie was going to take her cue from Wes this time. Because they were more than words on a page. She knew that now. She knew without a doubt that he loved her that night after his dad's apartment. He didn't need to say it. He'd shown her what she should have been able to see but was too scared to admit.

Now it was her turn to show him.

She threw on the mask.

"Let's go bid on some bachelors," she said, her voice muffled inside the donkey's head.

"You sound like an ass," Brynn said, giggling. "But a really hopeful one," she added. "I'll text Jamie and make sure Jeremy and Wes are on the upper level getting ready for the auction so I can sneak you in. Not that you're at all inconspicuous."

Annie took a deep breath.

Please be right, B. Not about the inconspicuous part. But about the hope.

Because hope was all she had left.

"Out," Jamie said when she and Brynn walked through the door and he saw his fiancée's Cubs gear. "Your kind is not welcome here," he added.

Annie let out a nervous laugh inside her mask. Jamie was decked out, head to toe, in a White Sox uniform, of course. Brynn ignored him, planted a kiss on his angry looking lips, and then whispered something in his ear.

His shoulders relaxed. "Well, I'm fucking powerless against *that*," he said. Annie didn't even want to ask.

"Who's the ass?" he asked, and Brynn snorted.

Annie wanted to stomp her foot, but then she thought that might be too asslike. But come on. There was a literary connection here. Plus, the metaphorical interpretation of her being an ass for not believing in Wes. But she should have known the night would be filled with donkey jokes.

Brynn whispered something in Jamie's ear again.

"Upstairs getting ready to parade themselves in front of generous donors looking for a good time."

Annie's throat tightened, and Brynn backhanded Jamie on the chest.

"*What*?" he asked.

Brynn pulled him and Annie toward his office. When they
got inside, Annie barely had room to move. Brynn must have
sensed this because it was she who lifted her mask off her
head.

"Christ," Jamie said. "I knew you were putting together
some crazy grand gesture scheme, but don't you think it would
have been nice to give your fiancé warning about *more* drama
happening in his place of business?"

Annie gave him a nervous smile while Brynn tried to
level him with her gaze.

"Remember what you whispered out there?" Jamie
nodded back toward the main bar area. "That was for your—
costume. But now that there's this?" He motioned between
the two girls with an accusing index finger. "I want it twice."

Brynn feigned a dramatic gasp, palm to her chest.

"You drive a *hard* bargain, Mr. Kingston."

Jamie raised his brows and nodded, a smile spreading
across his face.

"Ick," Annie said. "I'd really prefer not being a part of
your foreplay."

Brynn squeezed Jamie's cheeks in her palm and kissed
him.

"No drama," she said, then crossed her heart.

"Does your brother know?" he asked, looking at Annie
expectantly. She gave him a sheepish grin and shook her head.

"Jesus, Annie." He adjusted his baseball cap. "I want
whatever you're planning to do to work, but if it doesn't—and
I'm just considering all scenarios—is your brother going to
put a lawsuit on my hands?"

Crap. She hadn't considered Jeremy's reaction. The only
thing she knew about the Jeremy and Wes situation was that
Wes hadn't done anything drastic like press charges but that
he *had* moved out of the apartment, all in the span of five
days. She'd buried herself with work and avoided the bar and

her brother.

"You said they were upstairs together," Annie said. "That means they're getting along, right? Jeremy wouldn't have him in the auction if there was still bad blood between them."

Jamie shrugged.

"Wes kind of quit all of us," he said. "Left the apartment and called that night to tell me he thought it was best he stopped working here. Said he was heading back to New York next week anyway to finalize some stuff with his agent and publisher. I haven't seen him since your brother laid him out on my floor, and I *really* don't want to see that happen again."

Annie was finding it harder to breathe.

"Back to New York?" she asked, eyes wide. "Like, for good?"

"Shit," Brynn said under her breath.

"Shit?" Annie added, hearing the desperation in her own voice. "You didn't know about this?"

Brynn shook her head.

Annie grabbed her donkey head back, mustering up as much resolve as she could manage.

"I'm just here to bid on a bachelor," she said. "And I promise anything that happens after that will not put your bar in danger, Jamie."

She placed the mask back on her head, completing her ensemble.

The bar was safe. But her heart? That was another story.

Chapter Twenty-Seven

Wes looked Jeremy up and down, wondering how much cash he laid out just for the costume rental.

"It's pretty authentic looking, right?" Jeremy asked. "I had to watch a YouTube video, like, seven times to get the kilt right." He slid the tartan up past his knee and raised a brow. "Like what you see?"

Wes laughed.

"Do you even know what *Outlander* is?" he asked.

Jeremy shook his head. "I don't need to. I know women go crazy for the whole Scottish thing. And I'm not afraid to say this, but I think I'm even prettier than you tonight, Hartley. If your celebrity wasn't enough to bring in the donations, I'd accuse you of trying *not* to get bought."

Wes placed the fake nose over his own and situated the elastic band around his ears. "Cyrano?" he asked. Jeremy gave him a blank stare. "You ever see that '80s movie, *Roxanne*?"

He watched the lightbulb go on as Jeremy grinned.

"Yeah, yeah. The guy who says all the right stuff but isn't good-looking. Annie loves all those '80s movies. Made me watch them with her whenever she had a bad breakup. So, you know, I've seen a lot. Still waiting for her to invite me over for *Sixteen Candles* or something this weekend."

Wes's chest tightened. It felt like his ribs were trying to crush the vital organ that lay underneath. Was this a breakup? Could that happen before you even acknowledged the relationship? And Jeremy wouldn't understand the costume like Annie would. Cyrano said all the right things. Wes—the supposed wordsmith—never said the three that she needed to hear.

"She's really not coming, huh?" Wes asked, regretting the question as soon as it left his mouth. Of course she wasn't coming. He was auctioning himself off as a bachelor.

"She told me to call her tomorrow, that she didn't want to hear anything about tonight, even when it was all over. Sounds like a pretty emphatic *no*," Jeremy said.

Wes nodded.

"It's all for the best, right? You don't have to worry about your buddy messing around with your sister, and I don't have to worry about getting trampled to dust. Win-win."

Jeremy pulled at his fake nose and let it slap back at his face.

"Seriously?" His eyes widened. The swelling had gone down, but the skin under and around Wes's left eye was still an angry, mottled purple.

"Shit, man." But Jeremy was laughing. "I'm sorry. I have zero impulse control."

The buzz of the speakers interrupted them.

"Ladies and gentleman. Welcome to the first—and hopefully *annual*—Kingston Ale House Bachelor Auction benefiting Chicago's Food Bank. My name is Beth, your CFB representative and MC for the evening. I want to thank you in advance for your donations. Thanks to you, many families will have food this holiday season that otherwise wouldn't have."

Wes and Jeremy were lined up behind the bar at the back of the upper deck while Beth the MC stood at a table on the opposite end of the room, mic in hand.

Jeremy nudged him on the shoulder. "The real reason for my lack of impulse control," he said.

"You need help," Wes told him.

He laughed. "Yeah. You're not the first to think so."

Almost every seat at every table was taken, and still people were pouring onto the deck. Jamie stood at the top of the stairs, monitoring the traffic flow. Brynn was next to him, but that was it. Just the two of them.

He was leaving in a few days, anyway. This *was* for the best. He'd convinced himself of that when he bought the plane ticket, deciding to leave his bike in storage until he figured out where home was going to be.

They listened as the first bachelor was introduced, a local firefighter who was also, according to Beth, a gourmet chef. He was in uniform rather than a costume because, hell, he was a firefighter. The bids started before he could even get down the makeshift aisle between the tables.

"Fifty dollars!"

"One hundred!"

"One hundred and fifty!"

Wes turned back to Jeremy. "What's the real obligation as far as the date's concerned?" he asked. "I mean, I know the flyer says *date* immediately following the auction. But is *date* a euphemism?"

Jeremy shrugged. "It's open to interpretation. Just do me a favor and don't interpret where I can see you. I'm still your ex-whatever's brother."

"Yeah, of course," he said, his voice sounding distant even to his own ears. He scanned the room—a room full of beautiful women. Stacy could be out there. Or Oksana. Or anyone who was a part of his life before—before Annie.

What the hell was he doing? Maybe he blew it with her, but this wasn't the solution. And without a second more to think it through, he was stepping back from his place in line. He squeezed Jeremy's shoulder. "I'm sorry, Jer. I can't do it. I'll write a check, but I have to get out of here."

He paused a second, waiting for what he knew was coming, another fist to the face. But instead Jeremy just grinned.

"Go get her," he said. "Go find Annie."

Wes was already moving before Jeremy finished the second syllable of her name. But the place was so crowded that the only feasible way out was down the aisle. So he strode toward the opposite end of the room as bids for the firefighter came to a close. He was just about to slip behind a table in front of the stairs when he heard his name in surround sound.

"Wes Hartley, folks!" Beth said nervously into the mic. "You all know *New York Times* bestselling author Wes Hartley!"

He stopped in his tracks and noted all the women scanning their programs, listened to the mumbling about a change in order, and then Beth came over the speakers again.

"That's right, everyone. We're changing up the program because Mr. Hartley couldn't wait to meet his lucky lady." Beth motioned for him, and he had no choice. It would have been one thing for them to call his name once he was already gone. But now, with all eyes on him and the success of the event resting on Jeremy's shoulders, he couldn't be that selfish. So he ignored his easy out and made his way to the table where Beth stood. She covered the mic as the whispers from the audience began to die down.

"Getting cold feet, Cyrano?" she whispered. "Your friend promised you'd be on the auction block."

Wes shook his head. "Of course not. Just eager to get this over with."

He shoved his hands in the front pockets of his jeans and

painted on a smile.

She grinned back. "By all means." Then she uncovered the mic. "Well, everyone, now that we're all on the same page, I'd like to introduce again your next lucky bachelor, Wes Hartley. Mr. Hartley's debut novel has received critical acclaim while holding its spot on the *New York Times* list for its first two months of publication. Rumor has it the book will be optioned for film with Mr. Hartley penning the screenplay."

He narrowed his gaze at Jeremy back behind the bar who didn't even pretend to play dumb. He just shrugged and crossed his arms over his chest. He really was a man with zero control if there was a good-looking woman in the room.

"The starting bid will be—" But Beth never had the chance to finish the sentence.

"One hundred dollars!" a blond woman up front, dressed as Marilyn Monroe, called, holding up her paddle.

"One fifty!" This came from a pixie-haired brunette flapper just behind her.

"Two hundred," the first woman said, tossing an angry glare at her competition.

"Two fifty."

"Three hundred."

Wes watched the back and forth, both grateful that neither woman was someone he knew previously and at the same time slightly terrified that one of the tenacious bidders would be his date for the rest of the evening.

"Three fifty!" This bid was back with the brunette.

"A thousand dollars."

Gasps erupted from the crowd as everyone's heads turned toward the muffled voice.

Wes craned his neck to get a glimpse of the bidder, but he saw nothing more than the paddle, the black glove, and the gray sleeve.

Shit. This was it. He hadn't thought this through. It didn't sound like Oksana. But it could definitely be Stacy. If it was Lindsay—*engaged* Lindsay—well, then this night was more messed up than he'd expected.

"Eleven hundred," Marilyn Monroe said, a satisfied smile on her face as she held up her paddle and stared straight at Wes.

"Two thousand."

His eyes widened. He wasn't even sure he'd heard right. The bidder had to be wearing some sort of mask, but he still couldn't see the whole costume.

"Folks, we have a bid of two *thousand* dollars for an evening with Mr. Wes Hartley. Do I hear twenty-one hundred?" The whole room went silent, and apparently the rest of the bar had, too.

Wes glanced toward the staircase where Jamie and Brynn still stood. Jamie shrugged, and Brynn seemed to be trying to mask whatever it was she was feeling. He found Jeremy on the other end of the room, but Jeremy wasn't looking at him. His eyes were on the bidder, his expression *amused.*

"Two thousand dollars going once," Beth said. "Two thousand going twice. And sold to the—I'm sorry, but could the bidder in the back please stand?"

Slowly, she did. Or he. Who the hell knew? Because the person with the winning paddle who'd just made the Chicago Food Bank two grand richer—was a donkey.

"Sold to the donkey in the back row!" Beth said, her voice a little shaky. "Thank you for your donation. Your bachelor will escort you downstairs to the reception area."

The donkey gave an awkward nod and slid out from its table. First it tried to sidestep the remaining patrons from the outside, but as Wes found only minutes before, there was no easy path to the front other than the actual aisle. So he watched as Eeyore—or maybe it was Donkey from *Shrek*—made its way toward him to the awe of onlookers on either side, stopping in front of the table where he stood with Beth.

"Will you…take off the mask?" he asked.

"Why were you trying to leave?" she asked. Yeah, it was definitely a *she* in there, but she still sounded like she was underwater.

Wes looked toward Beth who shrugged. "We got our donation. So go ahead. Tell everyone why you were trying to sneak out." She handed him the mic.

More whispers and gasps. Wes simply groaned.

"Because I shouldn't be doing this when I'm in love with someone who's not here," he admitted. "I'm sorry," he said to the woman inside the donkey. "I'll hold up my end of the bargain, though. I'm your date for the remainder of the evening."

She placed a hand on her hip and cocked her head to the side, which would be so much less creepy if she wasn't, you know, a donkey.

"Will you take off the nose?" she asked. "For our date?"

His brow furrowed, but he nodded and removed the nose.

"I thought you'd be dressed as the Tin Man. Or maybe the Wizard," she said, and Wes almost knocked a chair over stepping out from behind the table.

"Take off the mask," he said, but she just stood there. "Shit, Annie," he pleaded. "Take off the mask."

She did, placing it on the table next to her.

And there she was. Red hair—her long, overgrown bangs matted against her forehead. Emerald eyes welling with tears as they stared back at his.

"You said *loved* the other day. Past tense. But just now—"

She couldn't finish the sentence, so he did it for her.

"I loved you that night." He took a step closer. "And the morning after." Another step. "And every day since you let me walk out that door." His hand was on her cheek. "And right now, Annie Denning. I love you *right now*." His thumb swiped at a lone tear that ran down her cheek. "Those words have never been simple for me, but I should have said it that night. Because magic is real, Annie. Between you and me it is."

She laid her gloved palm over his hand.

"Hearing you say those three words is pretty magical," she said. "But I should have trusted you anyway."

He leaned toward her. "I thought you'd be dressed as Dorothy," he said, his voice a low rumble in her ear.

"It's a metaphor, you know," she said. "Because I was an ass for not believing in you, and—"

He laughed, holding up his Cyrano nose. "And I'm the writer who can't seem to find the right words when they're not on the page."

She bit her lip. "The Dorothy costume, though? *That* one's at home," she teased, and he couldn't hold out any longer.

Jeremy pushed his way up to the front of the room and thrust the folded-up piece of paper at his sister—the one Wes had given him.

"What's this?" she asked.

Jeremy narrowed his eyes. "Maybe this whole commitment thing isn't for me, but hell if I'm going to watch you two put it off any longer. It's a list of people Hartley knows who've already committed to signings at Two Stories."

Annie sucked in a breath and stared at Wes. "How did you?" But her eyes roved around the room until she found Brynn and Jamie, and Brynn offered a guilty grin.

"You've got a lot of people who love you and who are looking out for you, Annie," he said.

"And you were gonna—" Her breathing hitched. "You were going to be one of those people even after I messed it all up?"

He nodded. "That's what happens when the heroine makes the hero fall in love, even when he doesn't believe in it."

Her hand flew to her mouth. "You read my blog?"

He raised a brow. "Kinda hard not to when there's a draft post left open on my laptop."

She made a move to put her mask back on, but he was done hiding—done letting her hide. Everything would be out in the open from here on out.

"For fuck's sake, kiss her already, Hartley!"

He couldn't help but laugh. Those were the last words he ever expected to leave Jeremy's lips. But who was he to argue? They were out in the open after all.

And then he took her in his arms, his beautiful, amazing, forgiving, and *forgiven* donkey, and lowered her into a dip, much to the delight of their audience.

"I'm gonna kiss you now," he said.

She smiled, that one small gesture obliterating him and building him back up all at once.

"I'm gonna let you," she said.

He pulled her to him, and she threw her arms around his neck. He kissed her with wild, grateful abandon, in front of a room full of people.

Applause and whistles broke out, and she smiled against his lips. Maybe Jeremy's lack of impulse control was infectious. Because when Annie was nearby, Wes couldn't imagine doing anything other than what he was doing right now.

He brought her back upright but wasn't ready to let go. So he kissed her once more and then laughed softly as he pulled away.

"What?" she asked.

He grabbed her hand and pulled her toward the stairs while Beth tried to redirect the crowd back to the remaining bachelors.

"I just didn't realize our first public kiss would be so— public. And that you'd be dressed as a donkey."

Annie was laughing, too, but she stopped him before they reached Brynn and Jamie.

"You okay?" he asked.

She nodded. "But before we officially have our date, I need you to know one thing."

He waited and worried as her face grew serious. But then her hand, or paw, or hoof—whatever it was—rested on his cheek, and that was all he needed. Wes knew that whatever came next, he'd get through it if it was with Annie.

"I want the happily ever after," she said. "But I want everything else that comes with it—the fear, the uncertainty, the work—too."

He grinned and reached for her hand, pulling off the glove so her skin was on his. Then he turned his head so his lips were on her palm, brushing her skin with a soft kiss.

"Happily ever after, huh?" He raised a brow. "Those things are for real?"

She smacked him on the shoulder. Then she lowered her hand and held it out between them.

"Shake on it," she said. "Admit it's real, and that you want a happy ending with me."

He smiled but didn't extend his hand. "I think we can come up with something better than a handshake."

She raised her brows and pulled him to the stairs, past a smiling Brynn and Jamie, and down to the first floor.

"What did you have in mind?" she asked.

He leaned close and whispered in her ear.

"Show me what you want," he said.

But he had a feeling he already knew.

Chapter Twenty-Eight

Somebody should have warned her how freaking hot it would be inside a donkey suit. The damp tendrils at the nape of her neck were cold on her skin, and the T-shirt and shorts she wore beneath the costume were plastered to her body.

"Are you sure you don't need any help in there?" Wes called from outside her bathroom door.

She reached behind her neck and found the zipper, letting out a relieved breath. This wasn't their first time, but it was going to be the first time with the whole *I love you* thing out there, and the last thing Annie wanted was for him to see her as a sweaty mess on what was turning into the most romantic night of her life.

"I'm good," she called back to him. "Out in a few. Just— uh, make yourself comfortable."

"Okay," he said, and she detected a hint of disappointment in his voice.

She looked at herself in the mirror, her red waves in various asymmetrical angles surrounding her face, some of them matted to her forehead. From neck to toe she was a complete and utter ass, and she couldn't help but remember Oksana from the wedding—or the pages she inhabited in Wes's first book. It wasn't that Annie wasn't a confident girl. He loved her. She knew it, believed it, and felt it in every vein as her heartbeat pulsed through her.

But what the hell was she thinking dressing up as a *donkey* to win him back? She wasn't exactly thinking about what came after the grand gesture when she'd set this plan in motion. You didn't just come home and sexily tear off an Eeyore costume.

But she wanted out of it now, so she tugged at the zipper and got it down a couple of inches before it stopped.

She groaned.

"Annie?"

She jumped, Wes's voice startling her so that her hand jerked the zipper back up to the top. And now it wouldn't budge at all.

"I thought you were making yourself comfortable," she accused, immediately regretting the annoyance in her tone.

She heard him laugh softly.

"Kind of hard to do if I'm not wrapped around you," he teased.

She had no choice. She threw open the door and crossed her donkey-clad arms and tapped her donkey-covered foot.

"I'm stuck," she said with a small pout. "How's that for comfortable?"

He bit back a smile, but she shook her head.

"Go ahead. Laugh." She threw her arms in the air. "This will be a great one for the book. Um…you know, if you're still working on the ending and are looking for a super sexy finale. I mean—if Jack and Evie get their happily ever after. Not that it's any of my business."

She groaned louder, expecting *this*, not her stupid costume, to be what ruined their reconciliation—reminding

Wes how she'd not only invaded his privacy but also assumed the worst of him when she did.

"Turn around, please," was all he said, and Annie was so caught off guard that she did.

He unzipped the costume with ease, and she stepped out of it as it fell to the floor. She turned back to face him, her white T-shirt that read FICTIONAL CHARACTER plastered to her chest. He ran a finger beneath the words, as if he was underlining them, and Annie's frown quickly morphed into an openmouthed gasp.

"You were never fiction for me, Annie," he said, his voice soft and insistent. "Even when I wasn't willing to admit it, you were always more. Words on the page are just that. But us?" He dipped his head and kissed the exposed skin on her neck. "We're real life. Maybe there is no yellow brick road pointing us toward Oz because, shit—I sure as hell have been lost for far too long. But I found it anyway, the Emerald City, and you want to know what it is? It's this girl who challenges me, who isn't afraid to show me what she wants, who calls me on my bullshit, and who's seen me at my lowest, my most broken, and loved me anyway. And donkey costume or not, she's the sexiest, most beautiful woman I've ever seen, and I'm still kind of floored she chose *me*."

He brushed the matted hair from her forehead, and she let out a shaky breath.

"*That*," she said. "That's why I didn't like the first book. Your hero hid himself away and never let anyone see cracks in his armor. No one ever truly knew him, which meant he could never truly be happy. And the hardest part of it all was that he *chose* that path, the one that never really seemed to have a destination."

Wes raised his brows. "That's not me. Annie. Neither is Jack. Not completely, at least. There's a little bit of truth in all fiction, but my fiction isn't my whole truth. You believe that now, right?"

She shrugged. "I might need a *little* more convincing."

He tugged at the hem of her shirt. "I already finished book two. Jack and Evie get their happy ending. Because you were right."

"About what?" she asked.

"There is such a thing as a happily ever after. But this one's just for us."

He kissed her then, and Annie's shoulders relaxed. She melted into him, forgetting that she was standing with a donkey costume pooled at her feet or that she'd ever been worried about how this evening would end.

She backed over the donkey and into the bathroom, pulling him with her as she did. She managed to keep her lips pressed to his as she reached to turn on the shower. She undressed him and let him undress her, and she took a few seconds to marvel at the beautiful man standing in front of her—the boy she'd known so many years ago.

"Everything okay?" he asked.

She nodded. "Only—I don't want a happy *ending*," she said.

He kissed her then, his tongue slipping past her lips, and she knew the end was nowhere in sight.

"I love you, Annie." He pulled her with him into the growing cloud of steam.

"I love you, too," she said, her hands splayed against his chest as beads of water pebbled his skin.

"Good." He kissed her again. "Because this is only the beginning."

• • •

Annie lay on the bed next to him, her pillow soaked from her freshly washed hair. He kissed her, his lips light on hers, tongue teasing but not entering. His hand traveled down her neck and over her breast, relishing the way her body moved in reaction to his touch, feeling her sharp intake of breath when his thumb grazed her peaked nipple. He didn't stop there, though, but kept traveling until his hand rested between her legs.

She sucked in a breath.

And he paused.

"Show me, Annie. Show me what you want."

She let out a soft moan, and he wasn't sure he'd be able to keep it together for this.

"You already know." Her words came out as a breath.

"It's different now," he argued, then softly kissed her neck.

She must have agreed because she placed her hand over his.

"Every time with you is like starting over," he said. "Because each touch reminds me how lucky I am that I didn't scare you away—how grateful I am that you fought for us." He kissed her again, this time more insistent. "I love you." Another kiss.

"I love you," she echoed.

And together they guided his hand down farther until he slipped inside.

"Once upon a time," he said softly in her ear, "there was Annie and Wes. And they were happy."

His lips found hers again as he moved inside her, Annie leading him every step of the way.

"Sounds like a pretty boring story," she said, and he felt her lips part into a smile.

He tilted his head up so his eyes met her emerald green gaze.

"Hey, watch it, there," he teased. "That's the story of my life."

She rested her free palm on his cheek and smiled the

sweetest smile, the kind he knew was only for him.

"Mine, too," she said.

He nodded. "Okay, then."

"Okay," she said.

He kissed her again because there was nothing more that needed to be said. The right words had always been there. The only thing missing—was her.

Epilogue

Eight Months Later

Annie signed the contract and slid it across her desk to Brynn. Brynn signed her name as well.

"There's no turning back now, Chandler. So I hope you're sure about this."

Her friend smiled. "It's time I step outside my comfort zone, too," Brynn said. "I've always loved this place, Annie. I'm honored you trust me with half of it," she added. "And with all the special events we've already had and the ones we have lined up for the next half a year, I'm predicting a mild uptick in revenue."

"A *mild* uptick?" Annie said, brows raised.

"Please," Brynn said. "With a financial genius like me in charge for the next six months, this place will be wallpapered with dollar bills when you get back.

"That's super tacky," Annie said. "Please don't do that. It won't go with the furniture. But if you want to redecorate your office? Have at it!"

Brynn swatted her on the shoulder.

Annie held out her hand, and the two women shook. "Partners," she said.

"Partners," Brynn echoed, and then she pulled her friend in for a warm hug.

Annie frowned. "Maybe I should postpone the trip, though. I mean, this is still so new, and it's going to mean more hours for you while you're planning the wedding and—"

"*Annie.*"

"Yeah?"

Brynn grinned. "You're coming back between each tour stop. I've got Tabitha and the new guy we hired. I'm here all the time as it is. Now I'll just push the merchandise a little harder. Plus you've got a wedding to attend in December. Actually, we're going to see each other too much in the next six months. Can we cut back on the visits?"

Annie giggled, and both of them stood and headed for the door, hand in hand.

"I'll be back every month," Annie said, convincing herself that would be enough, that everything would be okay, that she wouldn't miss Brynn and Jeremy and Jamie terribly, that this adventure with Wes—this was what came after the end of a romance novel. This was the start of their ever after.

Brynn kissed her on the cheek. "Now let's go enjoy the party."

They exited the office together, and then Annie followed Brynn down the stairs to the usually cozy reading nook on the first floor of Two Stories. Tonight it was bustling with caterers serving hors d'oeuvres, flutes of champagne, and, of course, bottles of Jamie Kingston's brews. She waved to Wes who smiled at her from behind his signing table, a line of patrons already forming just minutes after they'd opened the doors.

"I don't want to release the book in New York," he'd told her a few months before. They were lying in bed, and he was tracing lazy circles around her belly button, driving her mad like he always did.

She'd looked at him like he was crazy. "That's *the* place to release a book, Wes. That's where your publisher is, your agent. They've got you all set up to do that great indie store."

He'd shaken his head. "I'll still do a stop there, but it's not the place to *launch* the book."

And she'd known without him saying anything more, and her eyes filled with tears as he kissed her.

"The book launches where the story began—with *you*. And it's too late to say no because Max is already ironing out the details, so I hope you're up for the extra business."

She watched him now, about to embark on the biggest adventure of his life, and he wanted her to be a part of it. His dad and Sarah stood nearby, proudly holding their already signed books. Annie's mom waved from where she stood next to Theresa and Dad, the three of them apparently heading to a show at the Steppenwolf after the event. Doug and Dan had a coffee cart set up by the register, another partnership they were trying out. They'd sell coffee at the big events and would in turn give Two Stories shelf space at Hot Latte so that patrons who were looking for something to read might be inclined to buy a book—and to head down the block to see what else was available. Who knew? That could be her next partnership. When she returned, of course.

Everyone was here for her and for Wes—for his big night.

He stood when she got near, and her heart swelled to see him so happy, to *be* this happy herself. Wes Hartley wasn't a placeholder. He was all too real, and as much as that scared her, she'd also never felt more alive than when he was near.

"Folks," he said, reaching for Annie's hand and pulling her close. "*This* is Annie."

There were mild gasps, and some *ooohs* and *aaahs*. Annie's brows furrowed.

"What's going on?" she asked.

He grabbed the display book from his table and handed it to her. She'd read the book more than once, but in all the craziness of the past couple of months—of drawing up the papers for the partnership, getting ready for six months of on and off travel, she hadn't actually *held* the printed book in her hand. In fact, Wes never showed her an advance copy, and when the shipment came in a few days ago, he'd whisked her out for a celebratory drink while Tabitha and Brynn did the unpacking.

"I didn't want you to see the dedication until now," he said, a nervous grin on his face.

Annie's heart always seemed to speed up when he was around, but now it beat in overdrive.

"I don't—" she stammered. "I'm not sure I can read it in front of"—she leaned closer to him and whisper shouted—"all of *them*."

Quiet laughter filled the room, and while Annie didn't think anyone was laughing *at* her, she knew there was a punch line she wasn't getting.

He kissed her cheek and took the book back from her. "Okay. I will."

The patrons applauded. The small catering staff paused. Brynn had found her way to where Jeremy and Jamie stood against a shelf opposite the table. All their eyes were on Wes and Annie now.

He opened the book and read.

"For Annie." He looked up at her and grinned. She chewed her lip nervously. "For Annie," he said again. "We're not in Kansas anymore. Wherever we go from here, you'll always be home. The light that guides me. My Emerald City."

He looked up, and she wasn't sure if she was seeing him through the moisture welling in her eyes or if she detected a hint of wetness in his, too. He handed her back the book, and as she took it, he dropped to one knee.

The whole room was one collective gasp, Annie included.

"Marry me, Annie." She was sure he was holding up a ring, but she could barely see it through the rapidly falling tears. "It's time for *our* happy ending," he said.

She knelt down in front of him, glad Wes had insisted the party be casual, and only now realizing his perfectly fitted button-down was green. But now she wondered if the biggest moment of her life so far was going to happen while she was wearing jeans and a T-shirt that said CARPE READ 'EM.

Well, she wasn't wondering for long. Because *hello*? Wes was freaking proposing.

Her mouth formed the word yes, but instead she cried out, "Wait!"

He froze. The whole room seemed suspended in the moment.

"No happy endings, remember?" she said.

Wes blew out a breath, and she realized she must have scared him. He reached for her left hand, and she offered it to him willingly.

"No *endings*," he said, sliding the ring down her finger. "But a hell of a lot of happy," he added.

She nodded. "I'll say yes to that."

And then he kissed her to the sound of applause and catcalls from Jeremy and Jamie and Brynn.

"You know I have zero point of reference for how to do this, right?" she said in between tear-soaked kisses.

He shrugged. "That makes two of us."

"Yeah, but my mom will probably show up at our wedding with a guy half her age she met online that day. And my dad and Theresa just told us they have an open relationship and—have I mentioned how messed up I learned my teen years were?"

He cupped her cheeks in his hands.

"I love you, Annie. Didn't you say that was all that

mattered? That love would conquer all?"

He pressed his lips to hers, and her eyes fell shut as she nodded. "I did say that," she whispered against him. "I always thought those were three simple words, but I underestimated them—what it meant to say them. Or to have them said to me."

"They were the hardest words to say—until I said them to you."

"I love you, too," she said and felt his lips part into a smile.

"Then I guess we have an agreement," he said. "No endings."

She leaned her forehead against his.

"I guess we do."

THERE'S NO SUCH THING AS A HAPPY ENDING
by **HappyEverAfter admin** | Leave a comment

THIS POST IS GOING TO BE SHORT AND SWEET, EVERYONE. BUT I PROMISE TO POST FROM THE ROAD AND LET YOU KNOW HOW THE BOOK TOUR IS GOING. FOR NOW I JUST WANT TO SAY THANK YOU FOR SUPPORTING THE BLOG, FOR SUPPORTING MY STORE, AND FOR CHAMPIONING LOVE IN ALL ITS FORMS. READING ROMANCE HAS TAUGHT ME THAT LOVE CERTAINLY DOES CONQUER ALL—BUT NOT AT ONCE. WITH EVERY LITTLE OBSTACLE, LOVE HAS TO WORK ITS BUTT OFF TO TRIUMPH AGAIN AND AGAIN AND AGAIN. THE KEY IS TO NEVER BACK DOWN FROM THE FIGHT. HAPPILY EVER AFTER IS REAL. I LEARNED THAT FROM STORIES AND ALSO FROM MY OWN LIFE. BUT MOST OF ALL, I LEARNED THERE ARE NO HAPPY ENDINGS. ONLY WHAT COMES AFTER.

THE BEGINNING

Acknowledgments

Well, it took me eight books, but I finally found the characters who let me use their story to write a love letter to romance. Thank you, Annie and Wes, for showing us that love can conquer all and that happy endings are just the beginning.

Thanks to my agent, Courtney Miller-Callihan, for always being in my corner and for championing my ideas no matter how many shiny new ones I email you.

Karen Grove, you pushed me to turn an idea with potential into a story with real heart — and plenty of heat. Wes truly thanks you for the latter — especially in that wedding chapter.

Lia Riley, Megan Erickson, Natalie Blitt, Jennifer Blackwood, and Chanel Cleeton, I don't know what I'd do without our daily chats. You are my sanity keepers, my plot whisperers, and the most talented writers I know. I'm grateful to call you my friends. AWKWARD GROUP HUG.

Special thanks to Our So-Called Group and Kingston Ale House group members. Your support and daily shenanigans are the best.

Thank you to my Hideaway girls. Your guidance, advice, and Tingle-esque title contests mean more to me than you can imagine.

To all my readers, I am forever grateful that you let me keep doing this thing I love to do—making new stories.

And always, the biggest thanks go to S and C, for loving me infinity even when I'm frazzled, on deadline, and go for days without the laptop closed. You are my true heroes, and I love you most.

About the Author

A. J. Pine writes stories to break readers' hearts, but don't worry—she'll mend them with a happily ever after. As an English teacher and a librarian, A. J. has always surrounded herself with books. All her favorites have one big commonality—romance. Naturally, the books she writes have the same. When she's not writing, she's of course reading. Then there's online shopping (everything from groceries to shoes). And a tiny bit of TV where she nourishes her undying love of vampires, superheroes, and a certain high-functioning sociopath detective. You'll also find her hanging with her family in the Chicago 'burbs.

CPSIA information can be obtained
at www.ICGtesting.com
Printed in the USA
BVHW071106120422
634069BV00006B/235